DRIVEN:
Racing, Rivalry, Revenge

TM THORNE

Copyright © 2019 TM Thorne

All rights reserved.

ISBN: 9798643940319

ABOUT THE AUTHOR

TM Thorne lived in London for many years before giving in to property prices and the demands of raising a family, and now lives messily in the English countryside with her motorsport-mad husband and son and three demanding cats.

When not writing about her much-missed city, spending time with her family or tripping over engines and spanners littered around the house she likes to eat, drink and feel guilty about not doing enough exercise.

You can find out more about the author and sign up to her mailing list through social media or on her very own website:

Instagram: Instagram.com/tmthorneauthor
Facebook: facebook.com/tmthorneauthor
Twitter: @tmthorneauthor
Website: www.tmthorne.com

CONTENTS

1	An Inauspicious Start	1
2	Screwdrivers & Touring Car Drivers	7
3	A Familiar Stirring Sensation	14
4	Tousled Hair & Tiny Dogs	18
5	Psychos & Silver Spoons	24
6	Racehorses & The Living Dead	32
7	Abattoirs & Extra-Maritals	38
8	On the Side of the Angels	45
9	Lipstick & Ambition	52
10	A Rude Awakening	60
11	Drinking & Delusions	64
12	Steak & Lashings of Rain	71
13	Gummy Bears & Crash Barriers	84
14	Gaining an Advantage	95
15	Go Big or Go Home	102
16	Catching a Golden Goose	108

17	Sun, Sand & Total Seclusion	114
18	Back on Home Turf	119
19	Bacon Sandwiches & Broken Fingers	129
20	Motors & Moolah	133
21	Tea & Tantrums	140
22	Drop and Give Me Twenty	147
23	Windswept & Wild	154
24	Toppling Dominoes	162
25	The Morning After	183
26	Numpties & New Motivation	189
27	An Unexpected Adventure	197
28	Scuff Marks & Sex Pests	205
29	Wishful Thinking	212
30	Confrontation & Collapse	215
31	A Hospital Hangover	233
32	A New Beginning	240
33	The Big Finish	245
34	Sweat & Naughty Schoolboys	253

Copyright © 2019 TM Thorne
All rights reserved.

This book or any portion thereof may not be reproduced or used in any matter whatsoever without the express written permission of the publisher except for the use of brief quotations in book review.

This is a work of fiction. Names, characters, businesses, places, events and incidents are either the products of the author's imagination or used in a fictitious manner. Any resemblance to actual persons, living or dead, or actual events is purely coincidental and unintentional. Even when recognisable names appear, their actions are fictitious.

This book is unofficial and is not associated in any way with the Formula 1 companies. F1, FORMULA ONE, FORMULA 1, FIA FORMULA ONE WORLD CHAMPIONSHIP, GRAND PRIX and related marks are trade marks of Formula One Licensing B.V.

OTHER TITLES BY TM THORNE

FRANKIE FINCH BOOKS

Notorious:
Danger, Deception, Desire

Accused:
Stardom, Scandal, Survival

Driven:
Racing, Rivalry Revenge

Caged:
Rock, Ransom, Retribution

Made:
The Frankie Finch prequel (short story)

THE LONDON VAMPIRE SERIES

Spooked

Jinxed

Enthralled (short story)

1
AN INAUSPICIOUS START

"I'm sorry, Ben," said Rick Maberley, but he wasn't sorry, and Ben knew it.

The fat fucker sat there in his expensive shirt, open one button too many, showing a Lothario's amount of fleshy pink chest. His pitiless gaze locked on Ben. It was a gaze more suited to a mob boss than a businessman.

There wasn't an ounce of humanity in that piggy face. Maberley's words weren't an apology, they were a challenge, a test to see whether Ben would dare react.

Would he argue? Would he get angry? Or would he meekly accept the news and thank them for having considered him in the first place? Maberley knew the answer already. After all, he held all the cards, he had all the power, that was why he was team principal.

The day had started so well. Ben had even been looking forward to this meeting. He'd been a little nervous, perhaps - after all, it's not every day you get confirmed as an F1 driver. But they'd talked about this for months and today was just a formality to sign the contract for next season. What was there to be nervous about?

A rising star in the world of racing, Ben Redmaine had

worked damn hard to get where he was today. The long hours, the sacrifices, the constant pressure to win and deliver, it was all finally coming to fruition. For the past year he'd been a test driver for Pernice Bianca Racing and, after their current driver had failed to curtail his increasingly public gambling habit, Ben had been given the nod that the race-seat would be his.

Pernice Bianca were only a small outfit, certainly no Ferrari or McLaren, and they only had a fraction of the budget of a big team, but this was Ben's way in.

If he performed and got results, who knew what offers he'd get for the following season. This was his big chance. Either way, it was F1 baby! This had been the dream for as long as he could remember.

It was just before 10 that morning when Ben pulled into the car park, the car ticking as it cooled down from its sprint through the country lanes of Oxfordshire.

He strolled into the modern glass building, the smell of leather and car polish reassuringly familiar. In reception, with its immaculately polished floor, Ben passed between spotless historic racing cars and a case of gleaming trophies. He breathed in, relishing the surroundings. This was his world, where he belonged.

As he rode the lift up to the top floor, he took a deep breath, rolling his shoulders, and inspected his reflection, trying on a relaxed confident smile. It looked strained, unconvincing. A facsimile of his usual expression. He shook his head and snorted. What was he so worried about? He had this in the bag.

Rick Maberley gestured Ben towards a stylish, but uncomfortable, plastic stool and leaned back in his executive leather chair. It let out an unfortunate farting sound. At least, Ben thought it was the chair. Maberley was a porcine ex-racing driver-turned-motorsport mogul, who had run to fat since he swapped his driving seat for a large glass office some ten years previously. Ruthless and uncompromising, he was known as the Iron Hog, but only when he was out of earshot.

He steepled his fingers and flashed Ben a hard smile.

"Thanks for coming in today, Ben. You know we've been discussing next year for some time now and we've finally got an offer on the table for you." He paused. "There's both good news, and bad news."

Ben frowned. Okay, well as long as the good news was the news he was expecting.

"You know how hard it is to compete as a small team in this business, Ben. We're always stretching budgets, analysing where every penny is spent, and being the poor kid in the paddock is no fun. Having to choose between spending on development or producing spare parts isn't where we want to be. This year has been hugely disappointing, a tough year for everyone, which was why we felt something significant needed to change."

Ah, thought Ben, a smile tugging at the corner of his mouth, *he wants to re-negotiate my wages for next season. They want me to stay on a test driver's salary even though I'll be racing.* That wasn't ideal, but he could make it work.

Maberley was still talking.

"The exciting news is that we've signed a major new investor. They're making a substantial investment in the team, enabling us to compete at a higher level for the coming season. We may even be challenging for the top ten next year."

"That's great news, isn't it? What's the bad news?

"Well, Ben," Maberley cleared his throat. "I'm afraid the bad news, from your point of view, is who that investor is. You know Ted Cavendish, I presume?"

Ben's head dropped. His eyes briefly closed. Everything seemed to go into slow motion. Of course he knew Cavendish. Everyone knew Cavendish: the billionaire big oil tycoon whose son had gone from racing daddy's Ferrari

GT to winning F2. There had been rumours the kid wanted an F1 seat; in fact, they'd all joked about daddy buying him an F1 team for Christmas - after all, that was how he'd progressed his career until now.

Last year, Cavendish had taken over an ailing F2 team, staffed it with highly paid ex-F1 mechanics and ensured his son had every advantage, including an insane amount of track time, to ease him towards winning the championship. No one else stood a chance. It was whispered that his success had been secured thanks to favourable decisions from the stewards. Cavendish was a powerful man and everyone wanted to be on his Christmas list.

Christ, Ben recalled hearing that the kid had been on a round-the-world testing programme in an old F1 car over the winter. They'd all thought it was hilarious. It didn't seem so funny now.

In a daze, Ben barely registered the rest of what Maberley was saying. It only confirmed his initial suspicions. He wouldn't be moving to a race-seat; that would be taken by the incoming cash cow. And their other driver, who was bankrolled by the Columbian government and who had performed adequately, if not spectacularly, would be retaining his race-seat for the coming season. Of course he was.

They valued Ben enormously, he was an important member of the team, blah blah, and they hoped he would stay in his role as test driver. They were sure he could see that this was the best decision for the team, and this was a great opportunity for him.

"And after all," said Maberley with a patronising smile, "you're still young and there's always next year."

Feeling numb, Ben fantasised about grabbing Maberley by the shirt and punching him repeatedly in his fat, sweaty face. Then taking the uncomfortable stool and using it to smash his pretentious glass desk along with everything else in the office. That would feel great, up until the point where he was escorted from the building, sacked, and never allowed to set foot in a racing car again.

So, instead, Ben stood, shook Maberley's warm, damp hand and, resisting the urge to wipe his palm on his trousers, forced his most corporate smile and told him he understood. They had to do what was best for the team. And if anything changed, he hoped they would consider him for the race-seat again. *Hopefully when the rich kid had a bad accident in Round One*, he added silently.

It was only when he got back to his car that he dropped the act. Out of view, he took his frustration out on the steering wheel, punching and shaking it.

Fucking wankers! Sixteen years he'd been working towards this, only to be passed over by some over-privileged kid who didn't have an ounce of natural talent in his body. He was sick of this sport, it was full of sharks and crooks and all about money. Talent could get you so far, but when wealthy drivers were coached relentlessly and arrived bringing an obscene amount of money, he didn't stand a fucking chance. He thumped the steering wheel again, accidentally making the horn blare.

From the corner of his eye he spotted a startled employee standing looking at him in alarm, her mouth hanging open. He smiled and gave her a wave. *No, honestly, I'm not insane, I was just messing about. Nothing to see here!* The woman waved back tentatively and walked hurriedly towards the office. Ben took a few calming breaths.

OK, so he was stuck in the simulator for another year, at least. Hopefully it was just a temporary setback. That's if he ever got a shot at a race-seat again once it became known he'd been passed over for someone straight out of a junior formula.

He rubbed his face.

Not only would he have to sit on the sidelines and watch his new teammate under perform and fuck-up the drive that should have been his, but he'd be working hard to provide valuable data from the sim to help the fucker improve. His job would be coaching and facilitating the gilded cash cow, so he didn't make the team look too bad. Great.

Perhaps the season didn't need to be a total write-off, though.

Ben pulled out his phone, scrolling through his contacts for a number he never thought he'd need to call. He took a moment to calm himself and get into charm mode. By the time the call connected, he sounded confident and relaxed.

"Hugo, it's Ben Redmaine," he drawled. "Sorry it's taken a few weeks to get back to you about your offer. I wanted to think things through, to be sure I could give this 100%. I've managed to re-shuffle a few things and my answer is yes, I'll do it."

He contemplated the fabric on the ceiling of the car while Hugo droned on about his plans for the coming year.

After a few minutes Ben interrupted. "Yes, absolutely Hugo. That sounds great. I'd better dash, I'm just going into a meeting, but I'm excited to get started. See you next week."

Ending the call, he slumped back and let out a heavy breath. Thank goodness he'd had a backup plan. If Pernice Bianca weren't going to do anything to help him, he'd do something to help himself.

Besides, he was going to have a lot more time on his hands this year than he'd planned. He might as well put it to good use.

2
SCREWDRIVERS & TOURING CAR DRIVERS

Jake Golding leaned against the wooden fencing, oblivious to the cruel February rain, waiting for the lights to go out and the race to start. He cut a brooding and slightly ridiculous figure to the other parents who were watching from inside the clubhouse, a few of them sniggering at his stubborn determination to stand on the sidelines whenever his son was racing. Totally absorbed, Jake was unaware of their derision. There were thirty karts on the grid waiting to race and his son was stone dead last. It wasn't Max's fault. Jake still couldn't believe they'd had that puncture in the previous race.

Things like that always happened at the worst time, although there was never a good time for a tyre to blow. At least it hadn't caused an accident and Max had been able to limp back to the pits. Could he have run over a nail or something on circuit? Jake balled his fists in frustration. Why hadn't he checked the tyres on the grid? *That's what happens when you get complacent,* he thought, *and that's why Max was having to start from the back.*

His focus snapped back to the track as the engines roared and the lights on the gantry came on. There was a pause as everyone waited, breath held, for the lights to go out. Then the drivers hurtled off the grid towards the first corner in a billowing cloud of spray.

Max had gained half a dozen places before they hit the braking zone, but had to take to the grass to avoid a kid who lost grip and was sliding sideways towards the barriers. Jake winced.

"Somebody's run out of talent," he muttered as the careening kart almost caused a pile-up.

By the time he tore his gaze away from the first corner incident and looked for Max again, the racers were lost in a fog of rain on the other side of the track. Jake hunched his shoulders and peered into the mist, waiting to catch a glimpse of his son's gold helmet. As he came back into sight Jake let out a relieved sigh and the racers crossed the start/finish line for the next lap. Already up to eighth position, Max was making the kids around him look like novices as he carved his way up through the field, but his main rival was way out front by now.

Sam Cheavers was a chubby bulldozer of a child and was currently leading the race. Usually there was very little contest between them: Max beat Cheavers nine times out of ten on track. It was only when Jake got the setup wrong or they had bad luck that they didn't come away with the win. They just seemed to have more bad luck than most.

Three laps in, and Max's rival had edged a five-second lead over the chasing pack, which he was extending with every corner. Max was going to have to urge every bit of speed out of the kart to catch him in the remaining time. Jake glanced at the digiboard: his boy was currently fastest on track, going half a second a lap faster than Cheavers, but he still had a lot of ground to make up.

Jake squinted, trying to see the action on the other side of the track through the darkening gloom. He could see yellow flags waving furiously, so somebody must have come off. It was hardly surprising in this horrible weather; the track was like an ice rink. He just hoped it wasn't Max.

As Cheavers emerged onto the start/finish straight, Jake spotted Max at the front of the chasing pack and let out a shout of encouragement.

"Come on, son, just one more lap to go. Chase him down!" he bellowed, his voice carried away by the wind. No one else was there to hear him. He was the only person not watching through the steamy windows of the club house. Max was closing the gap with every corner until he disappeared from sight once more. Jake's heart pounded loudly in his chest as he waited for the leaders to come back into view.

After what seemed like an age, they reached the last corner with Max right on Cheavers' bumper. With a move that made Jake gasp, Max thrust his kart down the inside and pulled level. Taken by surprise, Cheavers threw a frustrated hand in the air and looked over to the clubhouse in indignation, enough of a lapse in concentration for Max to take the chequered flag by a couple of inches.

Euphoric, Jake punched the air and let out a massive whoop. Forgetting the cold and rain, he ran over to the pit lane where Max was climbing out of his seat. He scooped him up into a huge hug, swinging him round.

"You did it, son, that was awesome!"

Max slid his visor open, a big grin splitting his face. A shy, serious eleven-year-old when he wasn't behind the wheel, it was the best thing in the world seeing his face shine on days like this. As the other parents filled the grid around them, Jake spotted the hulking shape of Sam's dad, Rob Cheavers, and clapped him on the shoulder.

"Well done, mate, good battle."

Cheavers, who was fingering the screwdriver in his pocket and wishing he'd punctured Max's tyre for the final rather than the previous heat, gave Jake a dry smile.

"What have we got to do to beat you?" he grumbled.

Jake beamed, hair dripping into his face, and shrugged.

"There were only inches in it as they crossed the line," he said, as if that somehow made it better rather than worse.

As he turned back, he found himself enveloped in a cloud of wildly billowing, damp blonde hair. Flinging her arms around Jake's neck and planting a big kiss on his lips, Bambi Golding gave her husband a squeeze, then made room to include an embarrassed Max.

"Well done, boys, that was spectacular. I'm so proud of you both!" she squealed.

Releasing them, she turned to a surprised Cheavers, hugging him and giving him a gleeful kiss on the cheek. He shook his head with a reluctant smile. Though he couldn't stand Jake and Max, he had a soft spot for Bambi. In her early 40s, with an infectious smile, she had a habit of wearing low-cut tops which couldn't completely contain her wayward boobs, and the karting dads were all secretly rather fond of her. The wives of the karting dads weren't so enthusiastic.

Her real name was Emily, but everyone knew her as Bambi because she was hopelessly clumsy. Releasing the flushed Cheavers, she gasped as she remembered her exciting news and grabbed Jake's arm.

"Hey, you'll never guess who was watching the race with me! Come back to the van, there's someone that wants to meet you two."

Chase Ashcroft slouched against the van, sheltering from the rain. He dragged on his cigarette and stifled a yawn as he scratched the stubble on his jaw.

An ex-touring car driver and son of a famous racing driver, he ran Apex Motorsport, one of the largest teams in the paddock. More accurately, he fronted the team since, as his wife frequently pointed out, he couldn't organise a piss-up in a brewery. He'd grown up in the sport, never knowing anything other than a nomadic motorsport lifestyle, moving between circuits and only sleeping at home a couple of nights each week.

Chase was great with young drivers, partly because he'd never really had to grow up himself. He clicked with kids easily, finding ways to driver coach them without being patronising. His infectious enthusiasm for the sport remained undamped, even after twenty years of competing and working in it.

Seeing a bedraggled Bambi splashing towards him, he hitched up his low-slung jeans and got his game face on. He had a driver to sign up.

Ambling over to meet the race winner, he fist-bumped Max and gave him a lopsided smile.

"That was some driving out there, kid. Loved that move you pulled on the last corner."

Max, whose face was gritty and grimy and who was starting to shiver violently in his soaked race suit, smiled and looked down at his feet.

"Thanks," he mumbled, as Bambi bundled him off to get into some clean, dry clothes and warm up in the front of the van.

Chase turned to a dripping Jake who looked equally sodden.

"Let me take you for a coffee, mate. You look like you could do with warming up, and there's something I'd like to run past you."

Steaming slightly as he dried out in the café, Jake warmed his aching hands on a mug of tea. As the euphoria of the win wore off, he realised just how cold, wet and knackered he was, and to make matters worse he had to get up for work in the morning.

He looked out of the misted-up window and rubbed the glass with his sleeve. It didn't improve visibility. If anything, the weather seemed to be getting worse as darkness fell. What he needed right now was a hot bath and a cold beer, but he still had to pack everything back into the van and get home first.

Chase plonked himself down at the Formica table and Jake dragged his attention back to the conversation. This was a waste of time. They didn't need to join a team, they were doing just fine by themselves. He'd give Chase until he reached the bottom of his cup, then he was out of there.

By the time they finished talking and got back to the van, the rain had faded and darkness had enveloped the emptying paddock. After the cacophony of generators, power tools and race engines that had sounded all day, it felt eerily quiet, with just the occasional low crunch of gravel as a van eased its way towards the gates. Max, exhausted after a tough day's driving, was fast asleep across Bambi's lap in the van while she read a trashy paperback and munched her way through a packet of biscuits.

Laughing and sharing racing anecdotes, Chase helped Jake strip the kart down and pack everything away into the van. They got the jobs done in record time.

Chase shook Jake's hand. "See you next weekend, then?"

Jake shook his head and grinned.

"Sure, why not?"

"Great. Look, I know you're sceptical about doing the Nationals, but Max is a real talent. He should be pitting himself against the best in the country, not just at a little club like this. Bring him along to meet the rest of the team and see what you think. I know what you said, and it's true: there's a lot of money spent to gain drivers an advantage at top level, but it's not just about racing people's cheque books. I honestly think Max could take it to the big boys this year. This could be his big break."

Jake watched as Chase sauntered back to his car, a battered but sporty little hot hatch with a large dent in the bonnet and the trim missing from one side.

Climbing back into the van, he hummed happily. All the tiredness of earlier had been replaced with a growing feeling of excitement. He couldn't wait to tell Bambi. Maybe Chase was right, and he was holding Max back only letting him race at his local club. He'd read somewhere that Lewis Hamilton had been spotted by McLaren when he did the Nationals, so they had to give Max this chance, especially now he'd been scouted. Perhaps it would be the start of something big.

3
A FAMILIAR STIRRING SENSATION

In the words of Michael Caine: Fat Frankie Finch was a big man, but he was in bad shape. He lounged in his armchair, cigar smouldering in a heavy glass ashtray, took a slug of whiskey and sighed with satisfaction as he let one rip. With his t-shirt straining over his stomach, a pasty complexion and a gold chain nestling in generous chest hair, his appearance belied his reputation. Frankie wasn't a man to mess with.

He'd always enjoyed a scrap. As a young man, Frankie had been a fearsome bare-knuckle fighter and had spent the two decades since then establishing himself as a tough and uncompromising businessman. His East End empire was founded on extortion, armed robbery and a more recent expansion into recreational substances. Activities that were supported by a proclivity for casual violence and ruthless ambition.

Approaching forty and under pressure from his wife, he'd left the familiar streets of the capital for a mock-Tudor mansion in Chigwell and was starting to relax into his new suburban routine. Life was good, but as his sagging gut attested, he could do with getting back down the gym. Too much comfort was definitely making him soft around the edges.

He glanced down as *Stuck in the Middle with You* blared from his phone. He'd loved that song ever since he saw *Reservoir Dogs*. It always put him in the right frame of mind to handle whatever crisis was happening on the other end of the phone.

He muted the TV.

"Talk to me, Chris."

"We've got a problem, Frank. I've just seen Len and he says the shipment arrived short. I think he's having us on."

Chris Slaughter was Frankie's right-hand man. At six foot six, he was lean, menacing and built like a brick shithouse. He towered over most people, his wide shoulders accentuated by a well-cut suit, and with his naturally intimidating features he rarely needed to carry out a threat these days. Just his presence made most people pale and agree to anything. In Frankie's words, he was an absolute diamond. Chris rarely cracked a smile - he wasn't known for his light-hearted banter - but he was fiercely loyal. In fact, Chris was the only person outside his family that Frankie completely trusted.

"You've got to be fucking kidding me. You think he's been skimming off the top?"

"It seems more likely than the suppliers letting us down," said Chris.

"For Christ's sake, have a word then, will you? Tell 'em if they don't cough up the missing gear in the next 24 hours, they'll be getting a personal visit from me, and they really don't want that."

Frankie sighed. "Just get it sorted. I'm meant to be at a wedding tomorrow and Linda'll kill me if I'm late because I've had to go strong-arming Lanky Len."

Chucking his phone on the table he sagged back, taking a few slow breaths to relax the tightness in his chest. Eyes shut, he didn't see his wife watching him from the doorway.

"Seriously, Frankie, you better not be getting them chest pains again and not telling me," she said, hands on hips. "What did that doctor say about taking things easy and not getting yourself worked up?"

Linda Finch's heels clacked across the wooden floor. Dressed in tight leather trousers and a deep-cut silk blouse, he had to admit she looked sensational. She leaned in, giving him the full benefit of her ample cleavage. *That was money well spent,* mused Frankie, smiling to himself. She gave him a lingering kiss, her dark hair enveloping him in a soft curtain. Feeling a familiar stirring in his trousers, Frankie slid his arms around her and pulled her into his lap, bunching his hands in the smooth silk of her blouse. She sank into the kiss, losing most of her lipstick onto Frankie's face before punching him on the arm and wriggling out of his grasp.

"Later, Frankie," she said, exasperated, "I'm already late for the hen night, and we can't have the boss's wife turning up late with bed hair and walking like John Wayne, can we?"

"I don't see why not," he said, running a hand up her thigh.

"I'm sure you don't." She slapped his hand away, the ghost of a smile on her lips.

Tilting his head, Frankie watched her arse as it sashayed towards the door. After twenty years of marriage she could still drive him crazy.

"Chuck me a bag of crisps before you go will you love?"

She gave him a stern look. "Not likely! You're supposed to be on a diet. I'm not having your heart giving out on me. You can bloody well get out of that chair of yours and get some fruit from the kitchen if you're hungry. I've hidden all the crisps. Besides, I'm already late, gotta dash!" She blew him a kiss. "You're in charge of the kids. Ronnie's up in his bedroom on the PlayStation, and

Britney's upstairs revising. Stick your head round her door in a bit, will you? Make sure she's doing some studying rather than spending the whole night on the phone chatting about boys."

"Boys? She's only fifteen, Linda."

"Ha, don't you remember what we were like at that age? After all, we were married at sixteen."

"Yeah, but that was you and me Linda, times have changed. She's far too young to be interested in boys. For Christ's sake, it was only yesterday she wanted ballet lessons and a pony for Christmas."

"Uh huh, you keep telling yourself that, baby." She winked and wiggled her fingers at him. "Laters!"

Frankie frowned and shook his head. The kids were growing up fast. Ronnie was small for his age, but at twelve he was overdue a growth spurt. He was a right chip off the old block, so he was bound to shoot up soon. It had happened overnight with Frankie. One moment he'd been a skinny kid, the next he was towering over his mum and sounding like Bob Hoskins.

Ronnie wasn't handy with his fists the way Frankie had been at that age, but then he'd never needed to be. He was dynamite behind the wheel, though. Frankie looked over at the photo of Ronnie crossing the finish line, arms aloft in celebration, and smiled, raising his glass in a silent toast. Bring on the Nationals. This was going to be little Ronnie's year, he was sure of it.

4
TOUSLED HAIR & TINY DOGS

It was only as he reached 30,000 feet and the alcohol hit his bloodstream that Ben Redmaine's heart stopped pounding.

Closing his eyes, he savoured the cold prickle of the champagne as he drained his glass, then breathed a sigh of relief. A heavily made-up stewardess appeared at his shoulder to refill his flute. He rewarded her with a smile.

He hated flying, but tried to keep that quiet. He'd never live it down if his fellow racing drivers discovered his secret; his job was about machismo and having balls of steel. He could race fearlessly wheel-to-wheel at 200mph, but hearing jet engines roaring for take-off he was shaking like a fucking Chihuahua. It was embarrassing.

Stretching his shoulders, Ben settled back into his seat and closed his eyes, listening to the incessant hum of the plane and trying to slow his heart rate.

A smile played on his lips as he thought back to Eduardo and his sun-kissed Brazilian skin. He'd needed a break, especially after the devastating news about losing his race-seat, and the last week had been the perfect tonic.

Within hours of the meeting with Maberley, Ben had left the country. Angry and not trusting himself to keep his mouth shut, he grabbed a last-minute flight. Not caring where he went, he picked the first destination with guaranteed hot weather, beaches and plenty of bars. He needed a complete change of scene.

A small voice in his head nagged him to sit tight, just in case Pernice Bianca changed their mind and called him back for the job, but he knew that was stupid. He got on the plane before he could change his mind.

They met on the second day. Ben was lying on the beach, basking in the sun and lazily watching some local boys play volleyball. Spotting him, Eduardo had invited him to join them and they'd immediately hit it off, dividing the rest of the week between relaxing days at the beach and long, hot nights together at local clubs and in the hotel.

All too soon the holiday was over but it had done its job. Ben felt great, re-energised. He had a new-found enthusiasm and was ready to get back to work.

He surveyed the elegant first-class cabin. Secluded in his private cocoon he could relax, at least until it was time for them to land. Even he couldn't stay nervous for a full twelve-hour flight, and the alcohol had taken the edge off his anxiety.

The luxury of First was great, much better than the economy ticket he'd paid for, but it irked him that he'd had to rely on getting upgraded. If he'd been given the F1 drive, he'd be able to fly first class all the time. *Bastards*, he thought bitterly.

The corner of his mouth twitched as he remembered the flustered woman at the check-in desk. Wearing his team jacket and some designer shades had been a calculated gamble, which had paid off. The woman's eyes had widened. The killer smile he'd flashed helped too, judging by the pink flush that crept up her neck as she checked him in and shyly upgraded him to First.

Women had always been susceptible to Ben's charms, his tousled blonde hair, sleepy blue eyes and tall languid frame. It was good to see he hadn't lost his appeal. If a bit of gentle flirting could score him a luxurious flight home, then why not?

Well rested, he'd come to terms with being stuck in the sim all year, and was now focusing on his new project: starting his own race team.

Initially he'd been hesitant. He'd been approached a few months ago by the zealously ambitious parents of a young driver, who wanted him to set up a team around their over-privileged child.

Ben had spent his whole life having to race against spoilt, rich kids while he'd scrabbled for money every step of the way, so his first reaction was to turn them down. But that was when he thought he'd got the F1 drive.

Luckily, Hugo Aspinall was persistent and used to getting his own way. So eventually, after a lot of flattery, the offer of an obscene fee and his own race season going up in flames, Ben had agreed. He would set up the team and coach their precocious eleven-year-old to becoming British Cadet Champion.

Thinking about it, it was the perfect idea for this year. Last season, after the initial euphoria of being signed by an F1 team, Ben had found himself in the frustrating limbo of the test driver: not famous enough to be getting TV work or big sponsorship deals, yet hog-tied into his test-driver contract with the dangled carrot of a possible drive.

He had to remain super-fit and ready to jump in the car at a moment's notice, but without actually getting to race.

Now, with Cavendish bankrolling the team, and the other driver bringing in big Columbian money, he would only get the race-seat if one of their current drivers had to quit the season.

He needed an angle to get himself noticed, and the team idea was PR gold. Not only would it net him a lot of cash, but it would give him a philanthropic spin in the press, making him more desirable to sponsors who could help pay for that elusive drive.

He would be the young driver who, even though he was on the cusp of F1, had chosen to give selflessly back to grass roots motorsport. Even better, that he was coaching kids, something which could really raise his profile. At the very least it should get him a few TV interviews and a lot more followers on social media. It was worth a try.

The kid he would be coaching was supposed to be a good little driver, probably a bit of an arrogant brat, but having been in the paddock from a young age Ben had spent his life around the kids of the super-rich and was immune to them.

Plus, if he could attract other wealthy parents to his team, it could be a tidy little earner. It was all about who you knew in this game and finding a billionaire backer remained the dream. What better way than becoming a hero to their kids?

At 24, Ben had reached the glass ceiling in motorsport, where you needed serious investment to climb any higher. To be fair, being a test driver was well paid. He was the envy of a lot of his old racing friends who were stuck in nine-to-five desk jobs, only getting to go out on the occasional track day when time and budget permitted.

To all intents and purposes, he looked like he was living the professional racing driver dream. The truth was a bitter pill. He was frustratingly close to the success he craved, but it remained just out of reach.

He needed to get Ben Redmaine Racing (BRR for short) up and running fast, that meant a busy few weeks ahead. On his way to the airport he'd called his manager, who'd started putting in the groundwork for him. He'd booked Ben lots of meetings with people in the industry, officials who'd known him growing up and who now name-dropped him at dinner parties. They'd be delighted that a big name was getting involved with the sport.

He was also scheduled to do good deeds: giving out trophies at awards evenings for local clubs, taking top people out to lunch, inviting them for tours around the Pernice Bianca factory and giving out the few complimentary tickets he had to the British Grand Prix.

Basically, schmoozing and greasing palms. He knew how to play this game.

The pre-season test was only a few weeks away and Ben felt confident that he could pull his new team together quickly. He'd call in a few favours, one of the benefits of everyone feeling sorry for him after he'd been publicly dumped by his team.

He'd get the best mechanics and kit them out in a smart new team uniform. F1 standards all the way. They'd knock the socks off the other teams in the paddock.

Karting had changed enormously from when he was a kid. Back then, it was just him and his dad turning up with their Ford Sierra Estate, a kart squeezed into the back. Now budgets were escalating every year, with some dads spending upwards of a quarter of a million on a season's racing so their ten-year-old could run with a top team.

Thanks to his manager, who'd pulled out all the stops while Ben had been topping up his tan, BRR already had two drivers signed to year-long contracts: Aspinall, the driver whose parents had approached him, and North who was going to be Aspinall's teammate.

North wasn't the superstar that Aspinall was said to be, but the dad had deep pockets and that was the main requirement. Plus, she was a girl, and girl racers were great from a PR point of view. Once they'd given her the best power in the paddock, driver coaching and the benefit of being smiled upon by Ben's new-found friends in high places, she'd be running at the front. But behind her teammate obviously. She couldn't be allowed to beat Aspinall, not when he was bankrolling the team.

Ben smiled at the thought of the coming season. Not

only was he going to do very well financially out of this venture, but he also planned to raise the bar and inject a bit of F1 glamour into the karting paddock.

He'd be the man who turned karting into a premier formula of motorsport. All for a premium, of course. His budget was pretty much unlimited for this year. He'd get the best engines, his own dyno, the finest mechanics and even a new super-slick team awning, complete with catering. Everyone would want to be in his team. They were going to look the bollocks.

There was only one catch. With all that behind him, he had to make sure they won the championship.

Otherwise instead of this being a feather in his cap, he might find his reputation taking a real battering. Aspinall's parents were influential people and would make sure of that.

They'd made it crystal clear that he'd been brought in to ensure they won. In short, he couldn't afford to lose.

5
PSYCHOS & SILVER SPOONS

Jake and Bambi exchanged a wide-eyed glance as they drove through the security gate and saw the fluttering flags, smart race trucks and shiny team awnings. As their shabby van crawled through the busy paddock, they passed millions of pounds' worth of cars. Range Rovers, Maseratis and Lamborghinis were littered everywhere. This was a far cry from the pot-holed dirt paddock at their local track, which was full of transit vans and estate cars pulling scrappy wooden trailers.

Max sat bolt upright between them, eyes like saucers, silently taking it all in.

Easthorpe International circuit had never looked lovelier than early on that crisp March morning. Out in the barren wilds of the Lincolnshire countryside, it was bleak and windswept in the winter but, with the sun shining and the last frost of winter behind it, the track looked glorious. Flanked by fields on all sides, a pristine ribbon of tarmac wove through lush green grass scattered with candy cane curbs.

"Look, over there!" Max pointed, spotting the Union-

Jack-emblazoned Apex Motorsport awning. "I can see Chase."

Outlined against the smart red, white and blue livery, Chase was leaning in a patch of sunshine, a cigarette drooping from his lips. He spotted them and raised a hand in greeting.

They eased the van through the paddock melee. The place was teeming with mechanics heaving kit around, people standing chatting and kids zooming about on scooters and bikes.

Chase leaned in through the open window.

"Nice to see you, mate. Glad you could make it. Come and meet everyone."

Bambi, glancing down, noticed splodges of chocolate on her top from when she made rocky road early that morning. She grabbed a packet of wipes and started trying to dab it clean. She shooed Jake and Max out of the van.

"I'll be right behind you, boys, you go ahead."

Inside the awning there were already two karts set up, each with people clustered around them.

Flicking his cigarette away, Chase said, "Right everyone, this is Jake and his son Max. They're thinking about joining the team."

A wild-eyed kid with a shock of fair hair and a crazy grin barged into Max playfully.

"Hey, I'm Dommie. Wanna come and play in my camper?"

Max looked up hopefully at Jake, who shrugged.

Instantly friends, the way that only kids can be, the two of them charged out chatting and giggling. Jake chuckled softly. Well that was easy enough. Perhaps his worries about people being sniffy and standoffish at the Nationals were unfounded.

Striding towards him, hand extended, was a compact man who exuded success. His crisp, densely woven polo shirt was the colour of the Caribbean Sea, and he had the tan of a man who played golf on a regular basis. Jake had watched a programme recently about psychopaths and how, depending on their upbringing, they either went on to become ruthless killers or captains of industry. Jake suspected this man might fall into the second category. Smiling, but with an appraising gaze, the man grasped Jake's hand in a dry, firm handshake.

"James Carver, Dommie's dad. Welcome to the team. Chase said that Max is quite a driver. It's always good to have some new blood in the team."

He shot a sideways glance at a lean, rat-faced man on the other side of the awning. As if sensing their stare the man looked up, nodded brusquely at Jake and turned back to working on the kart.

"Since he's too busy to come over, I'll make introductions for you. That man is Grant Lillington," and in a lower voice, "and the kid next to him with the face like a smacked arse is his son Finn, who isn't allowed to play with anyone because he" - he mimed air quotes - "needs to be focused on the racing."

Jake raised an eyebrow.

"OK, good to know. Talking of racing, I guess I'd better get everything unpacked. It looks like you're all way ahead of me right now."

As Chase and Carver helped Jake unpack the van, they gave him the lowdown on the different drivers. Dommie Carver was a seasoned racer who had already done two years of Nationals. He was fast and a good driver when he was on his game, but had a tendency to get easily distracted and mess around. Plus, he was hot-headed, often losing his temper and getting red mist during races, earning him a reputation for being a hard racer, or an on-track liability, depending on your point of view.

If there were any penalties to be handed out, there was a good chance Dommie would be getting them.

This year, in an attempt to keep him focused, Carver had hired an up-and-coming racing driver to coach him and to stop him from losing his head.

"On a proper race weekend, all video games are being turned off and he'll have to get his game face on. Sugar and video games make him hyper. We got too many penalties last year, and this year his cards will be marked. He really needs to up his game."

"What about Lillington?" asked Jake.

"The kid's an OK driver," said Carver. "He finished ninth overall last year, which wasn't bad for his first season. The problem is the dad's incredibly competitive and takes it all far too seriously. Anything other than a win isn't good enough, and Finn just isn't at that level yet. The poor kid just looks miserable the whole time."

At 9am, the revving of engines erupted throughout the paddock as the first practice session started.

Chase took the boys to one side. Crouching down he gestured to Dommie and Finn.

"Right, I know you two have driven thousands of laps around this circuit, but this is Max's first time here, so we're going to use the first session to give him a chance to learn the track while you two find out where we are pace-wise. Run your tyres in, work out where the grip is, see how the kart feels and how your power compares to the other drivers out there.

"The three of you go out together: Dommie first, Finn second, then Max. Max, you follow their lines and try to keep up as best you can. Don't worry if they lose you, you're here to learn the track today."

Bambi, with damp patches on her top where the chocolate stains had been, headed into the awning, only to be knocked backwards by a tutting Lillington who was pushing the kart down to the grid and didn't appreciate her getting in the way. Flattening herself in the doorway, she was tugged back outside by a highlighted gym-bunny of a woman who gave her a conspiratorial wink.

"You must be Max's mum. Come on, let's leave the

boys to it. Come and have a sneaky cuppa, we'll only be in the way," said Iona Carver.

The Carvers' motorhome was chaotic and cosy with race paraphernalia scattered everywhere. It smelled deliciously of fresh coffee and bacon.

Bambi was nearly bowled over as a large, woolly dog pressed itself against her.

Iona laughed. "Don't mind Bentley, he's big and enthusiastic, but the soppiest dog you'll ever find."

"Oh, he's gorgeous!" cooed Bambi, ruffling his big, floppy blond ears. "I sometimes wish we had a dog; it'd be lovely to bring them along on race weekends. We've got a cat at home, but I don't think he'd be too impressed with that idea."

"Sweet, what's his name?"

"Lucifurr."

Iona guffawed.

"Oh, I know!" said Bambi, laughing, "We called him that because his eyes glow like a demon in the dark and he's always killing things, but it's so embarrassing when you have to call him in from the garden. I'm sure the neighbours think we're devil-worshippers!"

Shifting Dommie's helmet bag out of the way, Bambi gratefully took a mug of coffee. As she sat, Bentley plonked himself firmly across her feet and gazed up adoringly at her. Bambi grinned down at him, he really was lovely.

Wrapping both hands around the mug, she sighed blissfully and took a sip of rich, strong coffee. This was just what she needed. It had been an early start after a busy week at work and she was tired out. She was used to instant coffee in polystyrene cups at racetracks - this was a welcome improvement.

"Who was that awful man?" exclaimed Bambi, then gasped, horrified: "Oh God, it wasn't your husband, was it?"

"No, thank goodness!" snorted Iona. "That was Grant

Lillington. Don't worry about him, he's a bit up himself, but you get used to him. Well, you don't get used to him as much as just ignore him, frankly. Between you and me, I don't know how his wife puts up with him. She must have the patience of a saint to live with him 24/7.

"I think the only way their marriage lasts is because he's out racing every weekend and she has the house to herself."

Bambi sniggered. She'd been sceptical about doing the Nationals, but she was starting to think she might enjoy it. It was certainly nice to see other mums there, and if Iona was anything to go by, they might be good fun. She was used to it being mostly dads at their local track. The mums that came to watch had always been a bit hostile, if she was honest. It was really nice to discover such a friendly atmosphere and think that everyone got on well here.

Jake pushed the kart down to the grid, tailed by Dommie, who was busy giving Max the low-down on everyone in the paddock. They passed a short, pompous boy with white-blond hair and a disdainful expression. He was surrounded by immaculate mechanics and wearing a white race suit with a fluro yellow and turquoise BRR Motorsport logo emblazoned on the front.

Seeing Jake and Max, he sneered. "It's no surprise I'm going to be British Champion this year, just look at the competition." His entourage of mechanics sniggered sycophantically.

Dommie turned to Max and rolled his eyes.

"That," he said, "is Cosmo Aspinall. He's a total idiot. He's got the most money in the paddock and an F1 driver to coach him and it still isn't enough to get him up the front." The boys giggled and Dommie looked back over his shoulder and stuck his tongue out.

"How does he keep that race suit clean?" said Max, sounding awestruck. "My mum would kill me if I got a suit like that dirty! She'd probably only let me wear it when I was on the podium!"

"Yeah, well, he doesn't have to worry about mundane problems like that. He was totally born with a silver spoon in his mouth, he's probably got about ten race-suits, and a butler to fetch them for him. His dad will just buy him a new one every time it gets dirty. From what I hear, they're spending a massive amount this year trying to win the championship. And we're here to stop him." He flashed Max a big grin. "Come on, let's show him what real drivers can do."

Pulling on their helmets and sliding into their seats, the boys started their engines and sped out of the pit lane. Dommie gave Cosmo a loser sign as he raced past him. Chuckling inside his helmet, Max followed his teammates out of the pits. Soon, though, he'd lost sight of Dommie and was stuck trailing behind Finn, who was driving too aggressively and kept sawing at the wheel. Not wanting to cause trouble on his first day with the team, Max did what Chase had instructed and stuck dutifully behind him.

After a couple of frustrating laps, Finn ran wide in one of the hairpins and Max dove down the inside, glad to finally be able to open up the throttle. He started to chase down Dommie, who was now making his way through traffic. His lap times were getting faster but he'd got a huge gap to make up.

After ten minutes, the flag waved signifying the end of the session and the drivers made their way to the pits. As Max turned into the final corner, a kart appeared from nowhere in a flash of white yellow and blue and barged its way past, sending him off the track in a spray of gravel and dust. He just caught sight of Cosmo's lazy, middle-fingered salute before he disappeared into the pit lane.

Ugh, what an idiot thought Max, as he was forced to sit and wait for everyone else to file past before he could pull back onto the track. He found Dommie waiting for him as he finally climbed out of the kart.

"What happened to you? I thought you were catching

me!"

Max wrinkled his nose.

"That Cosmo kid happened to me. Punted me off as we were coming into the pits."

"He's such an idiot," said Dommie. "He's just trying to intimidate you 'cos you're new. Ignore him."

They both turned as they heard shouting, and watched Cosmo swearing and gesticulating angrily at a tall, handsome man wearing sunglasses, designer jeans and an immaculate BRR jacket.

"Oh my God," said Max, "is that Ben Redmaine he's screaming at? I thought you were joking when you said he had his own personal F1 driver!"

"Nope. Daddy Aspinall's paid him lots of money to come and set up a team around precious little Cosmo. Good to see he's not having an easy time of it, though. Bet he's regretting taking Aspinall on now!"

6
RACEHORSES & THE LIVING DEAD

"Oy Ron, look lively, son!" barked Frankie, glancing at his chunky gold watch as they swept into the paddock at an uncompromising pace. They'd made good time. It had only taken an hour and a half to get up to Easthorpe. Which was impressive as it was a 120-mile journey and they'd stopped for breakfast on the way. That was one good thing about early starts, the Old Bill were still in bed so he could keep his foot planted.

Ronnie looked up from his phone for the first time since he got into the car and slipped his headphones off.

Frankie shook his head. *What did the kid find to look at on that bloody phone all day?* He was like a zombie whenever he had that thing in front of him.

He parked his Jag outside a black awning emblazoned with a snarling orange fox and the words Fox Racing picked out in silver. Leaning on his horn Frankie drew peeved glances from onlookers, which cheered him. Fuck 'em. He wasn't here to make friends.

Danny Fox poked his head out of the awning and waved. He was a lean, fit young man with a racing-driver's wiry build, dark hair and a year-round tan. He would have been good-looking if his eyes weren't shifty, too close together and permanently bloodshot. In Frankie's words, there was more fat on a greasy chip than on Danny. He also had a racing driver's ego and a weakness for women and cocaine.

"Frank, bruv! Nice to see you. You ready to go out and win the championship this year?" He slapped Frankie on the shoulder and steered him into the awning. Ronnie's kart was set up on one side, the mechanic Aaron rubbing down the shiny new bodywork like the flanks of a prize racehorse.

Frankie nodded. Impressive. His boy would certainly look the part on track. Things hadn't gone their way last year. In fact, the wheels had come off Ronnie's season towards the end, sometimes literally as they suffered one mechanical problem after another. Frankie had started to doubt whether Danny was pulling his weight and wondered how much his reliance on sniff had affected their results. He'd even considered switching teams over the winter, but this all looked promising. Maybe he had misjudged him.

Running his hand along the bodywork, Frankie became aware of an annoying whine in his ear. He turned and found himself face to face with an earnest, birdlike woman. She had dark hair tied back in a bun and was wearing an oversized Aran sweater. Giving her an impatient look up and down, he noted her sensible hiking boots and freshly scrubbed complexion and inwardly groaned. She was an uber-competitive karting mum if ever he'd seen one, and he was not in the mood to make smalltalk.

"Frank, this is Julia Leech. Eden's mum," said Danny. Frankie glanced over at a scrawny kid with floppy hair and a jutting overbite gloomily munching on celery. That would be Eden. Danny continued with the introductions. "Eden's in his first year of Nationals so he'll be going for the rookie trophy this year."

"Well," simpered Julia, "he's actually terrifically talented. We think he could win the championship. He'd be the first ever child to become British Champion in his first year. The youngest too. If anyone can do it, Eden can."

"We'll see about that," muttered Frankie under his breath.

"Of course," she continued, oblivious to Frankie's growing irritation, "you have to take being an elite athlete super-seriously on all levels, don't you? We're so lucky that Eden is already so health-conscious. He'd rather eat fruit than sweets any day and being vegan really ensures he's only putting good fuel into his body. What you eat is a crucial ingredient to success. Don't you think?"

Fondly remembering the full English breakfast he'd enjoyed on the way up, Frankie grunted and strode over to the coffee machine to get himself a brew. He hadn't had enough caffeine to be dealing with these people. And that Julia was a real one-man crowd. Maybe he was getting soft, losing his edge. Ten years ago, there's no way some muppet would have been snapping at his heels bothering him. They would have known better. Perhaps handing over the reins to Chris wouldn't be a bad thing. He could retire and take the family over to Marbella. Get himself a big, fuck-off manor overlooking the sea and spend every day drinking beer and soaking up sunshine, with none of this shit to put up with.

Sensing someone lurking over his shoulder, he realised Julia had followed him. She waved a crumpled tea bag at him and proceeded to lecture him on the evils of caffeine.

"You shouldn't be drinking that poison! A black sesame and goji berry tea is so invigorating in the morning and calms your adrenals enormously. Are you sure you wouldn't prefer one?"

Eyebrows raised in surprise that she hadn't fucked off yet and damn sure his adrenals weren't in need of calming,

Frankie muttered, "Not a chance, love," and turned his back on her, hoping she'd disappear.

Closing his eyes, he took a gulp of coffee before swearing loudly and spitting it everywhere because it was fucking hot. He took a breath and offered up a silent prayer: *God give me the strength to deal with karting parents without actually murdering one of them.*

Frankie didn't hold with rudeness. Manners had always been a big winner for him, and he felt they were increasingly important in this rapidly changing world, but blanking Julia was better than punching her in the face, which is what he felt like doing.

He knew that was an overreaction, but these days his temper always seemed to be bubbling just under the surface, ready to erupt at the slightest provocation.

Julia decided Frankie wasn't a very nice man. Unused to such apathy, not to mention downright discourtesy, she turned to see where else she could project her energy. She spotted her husband chatting to Danny and strode over.

She suggested he should be putting a new set of tyres on rims rather than standing there gossiping and sent Eden off to get himself hydrated before the first practice session started. Honestly, nothing would get done if she didn't keep an eye on them.

Kevin, a well-groomed and patient man, shrugged at Danny and got to work. He was used to his wife's tyranny and liked an easy life.

If he was honest, he'd much rather have been down the gym than here.

He had a stressful job and worked hard all week and didn't have as much time as he'd like to work out afterwards.

But as, Julia took Eden's karting increasingly seriously, he was finding that even his weekend workouts were being severely hampered. Kevin took pride in his appearance, as the toned biceps peeking out of his tight white t-shirt showed, but he just had to ride this out.

Julia had always gone through fads. They could last anywhere from a few days to a few years, but she always eventually moved onto the next thing.

Besides, Eden seemed to enjoy this and it was good to be doing something as a family.

He also knew from experience that it was easier to give in than create a scene. He had enough stress at work, he didn't need more from Julia.

Danny sauntered over to Frankie and sniggered, throwing a look at Kevin over his shoulder.

"How pussy-whipped is he?"

Frankie gave him a level stare. Stuck between macho bullshit and a self-righteous health freak, Frankie grasped the only non-violent solution he could think of. He waved his phone at Danny and headed outside.

"Got a call to make. Business."

Dialling Chris, he was relieved to speak to someone normal. Straight-talking and no bollocks. Strictly speaking, Frankie hadn't needed to call him. He knew Chris would have everything under control, but it gave him a break from being in the awning.

He'd imagined that having the winter away from racing would have given him a chance to calm down, get some perspective. But he seemed to have just picked up where he left off at the end of last season. Pissed off with a short fuse.

He hated this fucking paddock and everyone in it. They were all out for themselves and you couldn't trust a soul. It was a right nest of vipers. He'd grown up on the tough streets of East London, using his fists to prove himself, but this was a much more vicious environment. People smiled and pretended to be friends with you while they plotted against you. There wasn't one person in the paddock who wouldn't fuck you over to gain an advantage on track.

Sitting in the tinted seclusion of his car, Frankie turned on the radio and tried to relax.

After fifteen minutes, he saw the Leeches heading down to the grid for the first practice session and heaved himself out of the car. He'd go and watch Ronnie - that was why he was here, after all. He couldn't be bothered to go into the awning and face more chat, so he leaned against the Jag and lit a cigar. He'd follow them down when they went.

As the minutes ticked by and his cigar burned shorter, Frankie became increasingly irate. Why were they still in there? They were going to miss the session at this rate!

Hearing the roar of engines as the karts headed out on track, anger flashed through him and he stormed into the awning.

Danny and Aaron were standing chuckling by the kart, with Ronnie still engrossed in his phone.

In a voice heavy with sarcasm, Frankie said loudly, "Sorry gents, am I interrupting you? Are we actually going out on fucking track today? Or am I paying you to just have a social?"

Aaron, who was a conscientious lad, jumped a foot in the air, turned pink and quickly nudged Ronnie to get his helmet on before jogging down to the grid. Danny, however, draped an arm around Frankie's shoulders.

"Don't worry, bruv, we've got loads of testing today, there's no hurry. Besides, Ronnie can drive circles around these clowns. He's rapid."

Frankie's eyes narrowed and he shrugged off Danny's arm. That might be true, but he was paying good money for Danny to do a job, not stand around taking fucking liberties.

If he was going to start taking the piss, they were going to have a problem.

7
ABATTOIRS & EXTRA-MARITALS

Savannah dabbed her face with a towel as she padded into the kitchen. She always felt better after working out. Grabbing a smoothie from the fridge, she slid onto a stool at the breakfast bar, enjoying the chill of the marble worktop against her arms.

She flicked through numerous selfies on her phone, glad she'd taken photos before she got all sweaty. Picking the most flattering picture - posing in her skimpy gym outfit, platinum hair cascading around her shoulders - she typed a message to Dave. I've been working hard. You? Adding a winky face and some heart emojis, her eyes sparkled as she pressed send.

She wondered how their day was going. She didn't know Parker very well yet. Dave's daughter had been packed off to boarding school to avoid getting involved in her parents' divorce and this was the first time she'd been out for a weekend since Savannah had moved in. She'd been apprehensive about how Parker would react to them living together, but she needn't have worried.

Dave had picked her up from school last night and,

despite Savannah's nerves, Parker had seem really laidback about it all. They'd all tucked into a takeaway in front of the telly and then turned in early, ready for their 6am start the next morning.

It was great they had a father-and-daughter activity to do together. Parker was a sweet-natured but awkward kid, she didn't say much, but according to Dave she lit up behind the wheel. At eleven, she was big for her age, taller than most of the boys in her year, but then Dave towered over everyone so perhaps that wasn't surprising.

Savannah didn't know the first thing about karting and Dave hadn't really told her much, but it was a shared passion of theirs, and it had to beat standing at the sidelines of a freezing cold football pitch all winter. Presumably.

It must have been hard for them both with the divorce. It sounded like things had got pretty acrimonious, so anything where they could go off and have some quality time together must be good.

Sipping her smoothie, Savannah stretched with a satisfied sigh and looked around the large, modern kitchen. She loved this room. With its stainless-steel appliances, open-plan breakfast room and big bi-fold doors, the space was bathed in sunshine on mornings like this. If only she could live between this room, the bedroom and the gym, because the rest of the house was as dreary as the interior of a 1970s pub. The spectre of Dave's ex-wife and her terrible taste in interior decorating hung like a malevolent shadow over the building.

Each room sported dark, swirling carpets, matching heavy drapes and a cluttered array of knick-knacks arranged in cabinets. Such was the pub vibe that she half-expected some rooms to smell of stale beer and cigarettes when she walked in. Dave had given her carte blanche to redecorate, but she felt uncomfortable. After all, it wasn't her house.

Still, there was no time like the present. With the rest of the day to herself she was determined to tackle the worst room of all: the sitting room. With the exception of the huge TV mounted on the wall, it was hideous. Not only was the carpet a churning mix of red and brown, reminiscent of an abattoir floor, but both the sofas and curtains matched. What had the woman been thinking?

She missed her friends on days like this, when she could do with a gossipy lunch and a spot of shopping, not to mention some genial encouragement. But there was no going back. Everything had changed the day she met Dave.

That's when she'd discovered they had never been her friends at all. She'd learnt that the hard way.

Initially she'd tried to make things work and keep the friendships going, but the final straw had been their reaction to her new boyfriend. Instead of being happy for her, they made snide remarks about his age and laughed, making nasty comments about him being her Sugar Daddy.

She suspected there was more than an element of jealousy in their reactions. It was true that Dave was well off, and she was living in this big house not having to worry about working or money, but for Savannah it wasn't about that. She hadn't had the best experiences with men in the past, but Dave was different. But her so-called friends just wanted to believe the worst.

Looking back, it was strange to think she had ever been happy with Chaz. Yes, he was young and attractive, albeit in a bit of a showy, over-confident way, and being the manager of the estate agents she worked in Savannah had been flattered when he showed an interest in her. It was only after a few weeks of drunken, after-work coupling and long, boozy lunches, which inevitably culminated in hurried sex in the properties they had the keys to, that she discovered he was married.

Thinking back, she should have realised before. The warning signs had all been there. He never stayed the night, he never invited her over to his house, and always had reasons for her not to call him out of hours. She'd only ever had his work mobile number, which he turned off most evenings.

When she finally confronted him, he'd been totally blasé about it.

"We're all grown-ups here, Sav, you know how this works. We've had fun, but you've always known it's just that." She hadn't, actually. It felt like a slap in the face. Shocked, she'd asked whether he'd ever leave his wife, which was clearly the wrong thing to do. By the end of that day, he had not only ditched her, but unfortunately had to 'let her go'.

Losing your boyfriend and your job on the same day. She hadn't seen that one coming. Nice going, Savannah.

Instead of offering sympathy, her so-called friends had been quick to say, "Well, what did you expect?"

"After all, he is married - did you want to be a home wrecker?"

Plus, it turned out he'd hit on most of them and apparently he'd started sleeping with the latest new girl in the office.

"Surely, you knew? Everyone else did."

It became clear that Chaz was well known for shagging every girl in the office who was stupid enough to fall for his charm. Savannah had been gutted.

Perhaps she should have expected this type of behaviour from a cheat like Chaz, but it was a shock to have her girlfriends turn on her at the same time. She sighed.

Turns out, it's easy enough to be friends when you're going out drinking all the time, but when the chips are down and you realise none of them give a damn about you, that's a real kick in the teeth.

It was at that point that Savannah had met Dave. She

was snivelling dejectedly at a bus stop, still shell-shocked after being fired and dumped in the same afternoon. To make matters worse, she'd had to return the keys to her company car, and she'd always hated public transport.

He sat down next to her and asked if she was OK.

Tall and gruff, with salt and pepper hair slicked back into an Elvis-style quiff, the big stranger startled Savannah at first. His random kindness was such a surprise that it prompted even more tears. This time it had been serious crying: sobbing, hiccoughing, snot, tears and mascara. The full works, all streaming down her face. Not her best look.

To his credit, he sat patiently with her, offering up a big, cotton hanky to mop her face with. She smiled fondly at the memory, *I mean, who carries a handkerchief these days?* Once she was all cried out, he'd nodded to the wine bar across the road and asked her if a glass of wine would help.

An hour later, they were onto their second bottle and her tears had turned to riotous laughter. Face swollen from crying and flushed from the wine, she must have looked a state, but she felt better than she had in a long time. Usually she'd be nipping to the toilets to check her makeup, not drinking too much in case she made 'a show of herself' and checking her phone for messages. That night she relaxed and had fun for the first time in ages.

This big, kind bear of a man had made her feel wonderful. Much later, both of them rather worse for wear, they shared a taxi, and once he'd seen her safely to her doorstep he climbed back into the cab and disappeared into the night.

Savannah had collapsed happily onto her sofa, hugging a cushion and grinning. Who would have thought such a horrible day would turn out so well? Her hand flew to her mouth. She hadn't got his number! She didn't even know his last name! She flopped back and giggled. Oh, who cared. She'd stalk that bus stop until she spotted him again, and this time she wouldn't have a tear-stained, blotchy face. She'd make herself look a million dollars and knock him off his feet!

She needn't have worried. The next morning, she was woken by a furious banging at the door to find an enormous bouquet of flowers standing on her doorstep.

Peeking out from behind them, a small delivery man chirped, "Somebody's a lucky girl today!"

That glow spread back over her face again. It faltered for a moment when she considered the flowers might be an apology from Chaz, but that was unlikely. Shrugging the idea off, she tore open the card. Reading it she grinned - she'd been sure she'd see Dave again! She copied his number off the card and sent him a text, agreeing to meet him that evening, then stretched, catlike, on the sofa, beaming despite her lurking hangover. Perhaps her life was turning around after all. What had been a horrible day yesterday might be the start of something really good.

Things had snowballed after that. They had seen each other practically every day since, and after a couple of months, when she still hadn't found a new job and her rent was overdue, it had seemed like a natural step for her to move in with him. She didn't like the idea of being financially reliant on him but, as he'd reassured her, it was only temporary and gave her the time to make the right decision rather than settling for a dead-end job just to keep a roof over her head.

That was a fortnight ago now and, bless him, he'd done everything to make her feel at home: filling the place with fresh flowers, stocking the fridge with champagne and the super-food smoothies she loved. It felt amazing when he was there with her, but it was a different story when she was there alone. She could almost feel his ex-wife's presence. It was as if she was skulking behind the hideous chintzy curtains giving her the evil eye.

The bedroom had been the first room they'd tackled: chucking out all the 1980s Laura Ashley bedding and turning it into a luxurious, modern sanctuary with lots of faux fur and velvet. It was gorgeous and waking up with him every morning felt like heaven.

What kept niggling away at Savannah was Dave's ex-wife. He simply wouldn't talk about her. She wished he would open up about what happened between them, why they had split up. They were still in the process of divorcing, from what she could tell, so it must have been a pretty recent development.

Her life was an open book to him, and yet every time she quizzed him, he clammed up and changed the subject. Recently she'd stopped asking, but she hadn't stopped wondering. All he'd said was that his ex had had an affair and he didn't want to talk about it.

Savannah really hoped he wasn't on the rebound. She'd fallen hard for him and couldn't bear the thought of him taking his wife back. The sooner she redecorated and eradicated all signs of Dave's ex, the better.

8
ON THE SIDE OF THE ANGELS

Chase tore the wrapper off a large tub of Quality Street, knowing the sound of sweets being opened would get the kids' attention faster than anything else. He rummaged around looking for soft-centres as the kids gathered. The back of the race truck had been converted into a smart little data centre, with a TV screen and laptop so he could go through data and video to help with driver tuition.

Dommie leaned round him to cheekily grab a sweet while his mum wasn't watching. Chase raised an eyebrow.

"You'd better not go hyper on me, Dom, or your mum'll tear strips off me."

Dommie pulled his most innocent face.

"What? Me, boss? Don't know what you're talking about," he said, his voice muffled with toffee.

"Hmm, of course you don't. Right, let's go through this data. In terms of lap times, Dommie was fastest but you two weren't far off him," he gestured at Max and Finn. He pulled up a graph on screen, showing the data from each driver overlaid so he could compare. "Looks like you got the hang of the track pretty quickly, Max. After the first few laps you were consistently banging in good, fast times. In fact, your last five laps were all within a tenth of a second of each other. Let's have a look at your on-board footage and see what your lines were like."

Switching to the camera footage, they watched the first few laps when Max had been behind Finn. Every time Finn missed an apex or went wide, Chase pointed out how he could have taken the corner differently, much to the annoyance of his dad who was lurking behind the kids.

As Finn missed a corner completely and Max finally passed him, he muttered, "Oh, for fuck's sake!" and stalked out. Dommie and Max exchanged a glance, and Finn looked down at his lap, eyes filling with tears. Used to the tantrums of zealous karting dads, Chase ploughed on regardless. There was no point him sugar-coating it if the kid was messing up. It was his job to help him improve.

It soon became clear that, once Max wasn't being held up, he was improving with every lap.

"Blimey," said Chase, "I don't think you put a foot wrong once you got past Finn. You're hitting exactly the right bits of tarmac every lap, no mistakes, and on a circuit you've never driven before. Impressive, very consistent!"

Max frowned.

"But if I'm getting it right, how come I'm still nearly half-a-second off Dom's laptimes?"

"Talent," coughed Dommie, grinning. Max shoved him and laughed.

The corner of Chase's mouth twitched.

"I think it's because your engine isn't very strong. We'll try a different one for the next session." Max, who knew he only had one engine, felt deflated. Chase obviously thought he had half a dozen different motors in the back of the van. He sighed quietly. Perhaps he wouldn't be able to do the Nationals after all. Chase would soon realise that they couldn't afford all this and would lose interest. What would be the point if he couldn't keep up with the others?

Chase, however, came up trumps. When they went

down for the next session, Max saw there was a different engine on his kart, courtesy of Carver, who'd lent them one of his spares.

"Right, boys, let's see what you can do out there!"

Engines roaring, they hurtled back onto the track.

Fifteen laps later, they pulled into the pits, sweaty and elated. Chase ambled over to Max, a big grin on his face.

"What did I tell you? Fastest on track that time! You definitely need to replace that motor and get yourself something better."

Max looked at his dad who was beaming with pride. But how were they going to afford a top engine? They were supposed to be doing this on the kit he already had. He knew money was tight. His mum and dad had made that clear before they'd agreed to do the test day.

Dommie came over and fist-bumped him.

"Well done, Max, you were rapid – and that was on my fifth-best engine as well! I'm going to have to up my game to beat you this season."

They grinned and walked off chatting, only going quiet as they passed Lillington, who was berating Finn.

"Pull your bloody finger out," he hissed. "You're a seeded driver, for Christ's sake, and you're being beaten by a nobody. It's embarrassing."

Dommie slid a glance at Max, who grimaced, and with their heads down they headed back to the awning. It looked like trouble was brewing.

Frankie glowered, his fists clenched. *Who did that balding little prick think he was?*

His earlier mood had lifted as he'd watched Ronnie on track and remembered how much he loved seeing his boy behind the wheel. He'd even felt a flutter of excitement about the coming season. Frankie loved the menacing new look of the kart, all dark and threatening. His boy looked the business out there, and it should put the fear into that toffy-nosed little upstart, Aspinall.

With Cosmo all in white, and Ronnie dressed head to toe in black, it looked like some biblical battle of good versus evil out there - only there was nothing angelic about Aspinall. Not unless you could pay your way through the pearly gates. *Besides,* he smirked, *who wants to be on the side of the angels – it's much better to be feared than loved.*

Frankie stood under a No Smoking sign and noticed his hand trembling slightly as he lit his cigar. He snorted in amusement; his adrenalin was pumping even after a practice session. Christ, he'd missed this. Enjoying the disapproving looks of other parents, he puffed away on his cigar and smiled to himself.

As he stood there, his heart rate gradually calming, Hugo Aspinall, Cosmo's dad, strode passed him and tutted mockingly.

"Such a shame, Ronnie just doesn't seem to have the pace this season, does he?" and, flashing him a smug grin, he walked briskly off.

Gobsmacked by the nerve of the man Frankie stood slack-jawed watching him walk away before scrolling through his phone looking for the timing screens. Shit! What had he been thinking, standing there congratulating himself because the new bodywork looked good? Ronnie's times were awful! He'd only been watching with a casual eye, not properly scrutinising the other people on track.

Why was Ronnie so off the pace? What the fuck was Danny playing at?

He stormed back to the awning, a familiar tightness growing in his chest. Stopping for a moment, he took a few breaths and made an effort to calm down. *No stress, the doctor said.* There was no need to go in all guns blazing, he'd give Danny a chance to explain. See what he had to say first.

Danny was standing smoking a cigarette and flicking through the messages on his phone when Frankie joined him.

"Ron's looking good out there, isn't he, Frank?" he drawled. "He hasn't lost any speed over the winter."

"He looks the business, Danny. Where were we on times? If you're this relaxed, I take it he's the fastest out there?"

Danny shifted slightly.

"Well, not quite. He was up there for the first session, and in that last one I clocked him on a 1:14.42. That's half a second faster than Eden."

"I don't care about being faster than Eden," said Frankie, his voice a low growl. "I'd expect Ronnie to be up the road from him, but it's not him we're here to fucking beat, is it? What about the front runners, like Aspinall and Carver?"

Danny, feeling that Frankie was being a bit unreasonable, pulled up the timings from the second practice session on his phone, which showed Ronnie fifth fastest.

Frankie looked at him, palms upturned.

"What the fuck? You call that fast? We're not here to be coming fifth!" He snatched the phone out of Danny's hands, jabbing at names with a stubby finger. "For Christ's sake, look at the kids in front of us! Both Aspinall and Carver are six-tenths faster, that girl Parker is ahead of us, and I haven't even heard of that kid? Who the fuck is Max Golding?"

Danny gave a dismissive wave of his hand.

"Oh, he's some new kid in Apex. It's only a practice day, Frank, I wouldn't take too much notice. They're probably messing about to make the kid look fast so he signs with the team. You know what it's like. Team bosses try all sorts of tricks to reel people in when they want them to join the team."

Frankie raised an eyebrow. Had Danny ever used tactics like that with him? He was walking a dangerous line if he had.

"I don't care what they're doing, we're not here to be

beaten by a fucking rookie. Stop brown-nosing the new kid and pull your finger out. What the fuck am I paying you for if it's not to get us to the front?"

Julia, who had been hovering waiting to speak to Danny, gave an indignant huff and marched back into the awning. Danny ignored her reaction. She'd just have to wait.

"Come on Frank, you know what it's like," shrugged Danny. "There are no rules on test days, no scrutineering, those kids could be running anything. They might not have the engine restrictors in, be running a dodgy fuel mix, they might have pasted stuff on the tyres to make them sticky. People will use all the tricks in the book to make the kids look fast just to get into our heads. Ignore them! Let's just do our own thing. They won't be able to do any of this once the Nationals start and everything's checked and controlled."

Frankie stepped back, giving Danny an unimpressed glare.

"If they're playing mind games with us, we don't just sit on our arses and play nicely. We up the ante and we make fucking sure we beat them. Pull your finger out, Fox. Get some pace sorted out and I want to see Ronnie at the top of the timings next session."

Hurriedly flicking his spent cigarette, Danny headed back into the awning. He pulled Aaron to one side and told him to take the engine restrictor out for the next session.

"What? Why are we doing that?"

"Frankie wants us to get into everyone else's heads," said Danny, rolling his eyes.

"Yeah, but don't we need to be finding some real pace rather than messing about? Nobody else out there is doing that, we're just off the pace."

"You want to tell him that?"

Aaron gave a half shrug and held his hands up.

"You're the boss."

As Aaron set to work, Danny was cornered by Julia, who had been waiting non-too-patiently for him to come and debrief Eden. Suppressing a sigh, he headed over to try and put the kid right on some of his driving lines, which were terrible.

He thought longingly about the wrap in his pocket. If only he could sneak out to the van and take a line, it would really take the edge off. Lord preserve him from pushy karting parents who all think their kid is the next Lewis Hamilton. They all want their child to be winning, but they can't take criticism and never want to hear that they're anything other than perfect already.

9
LIPSTICK & AMBITION

Jake twisted his wedding ring as he watched Bambi chatting to Iona. How would she react if he asked her to give up their family holiday so that Max could have a new engine? They had always agreed their holiday fund was sacred, not to be dipped into except in the most extreme of circumstances. It was there to ensure they could always take a well-earned break from the daily grind. That was important. But surely, she'd see how vital this was too? They couldn't let Max down, not when he was being given such an opportunity.

Bambi had been leafing through holiday brochures for the Greek Islands since Christmas and he knew she'd be disappointed, but he couldn't think of another way to find the money.

They'd had a good day's testing. Max had done his bit and shown everyone what he could do; he'd confirmed that he deserved a place at the front. They'd just have to find a way to afford this somehow.

Chase gathered the kids round before the final session.

"Well done today. You've all put in some great laps and demonstrated you're quick around here, but as you know it's not always the fastest driver that wins. You have to have the race craft to match that speed if you want to stay ahead. So, for the final session, we're going to have a race. The three of you against each other and whoever crosses the line first wins an ice-cream sundae with all the toppings when we go to the pub tonight."

He held out his fist. "I've got three straws here. Draw one each, and that'll determine the order you start."

The boys each took a straw, Finn managing to draw the longest, prompting a clenched fist and a competitive "Yes!" hissed under his dad's breath. Max drew the middle, and Dommie groaned as he got the shortest.

As they lined up on the grid, Lillington came over and crouched down beside Max.

"Good luck!" he said, clapping Max on the shoulder. Jake was surprised, perhaps he'd misjudged Lillington. The man had been a bit of a dick earlier, but Finn hadn't had the best day so perhaps that was understandable. He seemed to be making an effort now, though. Maybe he wasn't so bad after all.

"Right boys," shouted Chase. "Let's see who our winner's going to be!"

The boys roared out onto the track and the men jogged over to the fence to watch. The three karts hurtled around the first corner, under the bridge and out of sight. When they came back around, Dommie was ahead, followed by Finn, but Max was nowhere to be seen.

Jake's breath caught in his throat. *Where was he? Had he had an accident?* After a few tense seconds, Max reappeared but was going really slowly. What had happened while they were out of sight? Had he got damage? Had one of his teammates smashed him off? It took what felt like an age for Max to trundle slowly round to the pit entrance, shaking his head in frustration. Dommie and Finn were almost a lap ahead by now.

Chase and Jake ran over to see what the problem was. Looking at the engine, Chase shook his head.

"I thought so, the choke was on. He wouldn't even hit half speed like that." He crouched down to Max. "I've fixed the problem. Go do a warm-up lap, then come back in and I'll grid you all up for another start."

Jake ran his hand through his hair.

"How the hell did that happen? I always check I haven't accidentally knocked the choke switch."

"Lillington was talking to Max on the grid, wasn't he?" said Chase, raising an eyebrow.

Jake frowned.

"He wouldn't do that. Would he?"

Shrugging, Chase said, "Looks like he would. Probably his idea of a prank to play on the new kid."

Sure enough, when they got back to the fence Grant, smirking, pulled his best innocent face.

"What?" he said.

Jake glowered.

"Oh, come on, can't you take a joke?" Grant turned back to the track with a nasty smile.

Chase signalled Dommie and Finn to come into the pits so they could restart and Jake saw Lillington's smirk falter. Sending them all back out, Chase jogged over to join Jake by the fence.

Max, who was fired-up with frustration and wanting to prove himself, charged ahead of Finn on the restart, putting him on the grass as they went through the first corner. He was followed through by Dommie, who shunted him further off the track and left him bouncing across the run-off area.

"Oy, what the hell?" bellowed Lillington.

"Looks like a bit of payback to me," murmured Chase with a small smile.

"Seriously, that's how we're playing it, is it? Fucking ridiculous. They're supposed to be teammates." Lillington glowered over the fence, watching as Finn got back on track, now a few hundred yards behind the other two.

"Looks like someone can't take a joke," mumbled Jake

and he saw the corner of Chase's mouth twitch.

After the first corner incident, Finn dropped back further and further so the contest was just between Max and Dommie. They kept pace with each other, battling hard, each getting in front of the other whenever they could. But as they came to cross the line for the end of the session, Dommie was ahead by a nose.

Punching the air, he celebrated for the whole in-lap before coming into the pits and doing a full-on victory dance. When Max took his helmet off, he was laughing.

"Good battle, Dom, well done!"

Carver and Jake shook hands, smiling, but Lillington had stalked off incensed. Chase shrugged. He'd seen it all before. There was no point running after him. Most people weren't happy if they weren't winning, and some just couldn't accept getting beaten. It looked like he'd be having plenty of problems with Lillington in his team this year. There was no way he'd accept being the slowest driver in the team, but it looked like that was where he'd be.

Catching up with Carver and Jake, Chase said, "Come on, let's get packed up and head off to the pub. I could do with a pint."

Chase cranked up some music in the awning and with a banging soundtrack, it didn't take them long to get packed up and ready to leave. Jake was feeling pleased with how the day had gone, but was still shocked after the incident with Lillington. He'd never seen somebody behave like that in the paddock before.

Chase dismissed it as jealousy and said he'd have to get used to it, but to sabotage Max's kart? It seemed like a pretty cruel joke to play on a kid. If not downright spiteful. What if he'd done something that could have caused an accident? He'd have to keep an eye on Lillington from now on. It was going to be difficult being in the same team, but if what Carver said was true there were probably problems like that in every team.

As he took the kart out to load it into the van, he overheard Lillington shouting at a sobbing Finn while throwing the kit into the back of his van. Jake had seen plenty of tears and tantrums in the paddock over the years, but that was a bit much. Blimey, wasn't this supposed to be fun?

Perhaps Jake was just naive. With people taking it so seriously, the Nationals could be very different to what they were used to. If Chase was right, the way Lillington had behaved today was just the tip of the iceberg.

If he had done that on a test day, how far would some people be prepared to go for their kid to become British Champion?

"Oh dear, not so fast in that one?" gloated Frankie, who wasn't a gracious winner at the best of times. He slapped Hugo Aspinall hard on the shoulder, making him wince.

"Not looking so smug now, are you? Ronnie was a good six-tenths up the road from Cosmo in that session." He chuckled as Hugo stomped off, jaw clenched beneath his wobbling jowls. That was a good way to end the day. Ronnie had been rapid, just like he should be. That would get them all worried.

He headed back to the awning, a jaunty spring in his step. Clapping his hands together, he said, "Job well done, Danny. Job well done," and pushed a roll of £50 notes into Danny's hand.

"Aren't you coming to the pub, Frank?"

"Nah. I'm not here to make friends with these people. We're heading straight off. See you at Round One." Walking over to Aaron, he paid him too, then stood, his arms folded in satisfaction as he watched the mechanic meticulously check the kart over.

Stopping for a moment, Aaron twisted a rag between his hands and turned to Frankie.

"Mr Finch? Don't you think we should do some more

testing before the first round? Straight testing, so we know what our real pace is? Running with the restrictor out means we don't know how we'll fare against the competition when it comes to it."

Frankie chuckled indulgently.

"Don't be such a worrier. We'll be fine. Ronnie was fastest by a mile in that last session! Besides, Danny's taking the engines up to Biggs next week to make sure they're all top notch, so we've got nothing to worry about."

Aaron's forehead creased, and he wondered how much he could push his point with Frankie. He didn't see the point of being fast if you were running with illegal mods you couldn't use on a race weekend. He also hadn't been convinced by Danny's assurances that all the other fast drivers were doing the same. He wanted to say this to Frankie, but Julia had just joined the conversation, turning it back to Eden of course. Not wishing to say anything in front of her, he kept quiet and went back to checking the kart over.

Julia had been getting increasingly frustrated as the day progressed. She'd expected Eden to be one of the fastest on track, but Ronnie seemed to be getting further and further ahead with Eden making no real progress. Danny's placations that "he'll get there in the end" and "he just needs more practice" weren't what she wanted to hear. Her son was going to be British Champion this year, but to do that they required Danny's full support.

She needed to find a way of getting Danny to help Eden more if they wanted to beat their teammate, not to mention the rest of the field. The Finch family were definitely getting the lion's share of Danny's attention. Her fingers tapped on her thigh as she considered her options. As much as she wanted to shout at Danny right now, that probably wasn't the best way to handle him. She suspected he'd respond better to softer handling; after all, he'd had

Frankie bellowing at him all weekend so a different approach might be more effective. A smile tugged at the corner of her lips and she headed back to her motorhome. Emerging ten minutes later, she looked a different woman. The baggy jumper had been replaced with one of Eden's team t-shirts straining over her bra-less chest, her hair had been released from its tight bun and she was wearing lipstick.

Danny had finished packing up the van and was fingering the wrap in his jacket. Hearing footsteps behind him he spun guiltily on his heel, shoving his hands deep in his pockets and found Julia blocking his path. His heart sank; the last thing he needed was more moaning from her. To his surprise, she moved closer to him and, instead of complaining she murmured:

"Thanks for today, Danny, it's been good."

He inhaled deeply. She smelled of patchouli oil and soap, it was kind of sexy. She gave him a coy smile and toyed with a tendril of hair.

"Sorry for being a bit grumpy with you earlier. You were right, Eden does just need more time in the seat. Maybe we could sort out a practice day when it's just us?" She looked up at him through her eyelashes and ran a finger down Danny's chest. Leaning close to his ear, she whispered, "I'd love to do some one-on-one with you."

She heard his breath hitch and saw goosebumps prickle his arms. She smiled to herself. *Yes, this was definitely a better way of handling him.*

Danny leaned back against the van and looked at her, eyes twinkling.

"I'm sure I could sort something out. Call me during the week and we'll hook up". Julia nodded, a playful smile on her lips.

"OK, see you at the pub." She walked away, hips swaying. Danny watched her, mesmerised, till she disappeared around the corner, then shook his head. Checking his reflection in the van, he winked at himself.

He shouldn't be surprised. How could she resist the famous Fox charm?

10
A RUDE AWAKENING

Ben Redmaine was relieved when the last session finished. He'd planned to let the team pretty much run itself, but he'd already been dragged in far more than he'd wanted to be. So much for just being a figurehead and spending the profits. It looked like Hugo Aspinall wasn't going to let him off that lightly. The man was intent on treating Ben like a skivvy.

Ben had finally met Cosmo for the first time today and the kid had been everything he'd expected.

He'd taken both drivers on a track walk that morning, only to be informed by Cosmo that he knew everything already. The little show-off had ambled round in his fur-lined designer coat, bragging about everything he'd won and how fast he'd been during winter testing in Dubai.

Ben tried to bring Parker into the conversation, aware she was trailing silently behind them. But when she did speak, instead of asking a driving question, she'd asked Cosmo whether that was real fur on his hood.

Cosmo sneered back. "Of course it is. It's designer, not like your £10 Marks & Spencer coat."

Nice, thought Ben, as he saw Parker clam up, her eyes

narrowed. *Way to go alienating your teammate.* So much for team harmony. It was going to be a struggle to get these two kids working together.

Cosmo should realise he needed a helpful teammate, instead of thinking he could do everything by himself. He'd clearly been brought up believing he was superior and automatically entitled to win. Ben could see this was going to be an uphill battle. Cosmo could do with being knocked down a peg or two.

Ben tried gamely to advise the best line to take through a tricky double right-hander, but was dismissed by Cosmo, who said he knew the track like the back of his hand.

"In fact," the little brat had added, "I probably know it better than you do. When was the last time you drove this circuit in a kart?"

Ben gritted his teeth.

"Well, I expect you to be the fastest on track today, then. You've got no excuse, if you know it all already."

Unfazed, Cosmo had scoffed, "I don't think so. If I'm not fastest, that's your fault. That's what my dad's paying you for. If I'm not at the top of the timesheets you'll be in big trouble."

What a little shit, thought Ben. He's even worse than I expected.

Ben tried ignoring Cosmo and chatted to Parker, endeavouring to draw her out of her shell. He asked her about the braking zone and the line she would take, but Cosmo just talked over them, demanding their attention with an arrogance that was hard to ignore, showing them his new Rolex and wanting Ben to watch videos of him on a jet ski in the Caribbean.

Ben was sorely tempted to tell the kid to shut the fuck up, but he knew he had to keep his temper. He'd send a mechanic out to do the track walk next time.

The day hadn't really improved from there. To Ben's irritation, Cosmo had indeed been fastest in the first session. He'd been hoping Cosmo would mess up and have to admit he needed help.

More annoying still, it wasn't that Cosmo was driving well, but rather that he had enough power to get away with the mistakes he was making. When Ben suggested going through footage to see where he could improve, Cosmo had refused, saying he knew what he was doing.

Ben could feel a headache coming on.

As the day progressed, the other drivers improved and Ben's day deteriorated further. With Cosmo still steadfastly refusing to admit the problem could be him, Ben focused on Parker who, under his guidance, improved steadily with every session.

The Apex kids got faster throughout the day, as did Ronnie Finch. Instead of making Cosmo realise he needed to improve his driving, he'd thrown a tantrum, screaming about how bad the kart was, how down he was on power, and how it was all Ben's fault.

That, of course, had set Hugo off. In an effort of supreme self-control, Ben explained that Cosmo's kit was the best out there, that no expense had been spared. He was confident they'd got the best power in the paddock, the issue was that Cosmo needed to improve his driving. He needed to swallow his pride and take the time to look through the video and data, and take some advice on where he could improve.

Ben could see that Hugo struggled with this. While he could see it was the right approach, Hugo hadn't done a lot of hands-on parenting and Ben suspected he was a little frightened of standing up to his precocious offspring.

Hugo faltered, torn between blustering angrily at Ben that it couldn't be Cosmo's fault, and knowing that they needed every advantage if they were going to win this year.

In the end, common sense won out. After a hushed row, Hugo grabbed Cosmo by the arm and shoved him towards Ben to go look at the data.

Ben sighed. He'd hoped his work was done for the day,

but it looked like there was still some pain to go through. Cosmo wasn't going to take criticism well. Ben was going to have to earn his money the hard way.

11
DRINKING & DELUSIONS

The Carpenters Arms was a snug village pub, which had seen over a quarter of a century of daily drinking. Built in grey limestone, with a roaring fire in the grate, on a typical evening it had two regulars propping up the bar, which suited them just fine, thank you very much.

Alan, the landlord, was a generously proportioned man, who appreciated good bar food and always had a broad smile for his punters. He also kept a keen eye on the race calendar because on race weekends his pub transformed into the busiest in rural Lincolnshire. Only paying scant attention to the grumblings of one-legged Tom at the bar he spotted the first van entering the car park and rubbed his hands together.

"Right, gentlemen. We're about to be invaded. Any food orders, I'd get them in now before the crowds arrive and we're run off our feet." Groaning and mumbling half-hearted complaints, the regulars braced themselves for the flood of outsiders. Soon the pub was buzzing with raucous conversation and bright race jackets, standing room only.

Chase was quick to find the best spot, settling himself at a large oak table by the fire. While the rest of the team sat themselves around him, Bambi and Iona headed to the bar to get the drinks in. As they waited to be served, Bambi scanned the menu, eyeing the lasagne with garlic bread longingly. She sighed, her tummy rumbling, but decided on a chicken salad instead.

"I've put on so much weight over the last year or so. It's all the cheesy chips and bacon butties at racetracks, I just can't resist them! I think it's stress-eating."

"Not to mention all the wine!" laughed Iona. "I hardly eat on a race weekend; I get so nervous, even the thought of food makes me feel sick. I tend to replace it with prosecco on race days, it definitely takes the edge off my nerves!"

Julia, who was planning on working further on Danny that evening, arrived next to them at the bar and waved a £50 note at the barman. Eavesdropping shamelessly, she butted in:

"Oh, I simply must give you my recipe for lasagne. You'd never know it was vegan. Everyone who's tried it says it's impossible to tell the difference. Those excess pounds would just drop off if you cut out all that meat and cheese," she simpered.

"Thanks," said Bambi, colour rising in her cheeks. "That would be great." She was racking her brains trying to think who the woman was. She looked vaguely familiar. Where did she recognise her from?

Luckily the barman, who was fair to a fault, chose that moment to come over. He'd seen Julia barge her way to the front and made a point of ignoring her and the cash she was wafting around. Turning to Bambi and Iona, he gave them his most welcoming smile.

"Right ladies, what can I get you?"

Shortly afterwards, as Bambi made her way carefully over to the table under the weight of many pints of beer and a bottle of wine, all of which rattled precariously, she whispered:

"Who was that?"

"Uh, isn't she awful?" responded Iona, reaching to steady the wobbling tray as Bambi sloshed the drinks around. "That's Eden Leech's mum. They race at our local club and, to put it politely, she's intensely focused. Mega pushy and never shuts up about how perfect her child is. I think she's competing with Hillary Aspinall for most nauseating mum in the paddock."

Bambi frowned, taking a big gulp of wine.

"Oh, I don't think I've met her yet. Is Aspinall that blond boy in Ben Redmaine's team?"

"Yes. Wads of cash, that family, and they make sure everyone knows it too. She's another one who has a perfect life and can't stop telling everyone how blessed she is, even though her husband is a serial philanderer." Glancing sideways, Iona snorted and nudged Bambi. "Talking of philandering…" she jerked her head over to where Julia was flipping her hair and pouting at Danny Fox and they both collapsed into fits of giggles.

Bambi was having the most fun she'd had in ages. She hadn't eaten anything except a piece of rocky road today and the wine was going straight to her head. With Iona around, the Nationals could end up being fun. All this gossip made it a bit like being in a soap opera.

Oblivious to the girls' scurrilous chat, the men were discussing the likely winners of that year's championship. They analysed each competitor in turn.

"It looks like Dommie's in there with a good chance," said Jake.

Carver shrugged.

"He's been in with a good chance the last two years, but he loses his head too often. It only takes a couple of penalties or bad results and he'll be out of the running. We're trying to get the right people around him to calm him down this year so he can keep his focus, but as you can see it's going to be an uphill struggle." He gestured over to where the kids were playing pool, Dommie twirling his pool cue and roaring in a celebratory twerk after potting two balls in a row.

Carver gave a wry laugh. "Don't get me wrong, he's a good little driver, but only when his head's in the right place. If he can keep calm and focused, he could have a good year, but I'm not holding my breath. He's had too many run-ins with the stewards in the past, and he's earned himself a reputation. They'll be watching his every move this season."

Chase ran a hand through his hair, making it even wilder.

"He'll be alright, mate," he said. "Dommie just needs to keep it calm and he'll be fine." He turned to Jake. "As will Max after today's performance, but not on that engine you've got. We definitely need to get you on a Biggs engine."

Jake sighed, brow furrowed.

"It does look like we need a bigger engine."

"Ha, yes, that too, but I mean one from Biggs Racing Engines. Self-proclaimed best engine builders in the paddock. Although, to be fair, all the top kids are on Biggs engines. You won't get higher than mid-pack with the motor you've got now, no matter how well Max drives."

"It's true, Max was way faster when he borrowed your engine, Carver. I don't suppose you're selling that one, are you?"

"I could do." He considered for a minute. He had four engines that were better than that one, and he could do with the cash right now. Things had been a bit tight recently. He gave a half shrug and flashed Jake a smile. "Sure, why not."

Jake was flooded with relief. He'd been worried about being able to find a really good engine this late in the season. The relief was tempered by the nagging worry that this was rapidly becoming more expensive than they'd budgeted for. But, he reasoned, if they were doing the

Nationals, they may as well give it a proper go. No point just making up the numbers if they could run at the front.

He drained the last of his beer and readied himself to get the next round in. If only he wasn't driving. He could do with something a lot stiffer than an orange juice to take away the stresses of the day, especially with the way Lillington had been behaving.

"Is Lillington usually such a tosser about everything?"

Carver laughed.

"Pretty much. Nobody likes being beaten, but he takes it particularly badly, especially being beaten by a teammate. Your teammates are always your biggest rivals, more so when they're a newbie and it's their first day with the team."

"I guess so. I'm just shocked about that stunt he pulled with the choke; it seemed a bit childish."

"Not to mention vindictive. Be grateful you had a heads-up about him now. If he's willing to do that on a test day, he's probably capable of worse on a big race weekend. Lillington is desperate for Finn to succeed. Sometimes I wonder whether the kid even likes racing. I think he just does it so his dad can vicariously live out his F1 dreams through him."

Jake felt a bit uncomfortable. Is that what he was doing, too? He never got the chance to do any kind of racing when he was growing up. His dad banned anything with wheels after he came off his bike and broke his leg, aged eight. Had he pushed Max into this?

He shrugged the thought off. Even if he did encourage Max to begin with, the kid loved racing now and wouldn't give it up for the world. Plus, if the Nationals gave him a chance to get scouted…

He voiced his thoughts.

"Surely, though, some of these kids will make it into F1?"

Carver clapped him on the shoulder and laughed heartily.

"There speaks a true karting dad. The Formula 1 drivers of the future have to come from somewhere, right?"

Jake shrugged.

"Well, they do though, don't they?"

"Look. It's true that most professional racing drivers start out in karting - after all, it's the only racing you can do until you're fourteen - but talent can only take you so far in this game. Even at this age, some kids only do three-day weeks at school and spend the rest of their time being coached by the best drivers in the business.

"With the backing of massive teams and an unlimited budget they soon catch up with the naturally talented kids who can only afford to get in the seat a couple of times a month. Don't kid yourself, if you do progress further, a year in an entry-level single-seater class will set you back quarter of a million, and if that isn't small change to you, you certainly can't afford to get your kid a drive in F1."

Jake sighed, deflated. Talk about a reality check. So much for Max having a great year in the Nationals and being signed up by the Red Bull programme.

"Like Aspinall paying for his own private F1 driver to build a team around his kid, I suppose. Where does all his money come from anyway?"

"He's some fat cat city banker."

Jake laughed. "Is that rhyming slang?"

Carver grinned. "Pretty apt, eh? Sadly, Aspinall is one of the few kids in the paddock who does stand a chance of making it. His family have enough cash and sufficiently few scruples to screw over anyone that gets in their way.

"Don't kid yourself, Jake, they might call F1 the piranha club, but motorsport at this level is just as cut-throat. You'll find most people are smiling assassins who would do anything to get rid of the competition given the opportunity.

"A lot of this sport isn't about what's fair, it's about what you can get away with. Take last year's championship.

The kid who won was excluded from a race meeting mid-season for running an illegal engine, so everyone thought he was out of it. Then daddy hired an expensive lawyer and they managed to get it thrown out because some poor sod had filled in the paperwork incorrectly. So, a known cheat won the British Championship.

"Everyone in the paddock knows he cheated, but what does he care? It's only the people who were racing him that know, and he's still British Champion."

"You're kidding me? That's unbelievable! I had no idea it would be this ruthless. I guess that trick Lillington pulled should be the least of my worries."

Carver laughed.

"Now you're getting it! How you've lasted this long in karting being as trusting as you are, I don't know. You need to toughen up and keep your eyes peeled. You'll see a lot worse than Lillington and his petty tricks over the coming season, especially as it looks like Max is going to be running at the front."

12
STEAK & LASHINGS OF RAIN

Two weeks later, on the morning of the first round of the Nationals, Easthorpe International couldn't have looked more different. The sky was sullen, the track shrouded beneath a blanket of cloud like a child that doesn't want to get out of bed. Jake was exhausted.

After staying up in his garage into the early hours making sure everything was ready, he'd fallen into bed the previous night only to find he couldn't sleep. When he did finally doze off, his mind was filled with turbulent dreams and he kept waking in a panic that he'd missed his alarm.

By the time his clock finally buzzed at 6am, he felt more tired than before he'd gone to bed. Work had refused him the time off, so he had decided to pull a sickie. Needs must and all that. At least, when he had to call in 'sick', it wasn't much of a stretch to make himself sound convincingly dreadful.

Downing a hasty cup of tea, he'd bundled a drowsy Max out of bed and into the front of the van, where he promptly fell back asleep. Jake looked over at him, envious that he could nap so easily, and his smile softened. Max looked so young when he was asleep. All that attitude and energy fell away and he looked so young and innocent. He hoped he was doing the right thing putting Max into the Nationals. It seemed a bit of a shark tank compared to club level racing; he needed to be really vigilant to make sure Lillington didn't pull any more stunts to try and knobble them.

He'd caught Max watching old reruns of the Nationals on YouTube during the week, and they'd sat together watching them for hours, wide-eyed. Max really wanted this, so he'd do his damned best to make sure he got a fair shot at the title.

It was nearly 7.30 as they pulled into the paddock. Scrabbling around looking for his security pass, Jake held up a big queue of impatiently honking vans and race trucks waiting to get into the circuit. Max yawned blearily and stretched; he'd managed to sleep through the whole journey.

They'd never been to this track in the wet, so Jake was glad they had Friday practice before the real racing started on Saturday morning. They had a lot of work to do if they wanted to get up to speed.

Jake started unloading everything from the van and shouted Max to get his suit on. The first practice session was starting in half an hour and they couldn't afford to miss any track time.

Max poked his head round the door, his hood pulled up against the steady drizzle.

"Where's my suit, dad?"

"In the back near the kit bag."

"No, it isn't."

Jake sighed. That boy searched with his eyes closed most of the time. Reluctant to leave the kart unattended, he glanced around and saw Lillington was busy on the other side of the awning. The last thing he needed was that man tampering with anything. Why couldn't Max find the suit without his help?

He dashed out to the van and started tipping everything upside down, searching. *Where was it?* Jeez, they hadn't left it at home, had they? Rubbing his forehead, he dialled Bambi, hoping she hadn't yet left for work. He stood tapping his foot, listening to it ring. No answer. He sighed impatiently. Oh well, he'd have to get her to bring the suit up later.

"Just put your old suit on for now. We need to get out on track."

Seeing the crestfallen look on Max's face, Jake put a hand on his shoulder. "Sorry, son, I know you were looking forward to wearing it, but I'll just have to get your mum to bring it up tonight."

What a start to the day. Max had been so excited when his flashy new Apex Motorsport race suit had arrived last week. He'd never had a fancy, custom race suit before. It was red, white and blue with a large Apex Motorsport logo on the back and GOLDING spelled out in large letters across the shoulders.

When Jake had looked in on the sleeping Max later that night, he'd found him fast asleep wearing it. The last time he'd done that was with a pair of Lightning McQueen trainers with flashing lights when he was about four. He'd been so excited. And now he was going to have to do the first day of the Nationals in his scruffy old suit, which was fraying at the seams.

He so hadn't wanted Max to feel like the poor kid in the paddock. *Oh well, if the rain kept coming down, he'd be wearing his wetsuit over the top anyway.* Besides, there was nothing Jake could do.

Feeling he'd already let Max down Jake resolved to ensure the rest of the day went well. At least they had that fast, new engine to use. He frowned as he thought back to Bambi's reaction. He'd expected her to be angry, for them to have a row, but she'd just shrugged and said they could go on holiday when the season was done instead. After all, it was only for this year. He'd been glad she'd taken the news so well, but a little unsettled by it. The problem was, Jake wasn't so sure it would be just for this year. If Max had a good season, he couldn't see them just going back to racing at their local club once a month. This would be the start of an exciting journey. That reminded him, he needed to focus and make sure he didn't mess anything else up.

Chase wasn't anywhere to be seen before the first session, and everyone in the awning was frantically busy getting themselves ready, so he grabbed the only set of wet tyres they had out of the van and set about getting the kart ready as best he could.

Unfortunately, the first session was a disaster. Max's wetsuit was old and didn't really keep the rain out, so he came in cold and damp. The kart hadn't been fast, and he just hadn't had enough grip to keep it on the circuit, spinning off regularly. He hadn't been the only driver having problems but looking at the timing, Aspinall and Finch had been about two seconds a lap faster.

Where should he start? Was it the tyres or the setup that were so wrong? Jake rubbed his forehead wearily. What a start to the weekend.

Luckily, by the time they got back to the awning, dripping and disheartened, Chase had appeared. Jake slipped Max a fiver to go and get himself a hot chocolate and a bacon bap from the café while they looked over the kart.

Chase whistled.

"Man, I'm not surprised you were slow. Those tyres are shot. Plus, you're on the wrong gearing and your tyre pressures are way too low. Change the sprocket and put some new wets on and let's see how we go in the next session." Running his hands through his unruly hair, Chase said, "Sorry I wasn't here first thing, I overslept." He smiled that lopsided smile. "Don't worry, we'll get you sorted."

Sighing at the thought of shelling out money for new tyres just for the test day, Jake trudged over to the circuit shop. At least Chase seemed confident about what to do to get them up to speed. If they were doing this on their own, it'd be a nightmare to find the right setup.

By the time he got back Max was sitting in the front of the van with the heater on full blast, steaming up the windows as he dried out. He wished Bambi were there to help out. Why couldn't she have pulled a sickie like he did? He'd broached the idea a few nights ago, but she'd sternly reminded him that they couldn't even afford to go on holiday this year, so somebody needed to make sure the money kept coming in.

He felt a pang of guilt. They'd hardly seen each other over the past few weeks. He'd been spending all his spare time getting the kart kit prepped and she'd been putting in overtime to try and pay for that new engine. He thought back to the night before, when they'd gone to bed on a row. If he was honest, it was probably mostly because he was snappy and stressed about the weekend. He should call and smooth things over. He didn't like it when they argued, but right now he needed to crack on and get ready for the second session. Bambi would just have to wait till later.

That evening, when they finally got to the hotel, Jake and Max were both tired, grumpy and cold to the bone. Max had gone off to play with his new friends after the practice had finished, and after a long day of struggling with setup and standing in the rain Jake's mood plummeted fast when he had to trudge around the circuit in the dark trying to find him.

After half an hour of looking, when he did finally find Max he lost his temper and shouted at him in front of his new mates. Max had trudged unhappily back to the van and they'd driven to the hotel in silence. Jake was lost in his own thoughts. What with having to pay for the hotel, meals for the weekend, the new engine, race suit, and unexpected sets of new tyres, he was starting to realise the Nationals were a lot more expensive than he'd anticipated.

At least the hotel was on his credit card, so he wouldn't have to find the money for that straight away. Feeling guilty for shouting at Max in front of his friends, he smiled over at him.

"Come on champ," he said, giving him a squeeze. "It's been a tough day and we could do with a treat." He ordered them both steak and chips on room service, and they snuggled up in front of a movie.

By the time Bambi arrived after a long, congested drive up, she found them both cuddled up fast asleep, the TV still on, with trays and plates scattered all over the bed. Smiling to herself, she tucked the covers around them and put the empty dishes outside the door before climbing in beside her boys, exhausted.

Savannah frowned. Half awake, unfamiliar sounds filtered into her consciousness and it took her a few moments to get her bearings. As she opened her eyes and realised she was in the motorhome, confusion was replaced by a weighty feeling of dread.

Yesterday had been really productive. After Dave's encouragement she'd taken the plunge and finally got decorators in, getting the living room transformed from 1970s nightmare to something gorgeous and Instagrammable, but by the time the carpets were laid, the workmen had left and all the furniture was back in place, it was late. Much later than she'd planned. So instead of setting off mid-afternoon she'd endured a dark, late-night drive to the track through the back roads of Lincolnshire, which had been horribly nerve-jangling.

Torrential rain lashed down, making visibility terrible, and it hadn't helped that she was driving Dave's massive Range Rover. She wasn't used to driving such a big car, especially at night and in such awful conditions. The narrow lanes were full of blind corners and ruts and on main roads lorries barrelled past her, spattering her windscreen with rivulets of spray. Most of the driving she'd done in the past was around town in the company Mini when she was showing properties; nothing like this.

By the time she finally arrived, it was approaching midnight. Parker had been fast asleep for hours, and Dave had been anxiously pacing the paddock worrying that something had happened to her. Relieved and worn out, they'd shared a few glasses of wine and gone straight to bed themselves. It was such a relief to cuddle up under the duvet with Dave after that horrible journey, and even with the rain coming down and the wind buffeting the motorhome she fell asleep feeling that everything was alright with the world.

What the horrendous drive had achieved was distracting Savannah from the real problem facing her this weekend. Meeting Dave's ex-wife. Part of her was curious about the mysterious Cassandra, but she was also apprehensive. Dave was as reluctant as ever to talk about her, so she had very little to go on. She knew nothing about their breakup, other than it had been (and still was) acrimonious. Savannah was pretty confident that Cassandra wouldn't welcome her with open arms. Dave had shrugged it off as being nothing to worry about, insisting that his wife was 'ancient history', but she could tell he was nervous too. What had happened between them for things to go wrong? They had only split six months earlier, so something major must have happened. Could it be that Dave was on the rebound and would get back with his ex if he could?

Hoping that Cassandra would turn out to be some washed-out middle-aged frump, Savannah opened her suitcase and looked at the clothes she'd packed. What do you wear at a racetrack? Picturing the glamorous pit lane at the Monaco Grand Prix, but making a slight concession to the wintry weather, she picked out a figure-hugging jersey dress, with a deep side split and a leather jacket to wear over the top, finishing the look with some large sunglasses. No, perhaps it wasn't quite the weather for those. She slipped on a pair of wedges instead of heels as a nod to practicality. As her mum always said, it's always better to be overdressed than underdressed, and it wasn't like she was going to be getting her hands dirty doing oil changes or anything.

Dave and Parker were ready to head over to the team awning, but Savannah hung back, unsure whether to go with them or to stay out of the way. Dave slipped an arm around her waist, as if her tagging along was the most natural thing in the world.

"Come on love, come meet everyone."

Walking into the BRR awning, she was impressed with how professional it was. A large, airy, white marquee with frosted glass doors and vibrant yellow and blue BRR logos splashed across it, everything inside was spotless. Each kart was in a separate bay on its gleaming silver trolley, surrounded by fit, young mechanics in their smart uniforms, BRR bodywork shining under the lights.

Parker, who had been ambling a few steps behind them - race suit already on, headphones in, totally disengaged - strolled past and plonked herself in a plastic chair. Savannah smiled. That kid wasn't fazed by anything.

The one person Savannah recognised in the awning was Ben Redmaine, who was standing chatting to one of his mechanics. When he spotted them, he flashed one of his glorious megawatt smiles. With his year-round tan, which crinkled around his eyes when he smiled, and those floppy blond curls, he certainly was a good-looking boy. Just the kind she'd had more than enough of. Luckily, she wasn't getting any flirty vibes from him, so that was a relief. She didn't need that kind of complication, especially this weekend.

Introductions made, Savannah was startled to find a purposeful woman closing in on her. Sensibly Sloaney and armed with an overbearing smile she sported glossy auburn hair and an immaculate cotton blouse. Her corduroy trousers, which were tucked into Hunter wellies, strained over a generous bottom.

"Welcome to BRR, darling. You simply must come and have a coffee with me and tell me all about yourself," drawled Hillary Aspinall, linking her arm through Savannah's and steering her over to the little café area at the back of the awning. "Latte or Americano? There isn't much choice I'm afraid, it's a bit like East Berlin in here! I must have a word and get them to bring some chai latte and Earl Grey tomorrow. I don't see why we should be slumming it with the prices we're paying, do you darling?" She gave a braying laugh. "Oh, of course, I know it's Dave who's paying, not you dear, but he needs to feel he's in the right kind of environment. We don't want any instant coffee in polystyrene cups in here, thank you very much!"

Savannah wasn't sure how to respond to that, but luckily Hillary wasn't waiting for a response. She steamrollered on. "You must have heard of our little Cosmo, of course. He's the superstar of the paddock really, but still so humble, bless him. Everyone's tipping him to win the Nationals this year, we're just so proud."

Savannah reluctantly accepted coffee and a seat. She must make an effort. This was Dave's world and now they were together she needed to get comfortable in this environment. His ex-wife must have fitted in, so she had to try. She tuned back into Hillary.

"I've heard so much about you from Cassandra - I was simply dying to meet you." Savannah's eyes widened. She dreaded to think what Dave's ex-wife had been telling her. She was willing to bet none of it was flattering - or accurate, seeing as they'd never even met. As Hillary droned on about her tireless charity work for those less fortunate and how important it was to be giving something back to the community, Savannah pulled herself together. She could handle this. Hillary was a bit of a bore but was probably harmless otherwise. Luckily only minimal input was needed from her audience. Just the occasional nod and smile from Savannah seemed to be enough to keep her happy. The woman could talk for Britain; perhaps she was British Champion of that.

Tuning out the monologue, Savannah spied a portly man with a pink face, wearing Armani jeans and a striped business shirt, who was giving her a hungry look up and down. Seeing her glancing in his direction, he gave her a salacious wink and wiggled porky little fingers at her. Mortified, Savannah quickly turned back to Hillary. *Was that her husband?*

Oblivious, Hillary hadn't even paused for breath and was saying how marvellously blessed she was to have two such talented and kind children, who seemed to apply themselves with such a fabulous work ethic to everything they did. "Not only is Cosmo an incredibly gifted driver," she asserted, "but he's also an accomplished pianist. He inspires me every day with his positive attitude and dedication."

Glancing over at Cosmo, who was slouched in the corner eating blueberries while picking his nose, Savannah wondered if Hillary could possibly be talking about the same child.

I must try and make an effort, she chided herself. Hillary really does seem like a good person, and she's being very kind taking me under her wing. If only she could find a way to escape back to the motorhome. Resigning herself to being stuck for some time, she plopped a sugar cube in her coffee and took a croissant from the buffet.

"Naughty, naughty," admonished Hillary, earning herself a surprised glance from Savannah. "Of course, you're still at the age where you can eat anything you like. I used to be like that. Stick thin with a magnificent bosom. Sadly, as soon as you hit the dreaded Four-Oh, your metabolism grinds to a standstill. One serving of tiramisu and it takes a whole week of Ashtanga yoga to get back into my jeans. I'm sure you'll find the same when you get older, dear - just ask Dave." She laughed her annoying laugh and Savannah bristled.

Oblivious, Hillary ploughed on. "Of course, being a newbie in the paddock I don't suppose you know anything, darling. I'll give you a quick primer so you don't need to keep bothering Dave. Husbands get very grumpy if we get in the way on race weekends, they're just so focused.

"You missed the practice day yesterday, didn't you, dear?" she continued with a hint of disapproval in her voice. "Today we start with qualifying, which is followed by three heats, which are like little races. You get points for all of those, but the important day is tomorrow when you have the pre-final and the grand final – that's the one with the trophies, darling." Hillary lowered her voice conspiratorially. "I don't think you need to be worrying yourself too much about that, though. Parker's not really in with a chance of winning, so you may as well just relax and enjoy the ride!"

Savannah, who already knew perfectly well how everything worked, nodded absent-mindedly. Talk about patronising.

Everyone was getting ready to go down to the grid for qualifying, so she muttered an excuse and made her way back over to Dave.

Just then, like a whirlwind entering the awning, a woman who could only be Dave's ex-wife strode in cooeeing to everyone and ostentatiously air-kissing Ben Redmaine and Hillary. She was trailed by a handsome man with greying hair, who looked as uncomfortable as Savannah felt and who was presumably the new boyfriend.

"Hillary, sweetie! It's so good to see you!" she shrieked dramatically. "I've missed our little tête-à-tête's so much over the winter! I must introduce you to Patrick. He's my absolute rock and was just dying to come and see Parker race today." Patrick didn't look like he had been dying to come. If anything, he looked like he wanted to be somewhere else. As if suddenly remembering, Cassandra looked around for her beloved offspring. Spotting Parker sitting playing on her phone, she strode over and grabbed both of Parker's cheeks, planting a big lipstick kiss on her forehead. "Best of luck, darling!"

"Hi mum," mumbled Parker, wiping her forehead before pulling her helmet on. Cassandra threw her head back in indulgent amusement. "Oh, I don't know who she gets it from, she's such a tomboy!"

Arms linked with Hillary, and pretending that Savannah and Dave were totally invisible, she strode off to the grandstand to watch the qualifying, leaving Patrick to trail apologetically after them.

Savannah, who had frozen in horror throughout the whole episode, felt like she'd just been blindsided by a truck. Whatever she expected Cassandra to be like, it was nothing like that. She was a force of nature. A bitchy one. She may have been fifteen years older than Savannah, but swanning around in her designer jeans and pristine BRR polo shirt, acting like she was the sweetheart of the paddock, Cassandra had made Savannah shrink a little inside herself. Savannah was sure she'd overheard her whisper the words *slutty little gold digger* to Hillary as they left.

Dave caught Savannah's hand and shook his head, mouthing "sorry" with a sheepish grin. She let out a sigh of relief. At least he didn't seem bothered by her. Slipping his hand into hers, he murmured, "Come on, let's go and watch".

Thank goodness he was there with her.

Unfortunately for Savannah, Cassandra stayed in the awning for the rest of the day, hamming up being the heart and soul of the team and making Savannah want to strangle her. Dave did a good job of totally ignoring her, but it can't have been easy for him. Then again, perhaps he didn't find her annoying. After all, he was married to her for years, so perhaps that was part of the attraction.

Sadly for Dave that was not the case. He wasn't finding his

ex-wife's presence particularly easy to cope with. It was nice that she'd come to support Parker, and he'd never do anything to stop Cassandra from seeing her daughter, but he suspected there was another motive for her being here. She was making a complete show of herself, and he was mortified by her behaviour.

Not only had he overheard her making unkind comments to Hillary about Savannah being after his money, but he'd also heard her pointing out with mock concern the folly of letting a girl like that be around Ben Redmaine. It was obvious to anyone with a brain that she'd move onto someone younger and richer at the first opportunity.

He knew Cassandra was just being a cow, but this rattled Dave more than he cared to admit. He knew Savannah was out of his league and that his days with her were probably numbered, but he didn't want to lose her. Nevertheless, having a full-on row with Cassandra in front of Parker wasn't an option. The girl had seen enough of the two of them fighting to last her a lifetime, and she needed to focus on her racing. They should be supporting her this weekend, not point-scoring and squabbling.

He also had a niggling feeling that Cassandra was up to something. He'd seen her watching with a nasty smile on her face as Aspinall ogled Savannah's arse earlier, something Dave had also witnessed with some resignation. He would have to get used to that, he supposed. There was no point going all territorial and driving her away. Savannah was a lovely girl and was bound to get a lot of attention. All the same, he knew more than most how poisonous Cassandra could be and having her around felt dangerous. As much as he might try and shrug off his concerns, he was having trouble pushing down a rising feeling of dread. There was trouble brewing, he was sure of it.

13
GUMMY BEARS & CRASH BARRIERS

After a good night's sleep, Jake was feeling upbeat. The weather had dried and was looking brighter and Bambi had arrived, bringing with her Max's new race-suit, a positive outlook and a chocolate cake for the team to share. Even Lillington grudgingly accepted a slice, which was a small miracle. Any lessening of hostilities with that man had to be a good thing. The mood in the Apex awning was buoyant as they headed down to the grid for qualifying. The kids were bouncing around, hyped-up on sugar and excitement, and raring to get out on track.

Flags fluttered gently in the cold breeze and Jake paused to breathe in the atmosphere. This was it. The first round of the Nationals. Who would have thought they would end up here?

After months of conjecture and preparation everyone was keen to get started. There had been more than enough talk about who would triumph. It was time for the posturing to stop and the racing to begin.

Chase called the three boys over and gave them instructions.

"Right, boys. For qualifying, let's go out last and work through the field together. Round this track you get a faster lap time if you push together, so it's crucial you don't get split up if you want a good time. With some solid teamwork we could get top three, which would put us in a great track position for the heats."

High-fiving each of the drivers in turn, he left them to get their helmets on and into their karts. Dommie's leg jiggled impatiently as they waited while the rest of the karts pulled onto the racetrack, before hurtling out themselves; Dommie leading, closely followed by Max and then Finn, the three of them weaving to warm up their tyres.

Warm-up lap done, they approached the start line and dropped into formation. Driving nose to tail they soon caught up to the back of the pack. Overtaking, they worked their way up through the other drivers, Dommie ruthlessly diving into any gap and Max following him through. Leaning forward on every straight to minimise the aero drag, they stuck together like glue and soon caught up to Aspinall in his dazzling white BRR suit. The clock had counted down and this was their last flying lap. They couldn't afford to be held up by him.

Dommie, unhesitating, shoved his nose-cone down the inside of the first corner enough to unsettle Aspinall, which gave him and Max sufficient room to dive through. Heads down, pushing as hard as they could, they came around the final corner to cross the line, Max on pole and Dommie a hundredth of a second slower in second.

Arriving in the pits, they leapt out of their karts and hugged each other. Other drivers were still finishing their final lap and they stood nervously eyeing the board to make sure nobody managed to knock them off pole position. As the final driver went over the finish line, they high-fived each other and Max chuckled as Dommie launched into one of his outrageous victory dances.

They were startled out of their celebrations by a humourless official, who barked at them to get their karts straight into scrutinising. They sheepishly pushed their karts over to the bay, both still grinning wildly. As soon as the dads and mechanics were let into parc fermé, Jake ran over and swung Max around, giving him a huge squeeze.

"You did it! Pole on your first ever Nationals weekend! Amazing!" He turned to shake Dommie's hand. "Well done! You boys worked brilliantly together, great teamwork!"

A glowering Cosmo, who had qualified third, was lurking nearby. Refusing to take his helmet off, he stood with his back to his mechanic, arms folded.

Ben Redmaine watched him, knowing there was little point in saying anything. From his body language he could see Cosmo was only a whisker away from having a public meltdown, something Ben wanted to avoid at all costs. He needed his team to look as professional as possible, which meant Cosmo keeping his mouth shut until they got back to the awning.

Unfortunately, Hugo didn't have such reservations and, storming over, started bellowing at him.

"That was appalling! What the fuck am I paying you for exactly? We were slow out there! What the hell am I giving you all this money for if you can't even get us to the front?"

Ben wasn't used to being bawled out by anyone, let alone a portly, middle-aged banker who'd never driven a racing lap in his life.

He raised an eyebrow and pulled Hugo to one side. He muttered, "If Cosmo had driven better, he would have qualified on pole. Keep your voice down and go and look at the footage. He's completely messing up turn two; that's worth two-tenths a lap just on its own. Frankly he was lucky to get third. It was only because he managed to get a tow off these two that he qualified as well as he did. Two karts pushing together will always be faster than one on its own. This is going to happen if Cosmo continues to refuse to work with anyone else."

Hugo turned to a truculent Cosmo, who threw his arms up in indignation.

"Come on, dad, what was I supposed to do? The kart was shit," he whined.

Hugo huffed and stormed off, fuming. They were both making him look like an idiot. He wasn't paying Ben all this money to come third.

After the karts had passed scrutineering, Jake and Carver headed back through the paddock, chatting happily. What an amazing start to the weekend, especially after such an awful day yesterday.

Walking back into the awning, Jake was greeted by a frosty atmosphere. Lillington looked thunderous after Finn had got stuck in traffic and hadn't been able to keep up with the other two. He'd qualified down in sixteenth. The poor kid looked desolate and he'd clearly just had a roasting from his dad.

Chase bounded in and pumped Jake's hand enthusiastically.

"What did I tell you? I said Max has got what it takes, didn't I?"

"Thanks, he drove brilliantly. They both did. That was great teamwork."

Over Chase's shoulder he saw Lillington glowering and frowned. He turned to Chase and murmured, "Grant seems pretty annoyed. What happened to Finn?"

"He just couldn't keep up with you, that's what he's annoyed about."

Jake's eyes widened in concern. Chase winked. "Don't worry, it's just sour grapes. Besides, he'd have to catch Max before he could do anything, and after that qualifying he's got a lot of ground to make up in the heats. Besides, I think Grant's got his work cut out getting Finn's head in the right place to race later. He won't be thinking about knobbling you; you've got nothing to worry about."

Carver had rejoined them. "The boys worked well out there together," he said, then with a wry smile he added to Jake, "Let's see if you can hold onto that lead in the racing". Jake laughed but he noticed a steely edge to Carver's humour, which hadn't been there before.

He might be saying the right things, thought Jake, *but he wants to beat us as much as anyone does. What was it he said before? About your teammate always being your biggest rival...?*

As everyone returned to their respective corners of the awning, the atmosphere had changed. It suddenly felt very serious. Dommie was huddled at a table with his driver coach going through data and presumably talking tactics for the coming race, and Finn had disappeared. Max sat on a chair near his kart watching videos on YouTube and seemingly oblivious to the mood around him.

Jake took a deep breath and his mouth set in a grim line as he started to get the kart ready for the first race. This all suddenly felt very real.

Standing on the grid behind Max, Jake bounced anxiously from foot to foot. He didn't usually get nervous before a race, so this wasn't like him. It was brilliant that Max had got pole, but he now realised Max had a target on his back and every other kid would be gunning for him. As the marshal waved the karts out onto track and the engines roared, Jake ran over to the fencing to watch, his heart pounding in his chest.

Max completed the warm-up lap and lined up at the start. Jake could tell he was feeling nervous too. Whenever he was anxious, he always fiddled with the collar of his race suit as if it was rubbing on his throat. He was doing that now.

Just concentrate on the lights. Don't lose focus, Jake willed. A silence fell over the crowd, broken only by the throb of engines. As the lights went out, Cosmo, who was starting directly behind Max, was off the line like a rocket and was pressed hard against Max's rear bumper going into the first corner. Jake lost sight of him amidst the melee of karts, 32 of them all trying to fit through the narrow first turn.

Amongst the action, Jake saw yellow flags waving to warn everyone that a kart had spun into the barriers.

Hardly daring to breathe, he watched the karts roar through the corner, his heart sinking as he realised it was Max who was stuck at turn one, struggling to push his kart back out of the barrier. *So much for that great qualifying position.* Thankfully he got it moving again and jumped straight back in, racing back out onto the track.

By the time the leaders came around to start the second lap, Cosmo was out in front, followed by Dommie with Ronnie Finch close behind. The rest of the field followed, but Max was trailing about half a lap behind them.

Jake slumped forward against the fence. Oh well, there was nothing to lose now. Chin on his arms he watched as Max drove his socks off to try and regain some ground. Lap after lap went by with Max hitting every apex, squeezing every bit of speed out of the kart, and putting in fastest lap after fastest lap as he gradually started working his way back through the pack of traffic. But it wasn't enough.

The heats only lasted eight minutes and, by the time Max took the chequered flag, he'd driven brilliantly but only made it up to seventh position. Still, what a drive! It was a shame he'd come off on the first corner, but Max had put everything he had into minimising the damage and getting as many points back as possible. It would have been much worse if he hadn't managed to get the kart going again.

Back at the awning, Dommie and Carver were deep in conversation with their driver coach analysing onboard footage and data screens. Dommie had finished third behind Ronnie and Cosmo after battling throughout the heat and they were keen for him to get in front and stay there in the next one. Lillington was unpleasantly chipper because Finn had beaten Max, even though it was only by one position. He clapped Jake on the shoulder and said jovially, "It's not as easy when you're out there racing, is it?"

Jake's eyes narrowed. *What a tosser.* If they'd had another lap or two, Max would easily have got past Finn. Although, to be fair to Finn, he had kept himself out of trouble, which had made his race a lot easier and was more than could be said for Max. When Jake asked what happened, Max had shrugged. He wasn't sure. He just felt himself get tapped from behind as he was turning into the first corner, which was enough to spin him out. The next thing he knew, he was off the track and in the barriers.

Knowing Cosmo had started directly behind him, Jake wondered whether it was a professional foul designed to get Max out of the way early. He'd heard that some of the teams taught the drivers tricks like that, little ways of unsettling another driver's kart and making it look like they made a mistake. He wouldn't be surprised at Cosmo doing that - the Aspinalls were leaving no stone unturned to make sure he won this year.

It was a couple of hours until heat two and Bambi, after enveloping them all in tight hugs, had headed off to get bacon sandwiches and tea from the café, claiming that a good breakfast could fix most problems. Max, whose nerves were still jittery, took one bite and said he wasn't hungry, and Jake felt very much the same. They both ended up sneakily feeding the bacon to Bentley, who hungrily wolfed it down.

Bambi would go crazy at the thought of them not eating, but Jake's stomach churned even at the idea of food, so he couldn't blame Max for feeling the same.

The last heat had been a real baptism of fire, and to make things worse Max was starting on pole again for the remaining two heats. Perhaps qualifying first hadn't been such a blessing after all.

As the second race came around, Chase walked down

to the grid with an ashen-faced Max.

"Chin up, mate. You were unlucky in the last race, but you still managed to get back a lot of places and score yourself some good points. Remember, you weren't on pole by luck, you deserve to be up there, so don't let yourself be intimidated. Aspinall's a bit of a bully and all the kids want to win, but you mustn't let yourself be pushed around. Get out there and show them you deserve to be at the front. This time, be ready for some pushing and shoving into that first corner. You've got thirty-two karts all going full pelt into a sharp left-hander, so there's bound to be contact. Be ready for it. Hold your ground. And don't forget, you can't win the race in the first corner, but you can lose it there. Be prepared for Aspinall and try not to get knocked off again."

Max gave a solemn nod. He hadn't said much since the last heat and Jake could tell he was feeling the pressure.

If only he wasn't starting on the front row.

Engines rumbling, they got into their grid positions for heat two. This time when the lights went out Max hesitated, and the other drivers swarmed around and swamped him. He got through the first corner without incident, but by the time he'd come out the other side he'd dropped back to midfield.

"Come on Max, hold your nerve," muttered Jake.

The minutes ticked by and with each lap Max's confidence seemed to grow. He steadily made his way back up to the front, picking off one driver at a time, overtaking kart after kart until only Cosmo was left ahead of him. Jake held his breath as he saw Max make an audacious move around the outside of the hairpin to get into the lead, and then gasped as he saw Cosmo blatantly sideswipe him, sending Max's kart veering off track. He was vaguely aware of a cheer erupting from where the BRR mechanics were watching, but he was too busy running to notice. Red flags were out and the rest of the field pulled to a stop as an ambulance appeared on track.

Pushing through the crowds in the grandstand and vaulting over the fencing, Jake ran onto the track. Max hadn't moved and was still in the kart, which looked horribly crumpled and was still buried deep in the tyre wall. As the paramedics arrived, they checked him over and helped a limping Max out of the kart and into the waiting ambulance. Bambi came running over, hair flying nebulously in the wind. She and Jake swapped relieved glances that Max was up and walking. They clasped hands briefly before she climbed into the back of the ambulance with him and the door was shut. The emergency vehicle, lights flashing, left the track.

Now he knew Max was OK and Bambi was looking after him, Jake wasn't sure what to do. The rest of the drivers were being re-gridded for a restart. Pulling the kart out of the barriers, he wheeled it into the exit road and groaned in frustration. It was a total write-off. He knew he should get it back to the awning and start trying to fix it - after all, he had a hell of a lot of work to do if they were going to carry on racing - but with adrenalin coursing through him, all he felt like doing was finding Aspinall and those bloody BRR mechanics and starting one hell of a fight. He'd probably get banned, but right now it felt worth it.

After a thorough check-over by the paramedics, Max and a rather shaken Bambi headed back to the awning. By this time the race had finished, and all the kids crowded around Max who was suddenly a bit of a celebrity after his big accident. It took a while to walk through the paddock as they were stopped by everyone they knew, and a lot of people they didn't, who all wanted to make sure Max was OK. Having an accident was definitely one way to get yourself noticed. He was the anonymous new kid no longer.

Max was fine apart from a sore wrist and a few bruises

and was soon smiling again. Dommie bounded over and handed him a big bag of Haribo.

"Here you go. Glad you're OK, mate," he chirped. "Food of champions, at least that's what my mum says. My dad says I go a bit crazy when I have sweets, but my mum keeps a pack in the motorhome for if I have a bad day. She says there's a time and place to bring out the crazy and it's usually when I'm not doing very well." He crossed his eyes and pulled a face, making Max giggle. "I reckon you've more than earned the emergency sweets with that shunt. Reckon you'll be OK to go out for the last race of the day?"

"Dunno," shrugged Max. "My arm hurts a bit, but I think I'll be OK. I'm not sure they'll be able to fix my kart in time, though." He looked over to where Jake and Chase were standing, arms folded, by the mangled kart. The fact that they were just standing looking at it, rather than working, spoke volumes.

"Don't let it get you down, mate, it's happened to us all at some time. I'll get Cosmo back for you. He's going in the wall next race."

He grinned and Max laughed. Bambi, who overheard, was a bit shocked by what Dommie had said, although she told herself he was probably only joking. And she was grateful that somebody had got Max's back out there.

Max offered the open bag of sweets and Dommie, glancing around to check he wasn't being watched, grabbed a handful and shoved them in his mouth.

"Did he get a penalty?" asked Max.

"Who, golden-boy Cosmo?" replied Dommie, spitting bits of gummy bear everywhere. "Not likely. I reckon either his dad or Redmaine have paid off all the officials to turn a blind eye whatever he does this year. Bought themselves immunity."

"Surely you can't do that?"

Dommie raised an eyebrow. "How else do you explain it? I'd get a penalty if I even thought about taking somebody out."

14
GAINING AN ADVANTAGE

Over in Fox Racing the mood was chipper. Ronnie had won the first heat and finished second in heat two, and Eden was punching above his weight with two fifth places. What's more, that new kid had been put back in his box. Frankie smirked. Max Golding had ruffled a lot of feathers by poling it in his first round, but he was out of the frame now. They'd just heard that he wouldn't be going out for heat three.

As much as Frankie hated that jumped-up little prick Cosmo, he'd done them both a favour by putting the new kid in the wall. Golding would think twice before he got in the way of the front runners again. That was if he came back at all after this weekend. It sounded like the kid was racing on a tight budget, so the sooner they ran out of money and called it a day, the better. One less person to get in Ronnie's way.

Getting ready for heat three, he pulled Ronnie to one side.

"Right, son. Get out there and show that snotty little rich kid who's boss around here." Ronnie gave him a determined nod.

The race was rough from start to finish. With Max watching reluctantly from the grandstand, it was Dommie, Cosmo and Ronnie out front, taking chunks out of each other right from the get-go.

Ignoring a tightening in his chest, Frankie lit a cigar and bellowed his way through the whole race, shouting everything from instructions to encouragement to total outrage when Ronnie got a warning for shoving Cosmo a bit too hard.

It was only on the penultimate lap, when Cosmo gave Ronnie a hefty shove back and he spun off the track, that Frankie fell dangerously silent. The crowd around him continued to cheer and gasp as the action unfolded. *They sound like they're at a fucking fireworks display,* thought Frankie sourly. Danny put a sympathetic hand on his shoulder but quickly removed it when he saw the livid expression on Frankie's face. Cosmo had crossed a line. It looked like there was going to be trouble, and he didn't want to be in Frankie's line of fire.

Frankie watched with ominous calm as Ronnie tried to make up lost ground, but it was too late in the race and he finished trailing at the back, thumping his steering wheel in frustration.

In parc fermé, Hugo and Ben Redmaine were congratulating each other on their second win of the day when Frankie walked over. Hugo shot him a smug look and then turned back to Redmaine. Big mistake. Turning your back on a furious Frankie Finch is never a smart move. The next thing Hugo knew, he was pinned up against the wall with Frankie's face an inch away from his. A much bigger man, Frankie towered over him and quietly suggested he took his son in hand before he did it for him. Realising they were being watched by a horrified official, he put the red-faced Hugo down, gave him a steely stare and walked over to the official.

"I'll be waiting for the penalty Aspinall's going to get

for taking Ronnie out," he growled, before stalking out through the gates.

Regaining his composure, Hugo huffed in indignation, a spiteful look in his beady eyes as he went with the shocked official into the back office.

Back in the awning Frankie let off some steam. Ranting and swearing about "that fucking prick Aspinall" he then turned to Ronnie. "He was smashing you about all race, why the hell didn't you take him out first?"

Ronnie shrugged.

"I got a warning, dad. If I'd hit him again, I would have got a penalty."

Frankie sighed and bent down so he was at eye level with Ronnie. He put a hand on his shoulder and said firmly, "You never back down, son, do you understand? If you do, they'll think they've won. They'll think it's OK to push you around. You need to be respected in this game or they'll take the piss."

Danny, who had been listening, chimed in. "Now hold on, Frank, there's no point Ronnie getting himself excluded for the sake of a couple of points. It's better to play the game and keep collecting points – that's how championships are won, not by losing your temper and getting penalties."

Straightening slowly, Frankie raised himself to his full height, which was a good six inches taller than Danny.

"Did I ask for your opinion, Fox? Keep your fucking nose out. You never tell my kid to back down from a fight, do you understand? Especially with a privileged, toffee-nosed little shit like Aspinall."

Frustrated and intimidated, Danny beat a retreat to the seclusion of the back of his van after muttering some excuse about downloading data. He could do with a pick-me-up. It had been a long day. In fact, it had been a long weekend, and it was only Saturday. They still had another day's racing to get through.

He doubted Frankie would be able to get to the end of the weekend without going full-on psycho on Aspinall and he needed something to take the edge off. He found the wrap in his inner pocket and opened it carefully, using his key to scoop the white powder and sniffing a bit up each nostril. He closed his eyes and released a long breath. *That was better.*

Suddenly the back door of the van opened, startling Danny so he nearly spilt the little bag of coke all over the floor. He guiltily wiped his nose and spun to face the intruder. Julia poked her head round the door and smiled.

She had been watching the exchange between Frankie and Danny with interest and spotted an opportunity to get the upper hand. She knew damn well what he'd just been doing, but instead of showing her disapproval she stepped in and shut the door behind her.

"I just wanted to check you're OK, Danny," she purred, her head tilted to one side. "I can't believe how Frankie's behaving; he's not showing you the respect you deserve at all. It's totally out of order."

Danny visibly relaxed. Thank goodness she wasn't coming to have a go at him too. Julia moved a little closer.

"You look so stressed, Danny, maybe you need to relax." Looking slyly up at him she gently laid her hand on the crotch of his trousers. Danny's eyes widened. Cocaine coursing through his system, he didn't question his sudden desire and pulled her against him, kissing her deeply. He groaned as she unzipped his fly and reached to take hold of him, then suddenly there was a loud hammering on the door of the van. They both froze in horror, panting slightly and trying not to make a sound. Shit, the doors weren't even locked. The last thing Danny needed was to be caught with his trousers down.

From outside, Frankie's voice thundered. "Oy, Fox! You in there?"

Danny took a breath and tried to sound brisk and businesslike.

"Yeah, mate, I'll be right out."

"'Bout bloody time, you've been gone ages. I've been called to the steward's office; they must be doing something about Aspinall after all."

A smile playing on her lips, Julia sank silently to her knees and took Danny's cock in her mouth. Danny closed his eyes and groaned.

"Alright Frank, meet you over there. I'm just coming."

Waiting outside the steward's office was like sitting in a doctor's waiting room. It was stuffy and crowded, full of bad-tempered people who didn't want to be there, and who all felt they had much better things to be doing. Frankie tapped his foot impatiently. He felt a bead of sweat trickle down the back of his neck and tried to ignore the smell of B.O. that filled the room.

At least this meant the incident with Aspinall was being dealt with. The kid definitely deserved a penalty after smashing Ronnie off in that last heat.

After fifteen minutes of waiting, Danny arrived, flushed and surprisingly chipper. *Probably chemically induced,* thought Frankie. Everyone knew Danny was a bit too fond of sniff. What was taking all this time? Frankie looked along the rows of faces and couldn't see Aspinall. Perhaps they were waiting for him to turn up. It would be typical of that inconsiderate tosser to keep everyone waiting in this sweat box.

When his name was finally called, Frankie found himself facing a panel of three humourless officials only to be told in no uncertain terms that his behaviour in parc fermé had been unacceptable. They had footage of him on CCTV threatening another competitor, and while he was lucky that they were only warning him and putting six points on his licence this time, if it happened again he'd have his licence revoked and the matter would be referred to the police.

Frankie was so taken aback by this unexpected turn of

events that it took him a moment to react. The stewards, who believed he'd taken the news without kicking off, breathed a sigh of relief and tried to dismiss him before the red mist rose.

Forcing down his temper, Frankie said, "And what's being done about that fucking kid Aspinall punting my son off?"

Stone-faced, the Clerk replied, "I don't appreciate your language, Mr Finch. If you mean the incident between Aspinall and your son, we've reviewed the footage and it was deemed a racing incident. No further action is needed."

"Seriously? Are you fucking blind?"

"Please don't raise your voice, Mr Finch, and I won't warn you about your language again. You'll only make matters worse for yourself. As I said, we have reviewed the footage and no further action is being taken."

Exasperated, Frankie left before he started hurting people. It would make him feel better but getting a ban wouldn't help Ronnie.

Turning back, he growled, "I won't forget this."

Unimpressed, the Clerk raised an eyebrow.

"I can assure you, we won't forget this either, Mr Finch."

He strode out of the building feeling angrier than he had done in years. Trotting at his heels, Danny was asking him what happened.

"Fuck off, you little prick," said Frankie. How dare they treat him like this? He'd spent his life building up a formidable reputation and he'd got used to being shown a certain amount of respect. It was obvious that the officials were far more interested in kissing Aspinall's arse than was good for them.

It was a shock for Frankie to realise he wasn't as powerful in this environment as in his own manor. He knew how he would've got the upper hand in the past, but those tactics weren't going to work here. How was he going to get the officials onside and working in his interest?

The balance of power needed to shift or they didn't stand a chance of winning this year.

15
GO BIG OR GO HOME

Sunday dawned cold and bright and Jake, who had got to the track early, rubbed the back of his neck and stretched his shoulders. He was worn out. He and Chase had worked late into the night fixing Max's kart. After yesterday's damage they ideally needed a new chassis but, as Bambi had reminded him, they just couldn't afford that right now.

So, grimly determined, they'd done the best they could. They replaced the bent steering column, dented radiator and bent axle, and flatbedded the kart to try and straighten it. Luckily the chassis didn't look like it had cracked, but it had been so twisted in the accident they hadn't been able to completely straighten it again. It was the best they could do, but it was impossible to know how well it would drive today.

He'd also noticed a difference in Max this morning. He didn't seem his usual bouncy self. He'd been quiet and kept absent-mindedly rubbing his wrist, which was still a little sprained. He'd perked up as soon as Dommie appeared, but Jake wondered whether Max was feeling the pressure. He went over and crouched down next to him.

"How you feeling, champ?"

Max shrugged, "OK."

"Look, you don't have to do this if you don't want to. Nobody would blame you for wanting to sit out the rest of the weekend after that accident."

Max raised his eyes to the ceiling as if this was the most ludicrous thing he'd ever heard.

"Of course I want to race, dad."

"And you're sure your wrist is OK?"

"Uh-huh," said Max, eyes going back to the game on his phone.

Jake sighed. Sometimes talking to Max was like wading through treacle. Oh well, he'd tried. If he couldn't be bothered to look up from his phone to have a conversation, he couldn't be that worried about competing, and the paramedics had said his wrist was just sprained. As long as it wasn't hurting him, he was fine to race.

One consolation was that he was starting down in 28th place for the prefinal. He'd been surprised Max wasn't starting right at the back after a seventh place, a DNF and a DNS the day before.

He returned to check the kart over one last time before they went down to the grid. Suppressing his nerves, he hoped Max would be OK. If he had another day like yesterday it could ruin his confidence, not to mention their budget for the year.

Jake needn't have worried. Once the prefinal was underway, Max seemed to shrug off any apprehension and was back to his old self.

Starting near the back, Max steadily worked his way up through the field, although Jake couldn't help noticing his lap times were down on the previous day. Perhaps that bent chassis was slowing him down. They'd done their best to straighten it, but there was only a certain amount they could do.

By the time the chequered flag was waved, Max had worked his way up to twelfth position, which would be his starting position for the grand final. Not bad, thought Jake. He allowed himself a relieved smile. At least Max had finished in front of Finn. That would shut Lillington up. The man had been far too chipper after Max's shunt yesterday.

Sure enough, Lillington was glowering in his usual corner of the awning when they walked back in.

Oh well, he was just going to have to get used to that if they were in the same team. He certainly wasn't going to tell Max to slow down just to make Lillington feel better about himself.

There were four hours before the grand final and Jake had a decision to make. Max had made up a lot of ground in that last race, but he wouldn't be able to catch the front-running kids with the lap times he'd been doing. The kart clearly wasn't at its best. A new chassis would cost the best part of a grand. Jake chewed his lip thoughtfully.

They would need to replace it before the next round anyway. The money would have to be spent, whether it was today or in a few weeks' time. And there was no point even doing the Nationals unless they were competitive. He looked over at Bambi, who was drinking tea in a small patch of sunshine, wrapped in her big winter coat against the cold.

Calling Chase over, Jake asked whether he thought they could get a new chassis built up in time for the final.

"It's doable, mate, and I'll help you put it together if that's what you want. But it's a lot of work and a bit of a risk putting down a new frame when you haven't had a chance to test it."

Checking his watch, Jake considered for a moment.

"Let's do it. It might be a risk, but we know the kart we're on is going to be slow, so we might as well go for it. Is it OK if I pay you next week?"

He'd break the news to Bambi later. Right now they had a brand-new kart to build up.

That afternoon, as the karts lined up on the grid for the last race of the weekend, Jake hoped Max wouldn't have any problems this time. He was sure getting the new kart had been the right thing to do. It had been a tough first round, everything considered, and he would love it to end on a positive note. And ideally without damaging that new chassis.

Taking a deep breath and clapping Max on the shoulder, he ran to watch as they set off on their warm-up lap.

When the lights went out, Max was off the line like a rocket, hurtling past three people before he'd even reached the first corner. Jake winced as the thirty-two karts vied for track space in the tight left-hander, but they all got through cleanly.

He let out the breath he'd been holding and settled to watch, his heart thumping in his chest. As they headed into lap two, Max's lap times looked good, but Finn, who had started just behind Max and was following him as he worked his way forward, decided to make a last-minute lunge to overtake. Jake was sure Finn had been told to beat Max above everything else.

Chase threw his hands up in exasperation as Finn shoved himself in front and Max had to slam on the brakes to avoid a collision. Max glanced over at the pit wall and saw Chase giving them the signal to work together, so Max put his head down and, sticking to Finn's bumper, followed him round.

After a few laps Max, who clearly felt he was faster, took the opportunity and overtook Finn at the hairpin. Jake smiled to himself. *Good, Finn had been holding him up. Now he could just get on with the race and get himself to the front.*

As the laps tumbled, Max worked his way up through the drivers, picking them off one at a time, leaving Finn trailing behind. With only two laps remaining, the front three drivers had pulled a significant gap from the rest of the field, so he had little chance of catching them. His only hope now was to keep pushing hard and hope they started battling in front of him and slowing themselves down.

As hard as he pushed, however, it just wasn't enough. The front three raced hard and Cosmo, who was in front, defended so well it seemed his kart was twice its width, making it almost impossible for Dommie and Ronnie to get past and leaving them tripping over each other.

As they crossed the line, Cosmo was in first, with Dommie and Ronnie Finch neck and neck behind him. Max crossed the line three seconds behind in fourth place.

Jake sprinted down to parc fermé. What a drive! He was glad he'd put that new chassis down now. If only he hadn't been stuck behind Finn for those two laps Max might have made it onto the podium. Never mind, considering the trouble they'd had, fourth place was an awesome result.

Abandoning his kart, Max headed straight over to Dommie in the scrutineering bay and congratulated him for just beating Ronnie to second place.

"You too!" said Dommie. "That must have been a cracking drive. And you got some silverware on your first National final!"

"What do you mean?" said Max. "I came fourth. They only do trophies for the top three, don't they?"

"Top three, plus top rookie," grinned Dommie. "Which is you. And you've earned it this weekend. Nice result."

A big grin split Max's face. What a great way to finish their first big race weekend.

Jake smiled with relief. Max had driven his socks off, what a little legend! Hearing a fuss, he looked over and saw Julia Leech demanding the officials investigate Max for having shoved Eden out of the way. He frowned. *Max had made a clean overtake; she was just making stuff up!* About to go over and say something, he felt a hand on his shoulder.

"Don't worry about it, mate," said Chase. "They were hoping for the rookie award this weekend, it's just sour grapes. Some people will say anything to try and get their hands on a trophy. The officials know that. Max put in a good, clean drive; you've got nothing to worry about. Enjoy it."

And Jake did. The trophy presentation took place a couple of hours later, the boys spraying each other with fake champagne. When they came back to the awning, they were sticky and laughing, carrying enormous silver trophies.

"Wow, that rookie trophy is nearly as big as Dommie's!" said Chase. "Come on boys, let's take a team photo with them."

The three of them posed grinning against the Apex Motorsport awning, Dommie insisting they try and take the photo with him jumping in mid-air, making them all hysterical with laughter.

Lillington, perpetually annoyed, felt Chase had let Finn down by not making Max stay behind him, and after throwing everything noisily into the back of his van he left in a huff.

Chase shrugged and looked at Jake.

"Don't worry about him. Pissing off your rivals is a rite of passage mate. Nobody likes being beaten by the new kid and, besides, you're officially one of the championship contenders after this weekend's performance. There's no place to be faint-hearted if you're at the front."

16
CATCHING A GOLDEN GOOSE

"Woah," breathed Danny Fox, awestruck, as he pulled in through the ornate electric gates of Frankie's Chigwell mansion.

It was early evening, which at this time of year meant it was pitch dark, and the front of the house was floodlit in all its mock-Tudor splendour.

I knew he was minted, but I didn't know he was this minted, mused Danny, the corner of his mouth lifting. *Frankie can afford to pay me a lot more.* Walking up to the porch, his swagger was more pronounced than usual. He was clearly running with the big boys now.

Danny had been feeling a bit sorry for himself recently, resentful of Redmaine and his flash lifestyle funded by his golden goose, Aspinall. Not to mention that Dave North, who must be minted to have scored himself a fit girlfriend like that. He'd spotted her at the weekend, all tits and lip gloss, and planned to get himself a bit of that action at some point this season.

Maybe he wasn't so hard done by, after all, he just needed to make the most of the clients he'd currently got.

If Frankie had a pad like this, Danny clearly wasn't milking him enough.

He'd also just taken a call from Grant Lillington, who was furious after his fiasco of a first round with Apex and was thinking of jumping teams - so that would boost his income too.

Leaning on the doorbell, he got a fright when a colossus in a suit answered the door. This must be the infamous Chris. *Christ, he looked like something out of a fucking Hitman movie.* Feeling small and slightly less cocky, he followed Chris over to Frankie's den. Chris might be big, but he's acting like a glorified butler, thought Danny. Perhaps he isn't anything to worry about after all.

Walking into Frankie's den was like stepping back to the 1960s East End, apart from the massive TV screen. One wall was dominated by a framed boxing poster of the Kray twins, which looked like it had been signed by them, and on the other he was pleased to see a big canvas print of Ronnie on track in his Fox Racing livery. *Nice,* Danny nodded to himself. He could work with that. Fox and Finch. The dream team.

Frankie was settled in his leather recliner, cigar smouldering between his stubby fingers. He gestured to the sideboard.

"Have a drink, Danny."

Helping himself to a crystal glass and a couple of fingers of whiskey, Danny looked around for mixers. He'd much prefer a whiskey and coke, but it didn't look like that was on offer. He'd come to pick up Ronnie's engines to take them to the engine builder. Frankie wanted them put on the dyno to be tuned before the next round. Last weekend had been a good result for Ronnie, but Cosmo had looked rapid all weekend and he wanted to make sure they were getting maximum power.

Frankie reached into the pocket of his tracksuit and took out a roll of £50 notes, peeling off a stack of them.

"That should cover it," he said. "I've put a bit extra in

there. If Biggs has got any good new engines, make sure we get them before anyone else does and give him a bit of a drink too. It's always worth having your engine builder."

Danny pocketed the cash happily. He could use some of that to settle up his debts. His dealer had been on his case the last week or so, threatening to cut off his supply. With this he could give himself a bit of a treat and there would still be plenty left over to sort the engines out. That was if they needed sorting out at all. In truth, there was nothing wrong with Ronnie's engines; Frankie was just making a fuss. Not that Frankie needed to know that. Much better to take the money and keep him sweet.

Relieved that his supply was now assured, Danny produced a nearly empty sachet of white powder. Remembering his manners, he offered it to Frankie, who held a hand up in refusal. He never touched the stuff.

Frankie sat back, swilling a mouthful of whiskey around his mouth while he watched Danny bending over the lines of white powder on his table. He wished he hadn't bothered offering him a drink. He should have given him the cash and then got rid straight away.

By now, Danny was starting to run his mouth off about everyone in the paddock. Slagging off Redmaine and the rich kids, saying he reckoned they'd been greasing palms and bribing officials so they could get away with cheating.

"You wouldn't believe it, Frank. I heard a rumour that Aspinall had offered an official thirty grand to turn a blind eye to any problems Cosmo might have in scrutineering this season. It wouldn't surprise me.

"Apparently, they're pasting stuff on their tyres to make them sticky, adding stuff to their fuel, all sorts. But don't worry. They might have the officials in the palm of their hand, but all we've got to do is catch them out and put a protest in and they'll be screwed. In the meantime we just need to keep racking up those points. I'm not surprised Redmaine would do this kind of thing. You probably see him as this hotshot racing driver, but we used to race together and some of the stories I could tell you would make your hair curl!"

Frankie, who had been listening with a solid dose of scepticism, perked up, his interest piqued. A bit of leverage was always useful when you're trying to change the balance of power.

"Oh yes? Tell me more."

Danny grinned. "Redmaine's not the clean-cut golden boy he makes himself out to be. In fact, he's not the great driver he claims either; I used to beat him all the time. Where's the justice in that, eh? He's in F1 and I'm not even racing any more."

Frankie nodded with what appeared to be sympathy. He could totally see why nobody would want to sign a driver with permanent Columbian flu; he'd be a total liability.

"Go on, what's the inside story on Redmaine, then?"

"Now, I'm not prejudiced - I don't care what people get up to as long they don't expect me to join in - but whenever we would go out Redmaine always wanted to end the night at The Velvet Lounge. It's this gay club near where we grew up.

"Don't get me wrong, it's a banging club and we've had many a great night out there. There are some real fit birds in there, and although most of them are lesbians it's always worth a try, right? Every bloke loves a bit of lesbian action, don't they, Frank?" he pantomime-winked at Frankie, who somehow managed not to roll his eyes.

"Besides, there aren't many clubs you can go to where the women are nearly naked unless you're paying lap dancing prices, are there?" he sniggered.

"The difference was, the rest of us weren't gyrating with the trannies and queers on the dance floor. If he ever does properly make it to Formula 1, I'm guessing he won't want photos of those nights ending up in the tabloids. The only reason that hasn't already happened is that he's not famous enough. I've got a stack of photos on my phone ready to sell to the highest bidder as soon as he makes it big."

Danny grinned like a Cheshire Cat and chuckled.

Frankie nodded, nonplussed. He couldn't care less about Redmaine's sexual preferences. In his book, people could do whatever they liked behind closed doors, unless they were kiddy fiddlers of course. Bored, he checked his watch, wondering how much longer Danny would stay. He'd been hoping for better leverage than the fact that Redmaine preferred boys to girls once he'd had a couple of drinks. Nobody cared about that, the world had moved on - leaving Danny behind apparently.

Danny, meanwhile was in full swing.

"Another thing - it looks like that new kid won't be as much of a problem as we thought. From what I've heard he'll run out of money soon, especially if he keeps getting damage." He smirked. "And I'm sure we can do something about that. We'll make sure he doesn't get up the front again, eh Frank? He's probably lost his nerve after that shunt at the weekend anyway."

Frankie, who had tuned out Danny's rambling and wanted to watch Match of the Day, decided he'd listened to enough bullshit. He stood, clapping his hands together.

"Right then, those engines. They're in the garage. Chris'll show them to you on your way out."

"Oh, sure, right then," said Danny, surprised at being dismissed. "I'll just use your bog before I go." He leapt up, finding himself a little unsteady on his feet.

He stumbled off to the toilet, humming happily and thinking about the three grand tucked in his pocket, when he bumped into a pretty girl dressed in a pyjama crop-top and shorts. He stood and stared, drinking her in. Giving him a smile from beneath long dark lashes, she stood in her bedroom doorway, weight on one leg, twiddling a strand of long, dark hair around her fingers. This must be Britney. Danny knew Frankie had a daughter, but he didn't know she looked like that. *Blimey, no wonder he didn't bring her to the track, the boys would be all over her like flies.*

"Hey," he mumbled with a suave smile, playing it cool now that he'd regained his composure.

"Hey yourself," she murmured, biting her bottom lip and tucking her hair behind her ear. She walked past him to go downstairs, brushing up against him and making him very aware of the fact she wasn't wearing a bra underneath the thin t-shirt. He got an instant boner.

Danny stared after her for a few moments before bolting into the bathroom and locking the door. *Woah, out of bounds, man. Don't even think about going there. Christ, it was a curse being this attractive. But she's just not worth the risk.* He splashed his face with water and stood looking at himself in the mirror. There was a world of pussy out there. It wasn't worth finding yourself sleeping with the fishes over some teen jailbait.

He was glad Frankie or Chris hadn't seen that. Just the thought of their reaction was instant bonerkill. He dried his face off and shook his head. *Keep it strictly business, man. Don't fuck this up. It's your meal ticket.*

17
SUN, SAND & TOTAL SECLUSION

Savannah stretched and sighed contentedly, wiggling her toes in the soft, warm sand. She looked over at Dave snoring gently in the shade, slipped off the sun lounger and strolled down to the shore. She gazed out over the smooth turquoise lagoon, the heat of the sun on her skin melting away the stresses of the previous week. This truly was paradise. If only life could be like this all the time.

She considered waking Dave up for a bit of afternoon delight, but seeing him so relaxed she reconsidered. He looked so peaceful. Let him sleep. There would be plenty of time for that later.

The waves lapped over her feet, erasing her footprints as she walked, while her mind drifted back to the race weekend. It was never going to be easy meeting Dave's ex for the first time. Savannah just hadn't expected her to be such a bitch. It had been a nasty shock, and what with Dave seeming unusually quiet on the way home, she'd been concerned that seeing Cassandra again had affected him more than he was prepared to admit.

They had dropped Parker back at boarding school enroute back from the track and driven the rest of the journey home in silence. Perhaps Dave was sad about leaving Parker. It must still feel strange for him not having her at home. She'd only started boarding the previous September, so it was all still relatively new. However, she was more worried that his subdued behaviour was a reaction to seeing his ex.

She'd caught him smiling to himself at one point and, when she'd pressed him about it, he'd admitted he had something to tell her. But he refused to say anything more that evening, promising he'd reveal all the next day. Savannah snorted at the double entendre and ran a hand playfully up his thigh, but didn't get anything more than a tight smile in response and she'd reluctantly let the matter drop.

Dave was still being elusive the next morning, and to try and shake the feeling of disquiet Savannah headed off to the gym. She was probably overthinking things, but she felt uneasy. She was sure he was hiding something from her. After an hour of slugging it out on the treadmill, she felt brighter. Working out had been the right decision. Standing under the hot shower, she smiled to herself. She'd find a way to cheer Dave up and shake him out of this preoccupied mindset.

But when she walked into the bedroom, still wrapped in a big, fluffy towel, she froze. Why the hell was her suitcase on the bed? Had Dave had a change of heart after seeing his ex the previous day? Did he want her to leave? Had all this happened too fast for him and he was regretting asking her to move in? This must have been what he meant when he said he had something to tell her. Some bloody surprise! She stood rooted on the spot, not sure what to do.

Then Dave strode out of the walk-in wardrobe, his tummy protruding over the top of some ludicrously bright Bermuda shorts, sunglasses on, waggling a pair of airline tickets. What the...?

The relief she felt was so overwhelming, it seemed to push all the air out of her chest. She dropped on the bed and burst into tears.

"What on earth's the matter, love?" said Dave, suddenly worried there was something terribly wrong. "Don't you want to come to the Maldives with me?"

She laughed through her sobs, feeling like a total idiot.

"Of course I do!" she sniffed. "I thought you wanted me to leave."

Dave laughed and scooped her up in his arms, her towel coming undone and gaping open.

"You daft thing, why on earth would I want that? You're the best thing that's happened to me in a long time".

She looked up at him, beaming.

"Really?"

"Hell, yes! I can't believe you don't know that!"

Glancing hungrily down to where the towel had fallen open, he ran a finger slowly over her breastbone and murmured huskily, "And as much as I'd like to take full advantage of your current state of undress," he briskly drew her towel back together, "we need to get to the airport! Come on, the taxi's going to be here in ten minutes! Besides," he added with a saucy wink, "we'll have plenty of time to continue this when we arrive. It's going to be just you, me, and the most luxurious private beach you've ever seen for the next two weeks."

Savannah, who had never been anywhere more exotic than Spain before, let alone somewhere with a private beach, had no idea what to expect. After a mad dash round searching for her bikini, Dave persuaded her to just pack an overnight bag and buy everything new at the airport. They shared a bottle of champagne in the departure lounge, and after a long but luxurious flight (first class had been quite a revelation!), followed by a short, early-morning hop on a seaplane, they arrived at their destination.

The place didn't disappoint. It was the most idyllic spot she could have imagined. A beautiful private villa, fully stocked with every extravagance. The doors opened out onto decking, which led onto a secluded beach and the crystal-clear waters of the Indian Ocean.

She smiled and shook her head. What had she been thinking? She had to stop judging Dave by the behaviour of other guys she'd known. He was nothing like them. She couldn't imagine him giving her any reason to doubt him, but she was falling for him more and more, and the thought of everything going wrong frightened her. If only she'd met him before his hideous ex-wife had, their life together could have been so different. Just the two of them.

Her mind wandered back to the race weekend. She remembered the grim expression on Dave's face when his ex intimated she would go off with Ben Redmaine. Even though there was nothing in it, she'd felt instantly guilty. She wanted so desperately to show she wasn't interested in anyone else that she'd stopped even making eye contact with anyone male. Bloody woman, why did she have to stick her poisonous nose in? She knew exactly how to push Dave's buttons and play on his insecurities, and obviously wanted to do just that.

After whatever that woman had put him through, Dave was hesitant and seemed frightened to trust her, which meant that bitch could wind him up and make him doubt himself really easily. Savannah sighed. She needed a way to make him realise she didn't want anyone else.

Ugh! She shook her head in annoyance. She didn't want to spend a moment longer thinking about the bitch ex-wife while they were in this tropical paradise.

She glanced back over to where she'd left Dave snoozing, and saw him propped up on one elbow lazily watching her. She smiled to herself. There were definitely benefits to being totally secluded - she could do things she wouldn't dare do normally.

Holding his gaze, she slowly padded back towards the deck, tugging the strings on her bikini top and let it fall to the ground. Her teeth catching her lip, she slowly ran her hands over her breasts, sliding them down over her stomach and beneath the bikini bottoms. She slipped them down and deftly stepped out of them. Then, standing over him in the lounger, eyes heavy with desire, she gasped as his hand slid into the slick wetness between her legs. Letting her head fall back and closing her eyes, she moaned gently.

Time to get this holiday off with a bang.

18
BACK ON HOME TURF

Jake fumbled for his screeching alarm clock. Rolling back over, he reached for Bambi, hoping to lose himself for a few more moments before getting up, but found only the empty side of the bed. He sat up and rubbed his face. Of course, she would be on her way to work by now. She'd been working all hours for the past month, putting in as much overtime as she could to try and get some extra money in. They'd barely seen each other for weeks. More often than not he was asleep on the sofa before she got in, and by the time he woke and climbed into bed she was fast asleep.

When they did see each other, they both tried to avoid being snappy and impatient, but it didn't always work.

After hopelessly underbudgeting for Round One, they were in a bit of a mess. They'd looked at race fees and running costs, but hadn't factored how much it would cost with hotels, meals out, petrol and having to chip in for Chase's expenses too. Inevitably, perhaps, things had been fraught between them, especially after he bought that new chassis without her knowing. She conceded that Max would have needed a new kart, but was annoyed that he'd gone behind her back. What with that, Max's race suit and the new race engine, they'd gone through most of the money put aside for karting this year already.

Bambi wasn't one to have a stand-up row unless it was unavoidable, but he could tell from her grim silence that she was angry and seriously worried about their financial situation. They'd already had to sacrifice the summer holiday and dip into their emergency savings.

Jake had nearly joked that he wouldn't have enough annual leave left to take a holiday anyway, what with all the half-days and long weekends he was taking to do testing and development work, but he thought better of it. He wasn't that stupid.

Once he'd roused Max out of bed, thrown everything into the van and gulped down a quick coffee, they hit the road. At least they didn't need to stay in a hotel for this round as it was only half an hour away.

All in all, Jake was feeling confident. It might have been tough over the last month, but it would all be worthwhile. Round One had been a shock to the system, but they were at their local circuit this time, so he was sure they would have a home advantage. After all, Max had been club champion here for the last two years. He'd driven thousands of laps around this circuit. It was his home turf. What could go wrong?

Happily daydreaming of Max's greatest victories, Jake turned into Thorpe Hill circuit, as he had done many times in the past. To his surprise, he was greeted by a totally alien view. Gone were the pop-up gazebos and transit vans they were used to seeing; instead, the paddock was filled with shiny race trucks and flashy awnings. What a transformation! He barely recognised the place.

There was nowhere to park in the main paddock so they had to drive up to the top and park the van in the field there. Praying he'd be able to get back out of the mud again at the end of the day, Jake gave a heavy sigh. This wasn't the ideal start to the weekend. The Apex Motorsport awning was right down the bottom of the paddock, so they would have to unload and carry all their stuff down there. It would probably take him the best part of an hour. Oh well, the sooner he started the sooner he'd be done.

He turned up his collar against the drizzle and opened the back doors of the van. But, losing his footing in the mud, he slipped and landed hard on his bum, his spine jarring painfully. He groaned. Jeez, he wasn't as young as he used to be. He was sure that wouldn't have hurt ten years ago. Gingerly righting himself, he made himself keep moving. He didn't have time to sit around rubbing his arse - there was too much to do.

As he paused to catch his breath for a moment, his back complaining, he looked despairingly at the mud all over his trousers. Great. Luckily Max had hopped out of the van like a mountain goat and was now stifling a grin at the sight of his dad covered in mud. At least he'd brightened Max's day.

Once he was finally unpacked, Jake started to feel calmer. Even with all the window dressing of the Nationals around, the circuit was still the same and Max was always rapid here. They'd driven this track in every possible weather condition and knew how to set the kart up, so it was due to be a good weekend.

It helped that Max's confidence was on a high after a training day with the team the previous week. He and Dommie had gone out on track together, where he learnt to deal with some of the rougher driving he'd witnessed in the previous round. After all, if he could hold his ground with Dommie, who was renowned for being a bit of a bandit on track, he could hold his ground with anyone. They'd had a great day, and really enjoyed themselves, and were now ready to take the fight to the other teams.

Jake was glad they'd done it. The training had really

helped Max, who had started to doubt himself after that crash, but of course it had been another day of team fees, tyres and circuit fees on top of everything they'd already spent. *What was a few hundred quid more on the credit card, though? What did they say? In for a penny…*

Julia was feeling rather smug as she entered the Fox Racing awning. After working hard to build her special relationship with Danny (and she'd really been putting in the effort), she expected his full backing this weekend. She smoothed the fitted t-shirt over her chest and fluffed up her hair. It was nice to feel desired again.

It had been a while since Kevin had shown her any spontaneous attention; she sometimes wondered if he wanted to have sex with her. She was probably imagining it. After all, all marriages went a bit stale, didn't they? And a man's libido dipped when they reached a certain age. You couldn't expect that initial spark to last forever.

Smiling a self-satisfied smile, she strode over to the catering table. She'd brought along a fruit bowl and enough homemade granola bars and herbal tea bags for everyone. She felt she was at the top of the pecking order, now she had Danny wrapped around her little finger, and planned to take ownership of the awning and the health of everybody in it. It would make a great article on her blog: how she'd converted the team from burger-eating slobs into healthy, fit vegans. Especially that Frankie Finch. He was a poster boy for processed meat at the moment. She could just imagine the interview she'd post with a newly-slim Frankie evangelising about how she'd turned his life around.

Eyeing her handiwork, hands on hips, she nodded, pleased. Things were going to change around here. She inhaled deeply and took a moment to centre herself using a Pranayama technique. It was such a good way to calm your nerves. She hadn't seen Danny yet this weekend and had to admit to a fluttering of butterflies.

Just as Julia exhaled and re-opened her eyes, Danny sauntered in, fag drooping out of his mouth, chatting on a phone wedged between his chin and shoulder and carrying two massive bacon and sausage baguettes, one each for him and Kevin. As Kevin gratefully tucked in, Julia shot him a murderous glance. He had bacon grease dripping down his chin and a blissful expression on his face. What a betrayal! Didn't he realise how disloyal he was being?

Oblivious to the tension he'd caused by buying breakfast, Danny, having noted Julia's figure-hugging t-shirt with approval, thought back fondly to the night they spent in a hotel the previous week. Perhaps it hadn't been the wildest night he'd ever had - as wild as the missionary position in a Premier Inn could get - but it had been good to sleep in a comfy hotel bed rather than the back of his van for a change.

He couldn't believe his bastard of a landlord had chucked him out. He was only a month behind on the rent and he never thought he'd get evicted. Usually he could wangle a few more weeks before having to cough up the dosh, but not this time. The man was a tosser. He'd had to resort to dossing at friends' houses as much as he could since then, but his welcome was wearing thin even with his closest mates, and on nights when he had no other option he'd been sleeping in his van.

That was partly why he'd jumped at the chance to meet up with Julia when she called. She could be a bit of a whiner and never stopped going on about her perfect child, which was a bit of a turn-off, but it had been nice to check into a hotel after a couple of nights of roughing it, and that yoga she did all the time certainly paid off. Usually women her age were showing some middle-age sag, but she was as limber as someone half her years.

Lying in bed afterwards, giving her the perfunctory cuddle women expected after sex, Julia had wasted no time in bringing up her plans for Eden to win the championship and overcome their underwhelming start to their season.

She pulled out a detailed schedule. Danny was to give Eden extra one-to-one on-track tuition, take him to a racing sim to analyse his driving style and data, make sure their engines were the biggest on the grid, and look into every possible way of improving the performance of the kart.

Just to shut her up, Danny had agreed.

He wondered when she'd need to get back to her husband. Soon, surely? He half listened, agreeing to go along with her plans - after all, it was extra money for him - and thankfully after half an hour she'd showered and rushed guiltily back home.

As soon as the door shut, Danny had leapt joyfully out of bed. Finding the stash in his pocket, he'd cut a couple of lines while he scanned the room service menu. *This was going to be awesome!* For the rest of the night he'd been able to chill out, eat pizza, empty the minibar and take his fill of the porn channels, all on the credit card Julia had swiped at reception. It was the best night he'd had in ages.

Sleeping in the van in this weather could be bloody cold. Although, he should have plenty of cash again by the end of this race weekend. He'd have to get her to meet up with him again this week. He could get used to staying in hotels.

He glanced over at Kevin, who had polished off his contraband breakfast and was straightening the tools on his meticulously tidy workbench. Poor mug. Did he have any idea what his wife was up to?

Probably not. The guy was so henpecked, he looked like he just wanted a quiet life. Maybe Danny was actually doing him a favour by giving Julia something else to focus on. He smiled to himself. Yes, Kevin would probably just be grateful for the break.

Just then Frankie and Ronnie sauntered in and were immediately pounced on by Julia, who was conspicuously spending time with everyone except Danny to avoid arousing suspicion.

Ushering them over to her teabags and granola she gushed, "Ah, now you two look in need of a healthy breakfast. Can I tempt you with one of my famous homemade seed and nut bars? They're packed with protein and natural sugars and they're far better for you than all that nasty processed meat." She flashed them a condescending smile before shooting a poisonous look at traitorous, bacon-sandwich-eating Kevin.

"Nah, you're alright. I'm allergic to nuts," said Ronnie, deadpan, as he plonked himself in a chair and started scrolling through his phone.

Julia frowned.

"What?"

Frankie had to hide a surprised smile; that boy was a real diamond. Picking up the prompt, he turned to Julia in mock outrage.

"I'm surprised at you, Julia! Massively irresponsible to bring food like that into the awning. Even the smell of those could put him into anaphylactic shock."

Julia, who was used to being the most morally impeccable person in the room, was briefly dumbstruck. "Well, you really should inform people about any food allergies," she retorted angrily, before removing the offending items from the awning.

Frankie and Ronnie chuckled and discreetly fist-bumped each other as they watched her leave.

One annoyance dealt with, Frankie strode over to Danny.

"Nearly time for the first session, isn't it? What do you reckon? Did our engines come up to scratch?"

"Yeah, Frank," said Danny. "They'll be great. Biggs worked his magic on them and reckoned they were huge on his dyno, biggest in the paddock. Ronnie'll be fastest on track."

Excellent. He knew Danny wouldn't let him down. This was shaping up to be a good weekend, especially now that the irritating health nut had been put back in her box.

Frankie watched the first practice session with Aaron from the grandstand. After a lap or so, he could see Eden pulling away from Ronnie whenever they were on the straights. Frowning, he turned to Danny to ask him what the fuck was going on with these supposedly amazing engines, only to find he wasn't there.

Frankie felt his temper starting to boil. *Where the hell was he? If he was powdering his nose again, instead of doing his job, he'd punch him so hard he wouldn't be snorting anything for months.*

Checking the timing screen, Frankie could see that Ronnie and Eden were doing similar lap times, but only because Eden was messing up a couple of corners and losing speed through them. As soon as the session ended, Frankie stalked back to the awning to find Danny looking far too cosy for his liking with a giggling Julia.

"Sorry, Danny, am I interrupting something?" he said loudly. The two of them sprang apart and Julia quickly scurried off.

Damn sure Danny had been in the awning throughout the whole session, Frankie played the innocent.

"So, what did you think of that session, then?"

"Oh, Ronnie looked rapid out there. It's going to be a good weekend, I can tell."

Frankie raised an eyebrow, and after an uncomfortable silence he said menacingly, "No, Danny. No he fucking didn't. He looked fucking slow out there." He gestured over to Eden. "Even this little runt has got better power than Ronnie has. Care to explain?"

Danny, pulling up the timing screen on his phone, blustered. "Come on Frank, don't overreact. Look, our boys were the fastest two on track, we'll tweak the setup and we'll be right up there."

Frankie gave him a level stare, blinked slowly and, turning his back, walked over to Aaron, who had started checking the data and jotting the tyre pressures down in his little notebook.

"What do you reckon?" said Frankie. "Was the setup wrong?"

Aaron pursed his lips thoughtfully.

"Dunno, Mr Finch. We maybe went a bit high on tyre pressures, but apart from that we were pretty much spot on I think."

"So, it was the engine? We're down on power?"

"It certainly looks that way. I'm surprised Danny didn't take the motors to be looked at, to be honest. I know he took Eden's engines down to Biggs last week and they came back really strong."

"Oh, didn't he take this one to Biggs?" Frankie's eyes narrowed.

"I don't think so; it certainly doesn't look like it's been opened up." Over Frankie's shoulder he spotted Danny frantically shaking his head in panic and realised he might be dropping his boss in it. He stammered, "but I might be wrong…"

Frankie looked him in the eyes.

"Don't bullshit me, Aaron – I don't like bullshitters."

Aaron winced. He couldn't keep them both happy, so he may as well just tell the truth.

"No, Frankie, it hasn't been opened up."

"Tell me how you know."

Aaron shifted a little and looked uncomfortable.

"Well, I hope you don't mind, Mr Finch. The thing is, years ago when I was racing karts, someone tampered with my engine and it lost me a championship, so ever since I always put a line in permanent marker across the bolts that do up the engine. That way it's easy to tell if the engine's been messed about with. If the bolts have been undone, the marker will have been wiped away or the mark won't line up. I've been doing that with Ronnie's engines. This one hasn't been touched since the last round."

"You did that on all my engines?"

"Er, yeah?" said Aaron, looking anxious.

Frankie clapped him firmly on the shoulder.

"You beauty! You've just done me a massive favour. Check the other engines for me, will you, and let me know."

Frankie shot a look over at Danny who was standing in the doorway smoking a cigarette. Danny hadn't taken the engines to Biggs after all. Even after he'd given him three grand to do just that.

If Danny left them underpowered this weekend, he was going to regret it. There was no way Aspinall would be running a second-rate engine and, with the lead he already had in the championship, they desperately needed to beat him. Frankie clenched his jaw. Danny had been taking liberties, and you didn't take liberties with Frankie Finch.

19
BACON SANDWICHES & BROKEN FINGERS

Savannah lay on the sofa and surveyed the interior of the motorhome with a dejected sigh. With the bitch ex-wife not coming to this race she'd expected things to be better, but it wasn't turning out that way. That blissful holiday glow was fading rapidly. She had driven up with Dave on Thursday night to be here all weekend, but she was already starting to regret it.

The day hadn't started well when she'd popped to the café to grab Parker a bacon sarnie and found herself standing in the queue in front of Danny Fox. She would happily have ignored him had he not put his hand on her arse and murmured, "You're a sight for sore eyes, sexy" in her ear.

Furiously, she'd spun on her heel. Staring into his weaselly face with its bloodshot eyes, she hissed, "Well your eyes certainly do look sore, you slimeball. If you ever touch me again, I'll break your fingers, understand?"

Frigid bitch, thought Danny. *Must be time of the month.* He hadn't realised she was so highly strung.

The five minutes she'd had to stand fuming in the queue before getting served felt like an eternity. She wished she'd raised her voice more when telling him to get off, so that everyone realised what he'd done, but she didn't want Dave hearing that she couldn't even go to the cafe without being felt up.

They'd been so happy since the holiday, but she knew only too well that his confidence was fragile, and she didn't want to run to him with every problem. She needed to stand on her own two feet.

To make matters worse, she'd put on a few unwanted pounds on holiday and was now on a diet, which always put her in a foul mood. Hungrily inhaling the aroma of bacon, she'd cheerfully kill for a fried breakfast right now. Instead, when she eventually reached the front of the queue, she ordered herself a black coffee and skipped breakfast, holding out for the chicken salad she'd packed in Tupperware for lunch (and dinner). At least that way she could have a guilt-free glass of wine tonight. At this rate she was going to need it.

She gratefully escaped the café and hurried back to the awning. Parker accepted the bacon sandwich with a big friendly smile and a muttered "thanks" before tucking in. Everyone else was busy getting ready for the first session and Savannah felt a bit of a spare part. Thankfully there was no sign of Hillary this morning, so she went and stood by the coffee machine to keep out of the way.

Spying an opportunity, Hugo oiled his way over. "Well hello, my dear. I'm not sure we've been properly introduced. I'm Hugo Aspinall." He leaned in to kiss her on both cheeks.

She tried not to grimace at his stale alcohol breath and backed away as much as she could against the table. What a creep. Then, feeling his chubby fingers trail around her waist, she turned to him indignantly. *Seriously? What was wrong with the men in this paddock?*

Spying Hillary swanning into the awning, Savannah

firmly pushed Hugo to one side and rushed over to talk to her. She was definitely the lesser of two evils. With the younger of her two brats in tow, Hillary trilled a "Hello, Darling" at Savannah and air-kissed her theatrically, oblivious to her husband who was sidling off surreptitiously rearranging his trousers.

Unleashed, the younger child started hurtling around the awning on a scooter, ramming it into everybody's heels and generally making a nuisance of himself.

"Oh good, I haven't missed too much. Jago had his French horn lesson this morning, which we simply couldn't skip. It's the nanny's morning off. Such a pain." She rolled her eyes at the impertinence of staff and turned to the child. "Jago, darling, don't wear yourself out too much. Don't forget Anoushka's coming to take you to taekwondo later."

Turning back to Savannah, Hillary fanned herself affectedly.

"Oh, aren't they simply gorgeous at this age?" she cooed. "It's so important to let them express themselves, isn't it? They're just so full of joie de vivre!"

Yes, if *joie de vivre* is French for bad behaviour, thought Savannah impatiently. She watched in horror as Jago abandoned his scooter in the middle of the floor and started kicking a tennis ball at the backs of people's legs while shouting that he wanted sweeeeets. She could tell the mechanics were used to having to humour over-indulged kids, but she was willing to bet Dave's patience was wearing thin.

She realised Hillary was still talking.

"I just can't understand parents who let their children play on computer games and devices all the time. It totally stifles their creativity. I'm so proud of the thoughtful individuals that my boys are becoming, so independent and inventive. Here, Jago, have a macaroon."

"No. I want sweets!" screeched Jago.

"Nonsense, darling, you know macaroons are your

favourite."

Savannah glanced over at Parker, who had polished off her breakfast and who was sitting in the corner playing a game on her phone, seemingly oblivious to the commotion. Savannah knew which child she'd rather have. Unable to bear Hillary's staggering pomposity any longer, she feigned a migraine to escape the awning. After all, if she spent much more time listening to Jago shrieking about wanting bloody sweets, she probably would get a migraine.

That had been about half an hour ago. Letting out a deep sigh, Savannah stood and put the coffee machine on, savouring the silence broken only by the gurgle and splutter of the coffee percolating. Digging a magazine out of her handbag, she settled down to read, but her brain wasn't ready to let it go. *Who the hell are all these awful people?* Did Dave really like hanging out with them? Or was it just her? Had she just become really intolerant recently? She thought of Hillary and her smug, self-satisfied face. No, it definitely wasn't just her.

A short while later Dave popped his head around the door to make sure she was OK. She'd forgotten her migraine excuse. Feeling guilty that he'd been worried about her, she didn't have the heart to tell him she'd just wanted to get away from Hillary and her creepy husband.

Instead, Savannah said she was feeling better and joined him for the first practice session. Walking down to the stands she saw Bambi and Iona arm in arm, chatting and laughing on their way to watch, and felt a pang of sadness. She missed her friends - only, of course, they'd turned out not to be friends at all. In a way, that had been much harder than breaking up with Chaz. How could it have taken her so long to realise how fake they all were? Thank goodness for Dave. He really was the one good thing in her life.

20
MOTORS & MOOLAH

Danny paced restlessly as he left his third urgent message for Biggs to call him back. Shit. What was he going to do if Biggs couldn't get an engine for Ronnie? If only he'd taken his engines to be sorted out instead of doing bloody Julia a favour and concentrating on Eden. *That woman was more trouble than she was worth. She wasn't even that good in the sack.*

The problem was, he'd spent the majority of Frankie's money paying his dealer, getting some more gear, then splurging on beer and takeaways. Whenever money had been tight in the past, he'd lived on pot noodles and toast, but without a flat he'd been eating out or having takeaways every night.

Redialling, he got Biggs' answer message again and kicked the wall in frustration. It was nearly time for the next session and Frankie would go ballistic if they didn't find some extra power from somewhere. He had to think of something, and fast.

He could take the restrictor out again - after all, it was only the practice day. But Aaron would notice and would probably go running to Frankie about it. Unless... Danny's eyes widened and the corner of his mouth twitched.

Eden had strong engines. What if he persuaded Julia to run their second-best motor for the rest of the day? They needed to sign on two engines for race day after all. He could tell her to save the best one for tomorrow. That way, he could sneakily stick Eden's best engine on Ronnie's kart. She wouldn't notice - all the engines had the same Fox Racing branding on them; it was only the engine numbers that were different.

Besides, Julia had no reason to question what he was doing. A bit of sweet-talking and she'd be putty in his hands. That's what he'd do. It would get them through today and hopefully Biggs would be able to sort something in time for tomorrow.

He jogged back to the van and grabbed Eden's number two engine from the back. After all, it was only sensible that Eden should test both his engines. They'd both been rebuilt.

Handing the number two motor to Kevin, he took Eden's big engine back to the van. It had been rapid in the last session and, even if it was only a temporary fix, it would get him through the day.

Julia would need to give the scrutineers both those engine numbers ahead of racing tomorrow, but at least it would get Frankie off his back temporarily.

He would deal with tomorrow later.

He hung around the van for a few minutes to make it look like he was getting a different engine out. He needed to let this one cool down a bit too. He was just lighting a cigarette when his phone rang.

Finally, Biggs calling him back. Thank Christ for that!

Just then, he heard a roar of engines and realised he needed to get the motor on Ronnie's kart pronto or they'd miss the last session. *Why did everything have to be such a bloody nightmare?*

He shouted to Aaron and told him to get the engine on and out on track ASAP. Aaron frowned, wondering why the engine was warm, but with Frankie looking thunderous he just shrugged and got on with it. It was none of his business where the engine had come from, as long as it was straight and gave them a bit more power.

Danny cursed as his phone stopped ringing, redialling as he walked briskly away from the awning. This was a conversation he didn't want to be overheard.

Relief flooded him as Biggs answered the phone.

"Bruv, thank goodness I got hold of you. I've got a major problem down here. I've got Frankie Finch in my awning and he's not a happy customer. His engines are way down on power and he's starting to kick off. Between you and me, he's not somebody you want to get on the wrong side of. What can you do to get us some more waft before tomorrow?"

On the other end of the phone, Biggs chuckled.

"Are you for real, Danny? I haven't seen Finch's engines since last season and you're only telling me now he's down on power? What am I supposed to be, a bloody magician?"

"Bruv, you wouldn't find it so funny if you were here. Frankie's a fucking psycho and he's on the warpath."

"I'm not surprised. You're not laying this at my door. No engine builder in the world can keep engines tuned if they never see them! What do you want me to do? Tune them telekinetically?" He laughed heartily at his own joke. "Why didn't you bring them down when you came to the workshop last week?"

Danny's head dropped and he changed tack.

"Alright, bruv, I'll level with you. I thought his engines were fine, but I've been totally caught out, and right now Frankie's threatening to make earrings out of my bollocks. So can you help me out? It's the second round of the Nationals and our championship will be screwed if we don't get some power in time for tomorrow."

Biggs relented. Danny was a flake, but he'd brought a lot of business to his door over the years.

"Look, I've got a big motor here, which I've just finished building. It hasn't done much time on the dyno yet but it's already big. I can come and drop it down to you first thing, but if you want me to drive 200 miles to do that, you're going to have to pay top dollar to rent it. It'll cost you a monkey for each day you have it."

Danny frowned. *Fucking cockney slang. What was a monkey again? £500? Whatever.*

"Can't we just test this weekend and see how we go?"

Biggs snorted. "No chance. Not if I'm driving for hours to bring it up to you for first thing tomorrow. If you want a big engine at such short notice, you can damn well pay just like anyone else would. I should charge you a premium for having to come up with something at such short notice, but I'm doing you a favour. I'll charge you the same as I'd charge any of the front runners."

Danny sighed. What other option did he have?

"OK. Let's do it. Can you get it here by 8.30 tomorrow morning? Otherwise I'm in deep shit."

Slipping the phone back into his pocket Danny rubbed the bridge of his nose. Where the hell was he going to get that money from? He should have some by the end of the weekend when he got paid, but it wouldn't be enough. He'd have to think of a way of getting the money out of either Julia or Frankie.

Besides, Biggs couldn't expect the money up front, not when it was an unexpected expense. And at least it would solve Ronnie's power problem for the weekend.

The next morning saw Danny patrolling the track gates, anxiously waiting for Biggs to arrive. There were no practice sessions on Saturday. It was straight into qualifying, so he needed that new motor pronto.

He'd had to hand in Ronnie's scrutineering card already and, since you could only sign on two engines for the whole weekend, he'd had to take a risk and put Biggs' motor along with one of Ronnie's shit ones.

The problem was there was still no sign of Biggs. If he didn't show and Ronnie qualified badly, Danny would be in a world of crap.

He desperately wanted a bit of a pick-me-up right now, but he knew Frankie would be looking for him and his stash was back in the van. There was no way he could go back to the awning without that engine. He jumped as his phone rang. He rejected the call from Frankie. It would only make him angrier, but what else could he do? He glanced at his watch. Shit, only ten minutes until quali started. Where the hell was Biggs?

Frankie, meanwhile, was nearly apoplectic with rage. *Where the fuck was Danny?* Aaron still hadn't bolted an engine onto the kart, saying Danny had told him he would bring one over and they needed to get down to the grid. *What was the fucking hold up?* Just as Frankie was about to explode, a red-faced Danny burst into the awning, sweating and out of breath having sprinted the length of the paddock and handed an engine to Aaron. He stood, hands on his knees, panting and trying to recover. Frankie folded his arms. *Talk about leaving things to the last minute. What the hell was Danny playing at?* This motor'd better do the business. If Danny let them down today, Frankie was ready to kill him.

Heading down the grid Frankie passed Cosmo surrounded by his entourage of BRR mechanics. Cosmo sneered and gave him the bird. Frankie clenched his fists and made himself keep on walking. That kid made his blood boil. *Was everyone taking the fucking piss around here?* Hoping the little prick crashed, Frankie took his place in the grandstand.

He looked across at Danny swigging an energy drink, his hands trembling. He looked nervous. As well he should, the way he'd been behaving.

"Are we sorted?" growled Frankie.

"'Course we are, Frank! Why wouldn't we be?"

Turning to watch, Frankie rubbed the centre of his chest. He didn't need this stress. It was like everyone here was just trying to piss him off as much as possible. Hearing the engines roar, he turned his attention to qualifying.

Much to Frankie's relief, Ronnie looked fast. Whatever engine Danny had bolted on was good, thank goodness. By the end of the session Ronnie was in P2, only a tenth of a second behind Cosmo.

Danny breathed a secret sigh of relief and clapped Frankie on the shoulder.

"Nice job. I told you he'd be right up there."

Frankie nodded and turned to face him. "Not sure how much of that was down to you, Danny. I don't know what the hell was going on this morning, but if I ever find you've tried to pull a fast one on me again, you'll be eating through a straw."

Danny held both palms out, a picture of affronted innocence. "Don't know what you're talking about, Frank. You need to relax," he said and walked off.

Out of sight, Danny lit a cigarette and slumped against the side of his van. Taking a deep drag, he tried to calm his heart rate, all his energy sapped after the panic of sorting Ronnie's engine out. At least he'd get through today without getting kneecapped.

Hearing a distant squawking, he winced. That would be Julia on the warpath because Eden only qualified in tenth. Rolling his eyes heavenwards, he braced himself for the oncoming affront as she came looking for him.

"There you are! What the hell was that, Danny? You had poor Eden's kart setup totally wrong! We hardly even saw you before we went out on track! Tenth! I can't believe we came tenth!"

Danny shrugged, his patience at an all-time low.

"Well, suck it up, sweetheart. I thought he did well to get tenth the way he was driving, if I'm honest. Eden had the same setup as Ronnie and, with the engine he's got, he should have been one of the fastest out there. Don't blame me if the kid can't drive, he just messed it up."

Julia's mouth gaped in outrage. How could he talk to her like that? And to say such unkind things about Eden! She thought she had him on side!

Danny ploughed on. "If Eden hadn't made so many mistakes he could have been right up there with Ronnie, so he's got no one to blame but himself."

After weeks of working on Danny, and a not-insignificant amount of blowjobs, Julia was astonished that he could talk to her that way. Had it all meant nothing to him? It had always worked on Kevin whenever she'd wanted something.

Stunned briefly into silence, she gaped, mouth ajar. Danny took advantage to escape back to the awning. *For fuck's sake, what was wrong with everybody today?* It was only 9am and already he couldn't wait to leave the circuit.

He ran his hand through his hair, a sense of despair settling over him. They still had three races to go before the end of the day.

21
TEA & TANTRUMS

The weekend progressed without incident and by Sunday afternoon the sun was shining. Commentator Giles Winyard was feeling unseasonably hot and sweaty up in the commentary box. Wriggling out of his tweed jacket, he rolled up his sleeves and took a swig of tea. Ugh! he shuddered. Cold tea was vile but he needed something to whet his pipes before the finals started. Checking the mic was off, he straightened in his chair and did some quick voice exercises.

"Mah mae mi moe moo," he sang, gurning and exaggerating his lip movements to get himself warmed up ready for the task ahead. "Peter piper picked a peck of pickled peppers." He smacked his lips and took a few deep breaths. Right, he was ready. The cadet drivers were starting to line up on the grid, so he'd better start the show.

"Welcome to Round Two of the British Karting Championships. We're starting off today's finals with the cadet class, which is always guaranteed to give us some fantastic close racing, especially in such a busy field. We've got a full grid of kids out there today, and they're all hungry to get their hands on some silverware.

"On pole position, after a cracking weekend, is Cosmo Aspinall, the pundit's hot tip for winning the championship this year, followed by little Ronnie Finch. Young Aspinall is only eleven years old, and he's certainly living up to his billing so far. He's currently leading the championship by eight points. The big question is, can anyone beat him? Or can he extend his lead by winning here again today?

"Right then, off they go on the formation lap. Aspinall is, of course, running with the newly formed BRR team, run by our very own home-grown F1 driver, Ben Redmaine. Incidentally, Ben was kind enough to take me out to dinner last night. It was great to get the inside story on the professional setup he's bringing to the sport. It's not just about the driving in BRR, these kids have their own personal trainers, dietitians, a sim to train on. It's basically an F1-style regime to help them maximise all that potential and hone them into the Formula 1 drivers of the future.

"As they finish the warm-up lap and line up on the start line, we're waiting for the lights… which go out and go, go go! We're racing!

"Lovely start there by Aspinall, Carver follows him through, dropping Finch down to third place. Finch also looks like he might be in trouble from our new rookie driver Max Golding, who is already snapping at his heels. Golding, of course, took the rookie trophy in Round One, despite having a very difficult time of it earlier in the weekend, and he looks like he's ready to fight the big boys today.

"As they start lap two, Aspinall has pulled a lead from the other drivers who are squabbling amongst themselves. They really need to work together if they want to try and catch him. I can see him running away with the race at this rate.

"Oh, and Golding makes a move on Finch, putting himself behind his teammate! Now the question is, will they work together or will they fight amongst themselves? Aspinall's teammate Parker North is down in sixth position and quite a way behind, so he's all alone at the front, but superstar that he is Aspinall's not put a foot wrong so far. A classy drive from this young man.

"Ah, now Carver just glanced over his shoulder and Golding is giving him the signal to work together. Nose to tail, they're getting the benefit of bump drafting and they're starting to catch Aspinall. It won't take them long at this rate - two karts working together round this track are always faster than one, no matter who that one is."

Giles took a quick breather and a swig of cold tea, which he nearly spat all over the commentary box window as Carver made a bold move.

"Oh my goodness, Aspinall is off! It looks like Carver might have tagged him trying an overtake and he's spun off the track! He's wasted no time getting back on, and it looks like Golding might have been affected by that too as he's now dropped back into the path of Finch. Bit of a clumsy move there by Carver. I'm sure the stewards will be taking a look at that later.

"So, as we head into the final lap, the order has completely changed. Carver is out front on his own, followed by his teammate Golding in a surprising second place, being hounded at every turn by Ronnie Finch. Can the rookie take the pressure of having a seasoned racer like Finch on his tail? We only have one lap left to find out.

"Aspinall, meanwhile, is now back in sixth position behind his teammate. If only they had more time, they could work together to get back to the front. But, oh, Ronnie Finch makes the move on Golding and goes into second position as they come into the last corner. What a move! So, as they cross the line, the final positions are Carver in first, Finch second and Golding in third. Poor Cosmo Aspinall isn't going to be happy with that result, and we'll have to see what the stewards make of that move by Carver, which had such an impact on his race. Thrilling stuff from our young drivers out there today."

Giles slumped back in his chair, reaching for the Mars bar from his jacket pocket. That had been a hell of a battle. What a disappointment for Cosmo, though, and he sounded like such a nice kid. Ben had mentioned at dinner last night how much of a menace that Carver was. What a shame Cosmo's race had been ruined by him.

Over in parc fermé, all hell was breaking lose. Cosmo had hurled his helmet on the floor in a furious rage, screaming and shouting about how he'd been fired off by Carver. Ben Redmaine tried to calm him down without success, then turned to Hugo telling him to get Cosmo the hell out of parc fermé before he got himself a ban for bad behaviour. In an undertone, he added, "Don't worry, we'll get this sorted out in the office."

Dommie, Max and Ronnie were standing mouths agape as they watched Cosmo's spectacular tantrum. As soon as he was ushered away by his grim-faced father, the spell was broken and they turned to each other, laughing and gossiping, both boys congratulating Dommie on the win.

Dommie pulled a face. "Thanks. That's if I'm allowed to keep it. I dare say Aspinall's headed straight into the office to lodge a complaint."

"Yeah, but you didn't do anything wrong. I was right there. Cosmo just lost his head and panicked when you went to overtake. He spun himself out and managed to tag me in the process."

"I know," Dommie shrugged. "We'll see, I guess. I've had too many penalties to be optimistic. I reckon they'll want to make an example of me if what my dad says is right."

Unfortunately for him, Dommie was right. After fifteen minutes he was summoned to the stewards and was issued a one-lap penalty for 'driving in a manner incompatible with general safety'.

"Oof, that's harsh," winced Chase shaking his head.

Carver let out a sigh, shoulders slumped.

"Yeah, but what did we expect? Dommie always seems to get penalties, especially whenever he goes near certain drivers."

He turned to Max, who was looking shocked by all this, and extended his hand. "Well done to you though, young man. Our penalty puts you up to second place. Good to see you on the podium for only your second race at national level."

Max mumbled, "Thanks. It seems really unfair on Dommie, though."

Carver gave a dry laugh.

"Well, that's motorsport for you. Some people win on track, other people try to win in the office. We'll just come back and try again next time."

"I don't know how you can be so philosophical about it," said Jake, shaking his head. "I'd be livid. Can't you appeal the decision?"

"We could do, but there's no point. You can put money down to appeal it and it'll just get looked at by the same people who made the original decision. They're not going to change their mind. Plus, they have their favourites, and we're certainly not on that list. You're just throwing your money down the drain. Unless you have footage proving something and you're prepared to take it to court, you're better off just accepting it. You've got to pick your battles in this sport."

Chase clapped Carver sympathetically on the shoulder.

"Next time, mate. Come back and get the result next time."

Frankie Finch stood looking up at the podium, his heart swelling with pride. This was Ronnie's first win in the Nationals, and he looked great up there on the top step with his big silver trophy. He couldn't be prouder.

There was something bothering him, though. It had taken Aspinall being punted off and Carver getting a penalty for him to get the win, and that wasn't good enough. Even though Danny had found some more waft, he hadn't exactly done a great job this weekend and really needed to pull his finger out.

When Frankie had looked at the lap times, Ronnie was consistently slower than Cosmo. He simply wouldn't be able to win in a straight fight with the kit he'd currently got. Frankie wasn't prepared to rely on luck for Ronnie to win. Danny needed to do the job he was being paid handsomely to do, get the engines sorted, and get his brain out of his fucking trousers.

He'd spotted Danny and Julia all over each other again earlier. What on earth must her husband be thinking? Didn't he realise what she was up to? It had to be embarrassing for him. That aside, Frankie just didn't trust Danny any more.

All season, whenever Frankie had questioned their lack of pace compared to another driver, Danny's response had always been to say they were cheating. Frankie knew that was a possibility but it wasn't going to be true of everyone racing at the front.

Frankie had a nasty feeling he'd been taken for a mug, and he wasn't going to stand for that. Danny aside, there was also the issue of the blatant favouritism towards the BRR drivers. Cosmo was being allowed to get away with blue murder, with everyone around him receiving penalties. He needed to find a way to get that in check.

He would take Danny to one side and have a word. Reassert some authority around here. There was no way he was paying for this weekend, not after Danny left them without an engine until a few minutes before qualifying, and not after he'd lied about getting the engines tuned.

Besides, Danny had done fuck-all this weekend. It was Aaron who'd done everything. That kid had done a bang-up job on the spanners this weekend and proved his loyalties were in the right place. He'd pay Aaron and give him a bit on top too; he'd earned it.

That would get Danny thinking about who he needed to focus on instead of bloody Julia.

Frankie had already spoken with Aaron to make sure all Ronnie's engines, including the new one they ran this weekend, didn't disappear back into Danny's van.

Until he'd got that three grand back off Danny, he wouldn't be getting near their kit. He'd deal directly with Biggs from now on. Nobody mugged off Frankie Finch and got away with it.

22
DROP AND GIVE ME TWENTY

It had been a long time since Fat Frankie Finch had graced the inside of a gym, and he hadn't realised it would involve so much pain. *It didn't used to hurt this much to do exercise!* But today was his day to bite the bullet and start getting back into shape.

It was becoming hard to ignore his growing unfitness, especially since he was breathing like a bulldog in a sauna every time he went upstairs lately, and what with the constant nagging from Linda he had caved in.

If he was honest, it was an incident during the week that had really convinced him to do something. Every Wednesday night, he and Linda had date night. It was a tradition they'd started years earlier so they could have a break from the kids and spend some quality time together. The activities changed from week to week. Sometimes they'd go out for dinner, other nights they'd head out to a bar, stay overnight in a hotel, even just go for a walk, but it always ended the same way: in bed.

Frankie had always been a busy man. His chosen career path was a demanding one and could often drag him away from family life, leaving Linda feeling neglected and resentful - something he'd discovered during a monstrous row, which involved Linda throwing a great deal of their crockery at his head. After that, they'd decided date night would be sacred from then on.

This week, the kids were sleeping over at their nan's while he and Linda headed out to their local Italian. After a delicious bistecca fiorentina, followed by tiramisu and washed down with a couple of bottles of wine, they boozily meandered home, arms around each other, laughing and in high spirits.

As soon as they got in through the front door, the mood shifted. Linda turned to him, a sparkle in her eye, and started a slow striptease. Wriggling her dress to the floor and dancing backwards she beckoned him into the kitchen. Frankie's eyes widened. *The kitchen? They hadn't done it in there for years!* A slow grin spread across his face as he followed her, eyes glued to her toned behind as it swayed its way along the hall, by now only a tiny pair of lace knickers stopping her from being completely naked.

Biting her lip, she swung herself onto the kitchen counter, gasping as she felt the cold granite against her bare skin. She slowly slid her fingers inside the scrap of lace. Frankie watched her as he quickly shed his clothes - without any of the finesse she'd displayed and already at full attention. He moved between her legs, slowly kissing a path up her inner thighs, making her squirm as he moved higher.

Pulling the damp lace to one side, he breathed hotly, making her groan and she roughly grabbed his hair and pulled him in towards her. His tongue working hard, he glanced up at her. Head thrown back, tits gloriously spotlit as she bucked and moaned, she looked spectacular. Thrusting two fingers inside her, he increased the pressure and she grabbed the worktop as she felt her climax rising. He could tell she was close and kept up the pace until she reached a shuddering orgasm. "Oh my God, Frankie," she gasped. "Get inside me now." Not needing to be asked twice, he slipped inside her and groaned. Jesus, she felt good.

Picking up speed, he could tell it wouldn't be long before they both came together. The problem was, he was starting to tire. He found himself slowing, fatigue sweeping over him, as he struggled to catch his breath. He pushed on, gritting his teeth, sweat beading on his forehead. Knowing they were both so close, he put in a Herculean effort until they both came, clutching each other and shuddering.

Lying bonelessly on the sofa afterwards, he would usually have been happy and relaxed, but that episode had worried him. That was the first time in a while they'd had sex anywhere other than in bed and, thinking about it, Linda usually did most of the work. She liked taking charge. It was a shock how close he'd come to giving up because he was knackered, and that really wouldn't do.

One thing Linda wouldn't put up with was no Wednesday night delight. She'd assume he was seeing somebody on the side and he didn't want any more dishes hurled at his head.

That's how Frankie found himself in the boxing gym at 7am, getting beasted by Smiler.

He'd made a call to an old sparring partner after Linda had gone to bed and told him he needed to get back into shape fast. He'd been told that Tony 'Smiler' Collins was just the man for the job.

Smiler was a nice kid. At six feet four, he was 200 pounds of pure muscle and boasted a spectacular set of gold front teeth after his original, slightly goofy incisors had been knocked out in a street fight a few years earlier. They flashed whenever the kid opened his mouth.

On the exercise bike earlier, Frankie had found himself pondering who would win in a fight between Smiler and Chris. He needed some distraction from all this fucking pain. In the ring, where there were rules to be obeyed, it might be Smiler. But in the real world, where you put your opponent down the fastest way possible, it would be no contest. Chris would walk it. Somehow that made him feel better about the punishment he was suffering.

Frankie was on sit-ups now. He leant back on his elbows, trying not to let on how much his abs were screaming after doing three sets. The squats and the bike had been bad enough, and he was ready to call it a day.

After two minutes of rest, Smiler barked "Right, next exercise. Drop to the floor and give me twenty push-ups."

Frankie gave him a dangerous glare and considered telling him to fuck off. But Smiler just shrugged and flashed those gold teeth at him.

"Come on, man, this is what you signed up for."

He was right. Nothing about getting fit was going to be easy. Wearily, Frankie started doing push-ups. *Fucking hell, this was horrendous.* How had he become this unfit? Struggling through the exercises, arms shaking, he collapsed onto his back. His chest heaved. Smiler grinned and chucked a pair of boxing gloves at him.

"Take five minutes, then let's do some bag work to finish."

Finish? Thank Christ it was nearly over. He wouldn't be able to move tomorrow at this rate. Frankie heaved himself to his feet. Just then, his phone rang. He grabbed for it, breathing a sigh of relief. Saved by the bell.

Glancing at the screen he said, "Sorry, Smiler, I just need to take this". It was Biggs.

"Yes?"

"Hello, Frankie. Biggs here. I just got into the workshop to find your man Chris waiting here for me. About time I saw your motors! I was beginning to think you were taking them somewhere else. And while I'm delighted that's not the case, we've got a problem. I'm afraid I've still got an outstanding bill here for work I did for you towards the end of last year. I'll need that settling before I can do any more."

Frankie raised an eyebrow and took a calming breath. So, Danny hadn't paid his bills from last year, as well as pocketing all that money he'd given him to get the engines sorted. *Wanker.*

"It seems our mutual friend Danny Fox has been taking both of us for a ride. I've been giving him money to get our engines seen to and from what I'm discovering he's been pocketing the cash and telling you to put the work on account. Am I right so far?"

Biggs agreed.

"That's when he actually bothers to bring my engines in. I take it he didn't bring them in last week, like he said he did?"

"No. I did see him last week - he brought Eden Leech's engines in, but that was all. I figured you'd gone to another engine builder, mate, or I'd have let you know."

Frankie closed his eyes. "So, let me get this straight. When were my engines last looked at, exactly?"

He could hear pages turning as Biggs flicked through job sheets. He whistled. "It's actually been even longer than I thought. The last time I rebuilt your engines was back in June last year. They must be shot if you haven't had them looked at since then! Was that engine I brought up at the weekend any better? I saw you got a good result?"

So that's how they'd suddenly found some extra power for the racing. "Yeah, mate, that engine was good. Appreciate that, thanks. So how much do I owe you?"

"Well, the outstanding bill is for £1,600, then there's the bill for the weekend: two days rental at £500 a day. I'm not sure whether you're paying that or whether Danny is?"

"The rental is definitely Danny's expense. You'll have to get that off him, I'm afraid. I'll sort you out with the outstanding payment on my account and whatever you need for today. Pass me over to Chris and he'll give you the money. It looks like we'll both be chasing Danny for money this week."

"No problem, mate. Good to have you back on the books again. I'll get those engines back up to scratch for you and see if we can't get you some top power. I'm sorry to hear you've been fleeced. Between you and me, Danny seems to have gone off the rails recently."

"Tell me about it. That kid needs a short, sharp shock to bring him to his senses," said Frankie, "and I'll be more than happy to do that."

Biggs chuckled.

"I wouldn't like to be Danny when you next see him. He won't be getting any more credit from me either. I'll be suspending his account until he's paid for the rental, so he's going to be feeling pretty unpopular."

Frankie smiled. Good. Let Danny realise he couldn't fuck people over without there being consequences. "While you're on the phone," he said, "I'm constantly hearing from Danny that all the other front runners are cheating whenever they've got more pace than us. What do you think? Is that just bullshit to cover up for him not doing his job properly, or are they really all messing about?"

"Ah, that's the age-old question in motorsport, isn't it? People fly as close to the limit of the rules as they can without getting into trouble, and there are always people prepared to take things that bit further. But have I heard anything about this year? Nothing worth repeating. All I can tell you for sure is that no one is cheating with engines. I'd know - after all, it's my reputation on the line. And all the front-running kids are on my engines. As to other stuff, your guess is as good as mine, I'm afraid.

"My advice to you would be to just concentrate on getting Ronnie as fast as you can. Wondering what other people are doing is just a distraction, and one you don't need right now, especially if you want to catch Aspinall this year."

Fair enough, thought Frankie. *That sounded reasonable.* And he trusted Biggs a lot more than he trusted Danny. As long as you were paying Biggs he was working in your interest.

Gesturing another five minutes to Smiler, he dialled Danny. He wanted to see what the little shit had to say about not paying his bills. After a dozen rings, Danny finally answered the phone, a deafening noise in the background making him barely intelligible. He was clearly at a track somewhere.

Frankie asked him where he was. Danny couldn't hear him, so Frankie repeated the question, shouting. Not realising the trouble he was already in, Danny admitted he was out on a test day with Eden. "Getting some laps in at the circuit ready for the next round of the Nationals. I didn't think you'd want to come, Frank. I know you don't like Ronnie taking time out of school midweek, and let's face it, bruv, Eden needs the practice more than he does."

Frankie glowered and ended the call.

That confirmed it. The guy was a snake, and he was taking the piss. Not only was he shagging that sanctimonious Julia and giving Eden preferential treatment, but Danny had ripped him off. As much as he wanted to take the matter into his own hands and kick the shit out of him, he had to think carefully about how to deal with this.

He pulled on the boxing gloves, holding his wrists out for Smiler to do them up, all of his previous tiredness replaced with anger. He was in the mood to give something a good thrashing.

23
WINDSWEPT & WILD

Jake slumped on the sofa and cracked open a can of cider. It was 2am and he needed to be up early in the morning, but right now he just needed to chill out for a bit. After much discussion, he and Bambi had decided to buy a caravan. Staying at hotels was just too expensive and at least if they owned a caravan they could sell it again afterwards and recoup some of their money. It was big enough to sleep all three of them and had a large awning that could be unwound on one side. It had taken the last of their savings, but they were all quite excited about their first weekend in it.

As they'd set off for the track earlier that evening, it almost felt like they were going on holiday rather than to a race weekend. Plus, as Jake had pointed out, they could now have free caravan holidays. Bambi wasn't sure how keen she was on that idea, but tried to look on the bright side and not think wistfully of the quaint little gîte in France she'd had her heart set on.

Round Three of the Nationals was at Brompton Oak Circuit, in Kent. It was a track they'd never been to before and they'd had a baptism of fire on the journey. The news had warned of storms and high winds, but they hadn't realised just how hair-raising it would be towing a caravan in such wild weather. It was a good thing they were towing it with a large and fully laden van. Jake had felt the wind really catch the caravan a few times - had they been in a normal car, they might just have toppled over.

The Dartford Crossing had been one of the worst parts. A massive cable-stayed bridge high above the River Thames, the drop would have been dizzying in daylight. In a way the darkness was a blessing, but it didn't stop the buffeting winds. It felt like they were traversing a 500-foot-high tightrope as they were blustered around.

What made it worse was that speed was restricted on the bridge because of the weather. Jake would rather have just planted his foot and got over as fast as possible. It was no bad thing that Max was fast asleep across Bambi's lap. He wasn't keen on heights and this would have petrified him!

As they reached the other side of the bridge and more sheltered ground, they both let out sighs of relief. At least the way back was via a tunnel, although navigating a narrow, two-mile-long Victorian burrow under the Thames with a caravan in tow would bring its own challenges. That was a problem for Sunday night, though. They had a race weekend to get through first.

After what felt like an age, they pulled through the gates of the circuit to find the paddock deathly quiet and absolutely packed. Jake scanned the rows of tightly parked vehicles in despair. Where on earth were they going to plot up? All the teams had set up earlier that day, so there were awnings and race trucks filling every available space. Making things worse, the paddock was on a steep gradient. Built amid the rolling Kent hills, the rise was extreme from one end of the track to the other.

They crawled slowly along the bottom row of parking, only to find there wasn't enough room to turn the caravan around the corner and take it further up the paddock. As tempted as Jake was to just abandon the caravan where it stood, he knew that wasn't really an option. He climbed wearily down from the van, clothes flapping wildly around him in the lashing rain, and struggled up to the top of the hill, where he could see the Apex awning.

After five minutes he returned, soaked and shivering, to report there was no room up at the top, so they'd have to park along the bottom row wherever they could find a gap. After a further recce, Jake found a space just big enough to squeeze into. It was nowhere near the team awning, but they'd have to park there and carry everything up the hill manually first thing tomorrow.

Manoeuvring a caravan into a tight space isn't easy, especially when you've never done it before, and even less so when the weather, the darkness and your heightened stress levels are working against you. But eventually, after a great deal of frustration, they got it into the parking space, unhooked it and put the feet down. Bambi helped a bleary-eyed Max stumble from the van straight into bed where he immediately went back to sleep.

The caravan had one bedroom with a double bed, now occupied by a tightly curled-up Max, and the sofas in the living room pulled out to make a second bed. Sighing, and wanting nothing more than to join Max and give in to sleep, Bambi pulled her woolly hat down with grim determination and went back out to help Jake.

Shivering in the blustering wind, the rain now reduced to a mean, sharp drizzle, she helped guide the van into a tiny space between two enormous race trucks and wondered for the millionth time why they were doing this. Yes, she knew it was great to give Max the chance to race at the Nationals, but at what cost? They seemed to be getting more and more into debt, Jake's company was getting increasingly frustrated with him taking days off (although he insisted they were okay about it), and every time Monday morning came around they were all exhausted.

It wasn't just the Nationals either, it was all the race weekends they were having to do in between to stay competitive. The other kids were out racing every weekend, so they needed to be too. There were no such things as days off any more. This had taken over their lives.

Looking down, she realised with despair that she'd been standing in a rivulet of water and her boots were leaking. *Great. There was no way those would be dry by the morning. It wasn't as if the caravan had radiators you could leave them on overnight.*

Heading back inside, they both collapsed gratefully onto the sofa. Bambi sat hugging a large glass of red wine, wrapped in a blanket, while she listened to the howling wind and felt the caravan rocking in the storm. When she closed her eyes, she could imagine herself as a polar explorer huddled in a tent, listening to a blizzard blowing outside. At least she had a glass of wine. Shackleton wouldn't have had that. She should be grateful for a few home comforts.

The paddock was on too much of a gradient for them to level the caravan properly, so the floor sloped down wards. With everything on a kilter, walking around felt a bit like being at sea.

As she put her glass down on the table, it slid for a couple of inches before coming to a stop. Closing her eyes, Bambi hoped this would be a good weekend.

The next morning, the sky was bright and sunny, although the wind hadn't dropped and the trees around the top half of the circuit were shimmying wildly. It hadn't been the best night's sleep with the squally weather, but Bambi was grateful for a later start this morning.

At least they hadn't been up at 6am to drive to the track, like they would if they'd been staying in a hotel, and the fact that she could stay in her pyjamas frying bacon and drinking coffee while the boys heaved the kit up to the top of the hill was certainly a bonus.

Out of the window she'd seen Max racing back down the hill more than once chasing after a wheel or tool which had fallen off the trolley and was tumbling down towards the caravan. The paddock being on such a slant certainly wouldn't make Jake's job of pushing the kart around any easier this weekend. He'd be worn out and grumpy by the end of the day.

Savouring the smell of bacon, Bambi determinedly bit into an apple instead. She just seemed to be piling on weight recently, so a fry-up probably wasn't the ideal breakfast. Outside, she caught the sound of Jake's raised voice and, peering out through the blinds, spotted him on the phone.

"Of course I'm committed to the job, but I'm also committed to my family and I've had this day booked off for months." He pinched the bridge of his nose while he listened. "I understand that you're in a bind, and that it's urgent, but I'm also three hours away from the office and will be until Sunday night, so there's nothing I can do."

Oh dear, thought Bambi, *as if things hadn't been strained enough at Jake's work. The last thing he needed was a falling out with his boss.*

Despite his best intentions and his promise to Linda, Frankie Finch was already in a foul mood by the time he arrived at the circuit. Not bothering to look for a parking space, he abandoned his Jag in a disabled bay and strode with ominous purpose towards the Fox Racing awning. As he passed Danny's van, he overheard giggling from the back and glowered. *Nothing had changed, then.* He was contemplating banging on the side of the van when he spotted Chase, who gave him an affable wave. Perhaps it would be good to put some feelers out and see whether Apex was a team worth considering. He certainly needed to make some changes.

"How's it going, Frankie?" said Chase, shaking his hand.

"Not great, if I'm honest. The team's a right shambles at the moment."

"I'm not surprised. Rumour in the paddock is that Danny's in a bit of a downward spiral." Chase shook his head sadly. "I've known him since we were kids, but I've never seen him this bad before. He's always been one for partying, but since he lost his flat I think he's been spending all his money getting loaded. His judgement seems to be totally out of whack."

Frankie shrugged. "That's a pretty good assessment of it. I'll see how this weekend goes, but I'm not impressed with the way things are right now."

"Well, if you need anything, just give me a shout, OK? We'd be glad to have someone like Ronnie in the team."

Frankie chuckled to himself. Team bosses - they were always scouting. There was no loyalty in this game. He'd bet that Carver wouldn't be quite as welcoming as Chase if he knew Ronnie was thinking of joining Apex.

Danny, who'd made up with Julia and enjoyed a few more Premier Inn nights of passion over the previous weeks, overheard snatches of their conversation from the back of the van and had been frantically shushing Julia so he could listen. He swore softly under his breath. He'd been so wrapped up in keeping Julia happy, he'd taken it for granted that Frankie was onboard.

He hadn't heard from Frankie since the last round, except for that brief call while he was out testing with Eden when they'd got cut off. He shook his head. Nah, if Frankie was pissed off, he would have said something. He wasn't one to keep his grievances to himself.

All the same, he couldn't afford to lose the team fees Frankie was paying, especially since Biggs was suddenly being a tight-arse and had called in his debts. Danny fumbled hastily with his trousers so he could catch Frankie before he disappeared, leaving Julia dishevelled and indignant on the floor of the van. He needed to get Frankie back on side. If he didn't get his team fees for this weekend, he was screwed.

Jogging back to the awning, Danny ran it through in his head. Perhaps Frankie had cottoned on to the affair with Julia and that was pissing him off. Maybe he should cool things down a bit. She was starting to get on his nerves anyway, always lecturing him about having a cleaner lifestyle and settling down. He could practically feel the disapproval rolling off her whenever he lit up.

She was getting too big for her boots and had made some alarming comments about a future she was imagining they'd have together. He needed to put a stop to that idea before it took root and she did something stupid like leave her husband.

He spotted Frankie and Aaron standing by the kart, discussing their plan for the day, and clapped Frankie jovially on the shoulder.

"Frank, bruv, long time no see!" he interrupted. "Good to be back at Brompton, eh? Ronnie loves this track, doesn't he? I reckon it's going to be a brilliant weekend for him."

"Still," said Frankie, unsmilingly, "he could have done with some practice around here ahead of the weekend. You know, like you did with Eden?"

Danny chuckled and slung an arm around Frankie's shoulders, which Frankie immediately shrugged off.

"Ah, but Eden needed the practice, Frank. Man, he was crap around here. We all know that Ronnie's great on this track. Besides," he lowered his voice conspiratorially, "between you and me, Julia was banging on and on about getting him out here. I did it just to shut her up. She's such a nightmare. Won't leave me alone!"

"Well, perhaps if you weren't shagging her, she wouldn't be pestering you quite so much," Frankie growled.

Danny laughed, oblivious to Frankie's underlying

anger.

"Tell me about it! Wish I'd never gone there. You know what it's like, bruv, it all seems like a good idea at the time, especially when it's handed to you on a plate. And these older birds, they're always grateful," he leered.

Frankie remained stony-faced. *What a tosser.* Danny, meanwhile, wittered on, scrolling through his phone.

"Just look at all these texts she keeps sending me, she never bloody stops. Desperate, she is! *Hi Danny, What you up to, Danny? Miss you Danny, Can't wait to see you.*" He shook his head in mock disbelief. "But then, who can blame her," he said, running his hand through his hair and winking.

"Anyway," said Frankie, "things to do. You'd best get back to your girlfriend. She'll be looking for you."

With that, he turned back to Aaron, effectively ending the conversation. Danny sauntered back outside the awning to have a fag, grinning to himself. Everything seemed under control in there.

Brompton Oak was a tricky circuit, especially after the storm the previous night. Split across two levels, the top half of the circuit was overhung by trees, leaving the track permanently damp, whereas the lower part was bone-dry within minutes of the sun coming out. These differing track conditions meant that, while slicks were fast on the dry part of the circuit, you ran the risk of skidding off into the barriers at the top, and if you chose wet tyres they'd be destroyed within a few laps on the dry tarmac. There just wasn't an ideal solution.

Drivers had to be able to maintain control in slippery conditions as well as drive to preserve their tyres. It took real skill, so this round was always a challenge. Happily, today was just a test day.

Many of the dads fervently hoped that the track would be fully dry by the time they reached quali the next morning.

24
TOPPLING DOMINOES

After a frustrating day of being blanked by Danny, Julia had decided she needed to up the ante. On Saturday, she arrived at the track having put in maximum effort. Her hair was glossy and blow-dried, makeup carefully applied – if a little heavily for daytime – and she was squeezed into a tight t-shirt and jeans to show off her slim figure. Perhaps he just needed reminding of what he'd be missing if he didn't start paying her some attention.

By 10am, when qualifying was over (Eden had finished a solid sixth, which wasn't ideal, but she would overlook that), she strode purposefully back towards the awning. Frankie was deep in discussion with his mechanic on one side, and Danny was chatting to Kevin.

She bristled. Well, didn't they just seem to be getting on famously? Nice that Danny had time to lavish on her husband. Pushing down her frustration, she sashayed over, giving them the benefit of her sweetest smile.

"Well, what do we think of that, boys?" she said, trailing her hand across Danny's bottom as she walked past. To her irritation, he didn't react other than stepping slightly away.

"I was just talking to Kevin about that. It was a good result, wasn't it, bruv?" he said. To her annoyance, he was still including her husband in the conversation, rather than focusing on her.

She looked up at him through long, mascaraed eyelashes and, catching his hand, said, "Could I have a quick word with you, Danny?" She smiled before murmuring in an undertone, "In private...?"

Her smile hung for a few seconds, froze and was then quickly replaced with frown as Danny impatiently pulled his hand away.

"No, Julia, I'm working."

She stared at him, horror-struck, watching his back as he left the awning. *What the hell was he playing at?*

She felt a pair of hands rest gently on her shoulders.

"Let him go, love, you need to back off."

Her resentment boiling over, she spun on her heel and hissed.

"Oh, just fuck off, Kevin. What do you know, anyway?"

Kevin regarded her sadly. He'd known his wife for a long time and recognised that she wouldn't let this drop until it had blown up in her face - unless he stepped in. She'd always obsessively gone after whatever she wanted and had never been able to take no for an answer with any grace.

"I know it's time for you to stop this now," he said softly. "Whatever's happened in the past, you need to stop chasing him. He's been giving you the cold shoulder all weekend. You need to stop throwing yourself at him, it's getting embarrassing. He's just not interested any more."

Julia gaped at him. *What a horrible thing to say!* As if Kevin knew what he was talking about. He was just jealous. If he was more of a man, she'd never have looked elsewhere in the first place. She shook his hands off her, her eyes filling with furious tears. She spat, "What would you know? He's shown more interest in me than you have done in years! He's more of a man than you've ever been!"

Kevin sighed and looked at his feet. She was probably right. If he was honest, for years now he'd only initiated sex with Julia out of some feeling of obligation. He still loved her, but they just seemed to want such different things. She was on her militant health crusade, constantly posting a perfect version of their lives on Instagram, and when he wasn't working, he'd much rather be down the gym or chilling with Netflix and a beer.

Lifting his eyes to hers, he said, "I'm sorry if I've let you down, Julia. Let's get through this weekend and we'll have a fresh start. We're stuck here for the next few days, but I'll talk to a couple of different teams and we'll see what our options are going forward, okay?"

Julia truculently agreed. Perhaps that would be for the best. After all, they had to think about Eden's best interests, and he should definitely be qualifying higher than sixth place. It was probably down to Danny that he hadn't won a race yet. He was much better than that Golding kid and should easily be beating him.

Besides, if Kevin was prepared to make the effort, then she probably should too. Giving him a tight smile, she left the awning to get some air.

Frankie chuckled to himself, having overheard the exchange, pleased that everything was starting to tumble down around Julia. She should have known better than to try and disturb the balance of power in the team. Now, at least he would have Danny's full focus on Ronnie. The question was, did he still want it?

As dusk settled itself over the rolling hills of Kent, Savannah meandered her way happily back through the paddock, the mixed scent of barbecuing burgers and generator exhaust fumes hanging in the evening air.

With the bitch ex-wife away, she'd actually had a nice day. Parker seemed to have done well, and it was lovely seeing the pleasure Dave got from watching her on track. Savannah was beginning to understand why they both loved this sport so much. She'd even found herself shouting encouragement and yelping with delight during the last heat when Parker had made a particularly good overtake.

Dave and Parker would both be in the awning for another couple of hours yet, debriefing and getting everything prepped and ready for tomorrow, so she was heading back to the motorhome, planning to paint her nails and watch a bit of Saturday night telly.

At least that way she could avoid having to hang out with hooray-Hillary and horrible Hugo with his wandering hands.

Shaking her head to dislodge the flash of annoyance she felt thinking about the Aspinalls, she turned the corner and was knocked backwards onto the floor. Landing heavily, she heard a smash and realised she was covered in wine. She stared, shocked, at a madly apologising Bambi.

"Oh my God, I'm so sorry. I was lost in thought and totally didn't look where I was going!"

Savannah smiled shakily.

"Me too, please don't worry about it. Sorry about your wine!"

"I'm sure it was totally my fault," Bambi grimaced. "It's the first thing I've broken today, which is probably some kind of record for me!" She shrugged her shoulders with resignation. "Besides, it's probably not a bad thing if I have less to drink tonight. I think all us mums self-medicate with alcohol on race weekends, don't we?"

"I can totally understand that! It must be so stressful watching your child out there racing. Let me get you another bottle, we've got plenty in the fridge."

"It's fine, please don't worry," laughed Bambi. "We're always well stocked with alcohol! Do you want to come and have a glass too?"

Surprised, Savannah thought how nice it would be to

have a relax and a chat, especially as Bambi seemed refreshingly normal, but she'd need to change her wine-soaked trousers first.

"OK. Come in for a sec, let me grab some dry jeans. I seem to be wearing most of your wine," she laughed as she unlocked the motorhome door.

"Wow, this is fabulous!" breathed Bambi, stepping inside and looking around in surprise. "There's so much room in here! It's like a hotel!" She giggled. "We're a bit like sardines in our caravan!"

"It's nice, isn't it? I haven't really got used to staying at the track yet, though. I still wake up in the middle of the night wondering where I am. Until an engine starts revving right next to the window of course!" She wriggled into a pair of diamanté-spangled jeans. "It's all still a bit strange and new at the moment, to be honest."

She scrabbled around in some drawers for a pen and scribbled a note to Dave on the back of a race programme before grabbing a bottle of pink champagne out of the fridge. Linking arms, they picked their way over the uneven surface of the darkening paddock. Savannah's high wedges weren't the most practical footwear and Bambi was already slightly worse for wear with wine, so they both benefited from the support.

"My caravan's only around the corner," said Bambi. "It's always good to have a drink and laugh off the stresses of the day before the boys get back and start going on about karting again." She rolled her eyes in exasperation. "I'm guessing Dave is exactly the same as the other karting dads and pretty much talks about nothing else? It's up to us girls to keep ourselves sane in an environment like this."

Savannah grinned. *How refreshing to find somebody nice who didn't take it all so seriously.* She was looking forward to having a glass of wine, especially after having been with the Aspinalls all day. She'd go for one quick drink and would be back before Dave had finished in the awning, hopefully with some paddock gossip to share.

Entering Bambi's caravan, she was greeted warmly by Iona, who was swiftly designated as the champagne opener, something she accomplished with screwed-up eyes as she shrank away from the exploding cork. With a delighted squeal they caught the bubbling overflow and clinked glasses with a collective sigh.

"Here's to us all having something to celebrate tomorrow, girls!" said Iona, and they raised their glasses.

"Now," Bambi turned to Savannah. "You must tell us how you're finding being in a team with the lovely Hillary Aspinall."

Savannah's eyes widened, unsure how to respond, before realising they were joking, and they all collapsed into giggles.

Iona groaned theatrically, "God, that woman is awful. I've heard that they pay so much money in team fees, she pretty much gets her pick of the mechanics in there." She wiggled her eyebrows suggestively to a chorus of "No!" and "You're kidding me?"

"It's true! It's part of the deal, apparently. The mechanics have no say in the matter. It's kind of an unwritten clause in their contract that they have to keep her sweet. Take one for the team," she guffawed loudly. "I suppose it must ease the pain of having such a slimy husband, and it certainly explains why she's always at the track."

Savannah giggled. Thank goodness she wasn't the only one who couldn't stand the Aspinalls. Hillary's smugness wouldn't seem quite so intimidating when she saw her tomorrow.

As the wine flowed, the conversation inevitably turned to the latest paddock gossip and the fact that Iona had spotted Julia and Danny Fox in a steamy clinch the previous weekend.

Savannah felt herself begin to relax and unwind. "Ugh, no!" she shuddered. "He's so sleazy, why would she do that?"

"I know!" squawked Iona, raising her eyebrows. "You'd think she'd know better, especially after what happened last year."

"Why, what happened last year?"

Bambi and Iona exchanged glances.

"You mean, you don't know?"

"Know what? I've only come to the last few race weekends."

Iona grimaced awkwardly. "Well, about Dave's ex-wife?"

Savannah's heart sank. Biting her lip, she admitted, "Actually, I don't really know what happened between them." She studied her nails, noticing the polish had chipped on her index finger. "I know she cheated on him, but Dave doesn't want to talk about it and, well, I don't want to keep pushing the subject."

"Ah, well, I don't blame him, but I guess you should probably know what happened." Iona glanced at Bambi, who nodded. Topping up their glasses with a fresh bottle of much cheaper wine, she explained, "To cut a long story short, Dave and Parker were running with Fox Racing last year and the mum was having it off with Danny Fox for months."

Savannah's eyes widened in horror. *Not Danny Fox? That awful sleaze bag. What had his wife been thinking?*

"It was going on for ages," continued Iona. "Basically, everyone in the paddock knew about it because, well, Fox isn't one to keep his mouth shut, and she wasn't exactly being discreet... So it was a bit of an open secret. The problem was, nobody knew whether Dave knew and was just turning a blind eye, or whether he was just oblivious, so nobody wanted to be the one to say anything. I mean, how do you bring something like that into a conversation?"

Iona paused, taking a swig of wine. "And then, like everything else, it became old news and everybody moved onto the next bit of gossip." She pulled a face. "Sorry, it sounds incredibly callous saying it like that, but I didn't know Dave well enough to say anything and, well, you're not going to get thanked for pointing something like that out, are you?"

Savannah nodded, twisting the stem of her wine glass in her hands, which suddenly felt cold and clammy.

"So, how did he find out?"

"Well it was pretty awful actually. I've only heard this second- hand but, from the stories that went around the next day, it sounded like he walked in on them having sex in the motorhome. He threw them both out stark naked in the paddock and has only really spoken to her through lawyers since."

"Oh my God, yes, I heard about that!" gushed Bambi. "I didn't realise it was Dave that happened to, though. Although I did hear that he threw her a jacket, so she wasn't completely naked. His wife really can't have been fussed about keeping the affair quiet. She must have wanted to get caught. After all, why would you risk doing it in your own camper when your husband could walk in at any minute?"

"I had no idea," said Savannah quietly.

Iona nodded gravely. "Some people did wonder if she'd wanted to get caught to force Danny into making things public. From what I heard, she wanted to leave Dave, but Danny didn't want to rock the boat. He wanted to keep Dave paying team fees while screwing his wife on the side. I heard she expected to move in with Danny after Dave chucked her out. She assumed they would make a go of it, but it turns out he only ever wanted to get his leg over.

"Rumour is, after Danny gave Cassandra her marching orders that day, she turned up on the doorstep of Dave's best mate with a huge taxi fare that needed paying. She was in floods of tears, still wearing just a coat with nothing underneath, with a sob story and puppy dog eyes. It sounds like this bloke had always had a soft spot for her, which I'm sure she knew. He never stood a chance. They've been together ever since."

Savannah's eyes filled with angry tears. That must have been the boyfriend she'd been parading around a few weeks ago. No wonder the man had looked uncomfortable! How awful for Dave, especially as she'd shacked up with his best friend. And to think how the bitch ex-wife had lorded it over her and tried to make her feel awful. Just wait till she saw that cow again. She had a few choice words she'd like to say to her that would wipe the smug smile off her face.

Topping up her glass, Bambi gave Savannah's hand a squeeze.

"Hey, don't feel bad. If that hadn't happened, he'd never have met you, and you're lovely. So, even though it must have been awful at the time perhaps it was for the best!"

"I suppose so. I just hate to think of everybody knowing and talking about it behind his back. It must have been horrible when he found out."

"True, but even the hottest gossip in the paddock is old news the week after. There's so much going on, everyone moves on and finds something new to talk about. It's like EastEnders, there's always a new scandal to eclipse the previous one. Besides, plenty worse things have happened. If I had a pound for every bored karting mum who'd ended up screwing the engine builder or one of the mechanics, then racing would be a lot more affordable!" laughed Iona.

"Racing's like a drug. Getting faster and getting that next win starts to take over every waking thought, and when husbands are so obsessed with winning, they forget their wives need a little attention too."

"Tell me about it," groaned Bambi. "I've hardly seen Jake for the past couple of months, let alone got any action," she blushed. "Honestly, if he isn't working, he's reading books about engine performance or watching bloody karting videos on YouTube."

"Maybe you should join Predator," nudged Iona, winking salaciously.

"Oh, shut up!" snorted Bambi, wine coming out of her nose, as she grinned over at Savannah. "The Aspinalls might be bad, but you've got to be glad you're not in that team."

"Why?" asked Savannah.

"Well, there are about half a dozen people running in that team and rumour has it, on Saturday nights, all the wives put their car keys in a bowl, then…"

"No!" squealed Savannah. Bambi and Iona both nodded seriously before their raucous laughter filled the caravan.

Dave was smiling as he entered the motorhome. It had been a good day. They'd been quick, and the atmosphere in the team had been much better without Cassandra around. He was ready for a drink and a quiet dinner with Savannah. Parker was off playing video games in a friend's caravan and wouldn't be back for a while.

"Sav?" he called, a frown creasing his forehead. Where was she? Opening the fridge, he took a beer, spotted her scrawled note and scowled, a sense of unease growing in the pit of his stomach.

He took a deep swig and plonked himself down on the sofa. Who had she gone for a drink with? The only people she knew were the Aspinalls, and he couldn't see her going for a drink with either of them. Unless it was that creep Hugo. His stomach twisted at the thought. He turned on the TV and resolved to wait till she came back. After all, she said she was only going for a quick drink, she'd be back soon. And he had no reason to doubt her. As he kept reminding himself, she wasn't Cassandra.

But as he sat there, the mindless talent show failing to hold his attention, his memory kept flashing back to that night, last year, when he'd walked in to see Danny's scrawny arse pumping away, his wife's legs wrapped around him. Dave stood and looked out of the window, trying to rid himself of the mental image. *Savannah isn't Cassandra,* he told himself firmly, and it wasn't fair to think she'd do the same thing.

Giving up on the television, he paced the length of the motorhome, glancing anxiously out of the windows. What should he do? After all, Savannah was a vibrant young woman, and she could probably do with a night out after spending weeks on end just with him. She may have been bored senseless having nobody else to talk to. He glanced at his watch again. It was getting late. He drained his beer and took a deep breath. He couldn't stand here wondering any longer; he needed to get out and do something. He'd go for a stroll around the paddock.

There was no bar or clubhouse at this track, nothing that would be open at night, so Dave slowly walked along the rows of vehicles, past smouldering remains of barbeques, not knowing what else to do. His mind wouldn't stop racing. He could almost hear Danny Fox taunting him. "Lost your girlfriend have you Dave?"

His fists clenched and he marched on. There were traces of music over the hum of generators and faint noises of people unwinding as he passed by, but no sign of Savannah. With a heavy sigh, he turned and started to head back to the motorhome. Perhaps she'd be back by now.

As he rounded a corner he came to an abrupt halt. Tilting his head to one side, his heart pounding, he listened. He could hear Savannah laughing. Her laugh was a bit of a donkeyesque bray - which he considered utterly charming, but it was also really distinctive. That had to be her! He crept towards the caravan where he'd heard the noise, unsure what to do next. He felt foolish, acid rising in his chest, but if something was going on, he had to know. He wasn't going to be the last person in the paddock to find out - like last time.

His mouth set in a grim line as he knocked on the

door, but there was no answer. Now he was closer, there was so much noise coming from inside he wasn't surprised they didn't hear him. Bracing himself for what he might find, he opened the door and was hit by a waft of warm, boozy air and the sight of Savannah, Bambi and Iona, sloshed and laughing, surrounded by empty wine bottles. Feeling the cold draft, the girls turned and gave a drunken cheer of welcome as they saw Dave filling the doorway.

Savannah, delighted to see Dave, flashed him a huge smile. Then her hand flew to her mouth. Shit! She'd only meant to pop out for one drink and she must have been gone for hours! Even after a few drinks she was aware of the tightness in Dave's face as he'd opened the door. He might be grinning and looking relaxed now, but he'd obviously been worried. And after what she'd just learned about his ex, she didn't blame him.

Wobbling slightly, but firmly ignoring his insistence that she stay and have fun, Savannah stumbled to the doorway. Dave caught her in his big arms and roared with laughter. She was totally smashed. Christ, he loved her.

As they left, Dave supporting the unsteady Savannah, he passed Jake who had just got back to the caravan after finally packing up. They swapped wry glances and Dave grinned. "Best of luck in there mate."

Jake shook his head; he could hear the laughter from inside. It sounded like a hen party.

As they meandered slowly back to the motorhome Dave felt a mixture of relief and irritation with himself. He should have trusted Savannah. It was really unfair that he'd assumed the worst, and it was nice that she'd found some friends. It wasn't good for her to be so reliant on him and he'd been feeling bad that she didn't really know anyone.

He resolved to try and lighten up. She didn't need him crowding her and he decided never to think the worst of her again.

The following morning, Savannah woke to the sound of

two-stroke engines screaming outside the bedroom window. Groaning and pulling the pillow over her head, she heard Dave chuckle softly.

"The paddock's not a great place for a hangover, love. I'd take a couple of painkillers and go back to bed for a bit if I were you." Giving her a loud smooch in the ear, he was rewarded by a screech and a thump with the pillow. Dave grinned as he got out of bed. *Even hungover, she was gorgeous.*

Savannah must have drifted off to sleep again because the next thing she heard was the door slamming as Dave and Parker headed off to the awning. She groaned. What had she been thinking having so much to drink last night? Still, it had been fun. She wondered if Bambi and Iona were feeling equally rough. Sighing, she heaved herself upright and, squinting against the light, went in search of some aspirin and a cup of coffee.

Catching her reflection in the mirror, she scrunched up her nose. All the makeup in the world wasn't going to stop her looking dreadful today. Over the tannoy she heard the first race being announced and hurriedly pulled on a pair of jeans and a sweatshirt, ran a brush through her hair and, after rooting around in her handbag, triumphantly produced a pair of sunglasses. That should mute the day enough to be manageable and cover up her puffy eyes. After quickly brushing her teeth and adding a dab of lip gloss, she decided that was the best she could do and headed down to the awning.

As soon as she walked in, she regretted her decision. What with engines being started and Jago riding around the awning on a plastic motorbike, making engine noises at the top of his lungs, she nearly turned on her heel and strode straight back out again.

To make matters worse, she was instantly swooped upon by Hillary. Stretching the truth, Savannah claimed she had a migraine - after all, her head genuinely felt like it could explode at any minute - and Hillary was instantly full of gushing sympathy.

"Oh, migraines are simply awful, aren't they?" she trilled loudly over the cacophony. "And being at a racetrack too, so unlucky! When I feel one of my heads coming on, I simply swear by a good massage. It totally nips a migraine in the bud, and I haven't had a really bad one for years now. I have the most marvellous masseur on call. He's an absolute godsend. He comes straight to your house in a jiffy, sorts you out and then I have a few large glasses of water and sleep the whole thing off."

Savannah nodded and chuckled to herself, wondering whether Hillary's masseur did more than just rub her shoulders after what she'd heard about her appetite for team mechanics.

Hillary ploughed on relentlessly. "Of course, I don't believe in taking pills. Filling your body up with chemicals just masks the problem and it's so unhealthy. It's much better to take an holistic approach."

"You don't believe in a lot of things," muttered Savannah into her coffee, jumping to one side to avoid Jago hitting her shins as he careened past on his bike. "Like controlling your bloody kids."

Having just downed a couple of Neurofen and an Alka-Seltzer, she now really fancied a greasy sausage bap. Sod the diet. If only she had earplugs and some Prozac, she might have the patience to cope with Hillary and her bloody children. Stepping outside for a breath of fresh air, she took a deep breath and gagged slightly. It was all well and good being surrounded by this beautiful countryside, but the pervading smell of cow shit and petrol really wasn't helping her roiling stomach. She'd watch this race and then stay hidden in the motorhome with a pot of strong coffee until the final.

That was exactly what she did. As three o'clock came around, Savannah heard a tap on the door. Heaving herself off the sofa and praying it wasn't Hillary on the other side, she opened it a crack and was faced with a peaky-looking Bambi.

"Oh God, you look about as good as I feel," Bambi laughed. "Are you coming to watch the final?" As Savannah grabbed a coat and locked up behind her, Iona bounded over to them, full of beans, and they headed towards the grandstand.

"How the hell are you so spritely today?" she muttered resentfully.

Iona grinned. "Who knows? Just call it nervous energy. It's all that keeps me going on a race weekend!"

She lowered her voice. "Plus I've already had a glass of fizz to take the edge off. Hair of the dog - it really helps with both the nerves and the hangover."

"Christ, you're like the bloody Duracell bunny," laughed Bambi shaking her head. "Wish I could shrug off a night's drinking as easily. I was sick as a dog this morning!"

Standing in the grandstand, waiting for the final to start, Bambi looked pale and shaky. Unsure whether it was nerves, the hangover or a toxic combination of both, she would be glad to be on the way home.

She always got anxious when Max was out on track, but somehow it was worse with the Nationals. The racing was harder and, after Round One, she was worried that Max would have another accident. She glanced sideways at Iona, who was jiggling from foot to foot and crossing herself. She smiled to herself; she hadn't realised Iona was Catholic. It was funny how everyone had their little rituals on race days. Catching her eye, Iona reached into her pocket and pulled out a hip flask.

"Bit of Dutch courage?"

Bambi shook her head vehemently and turned a little green. Iona shrugged and took a swig. Savannah gave her a nudge.

"Hey, come on, don't worry. We've only got to get through one twelve-minute race then we're done for the weekend. Besides, Dave says Max is a really good driver, so I'm sure you've got nothing to worry about."

As the karts lined up on the grid, Bambi tried taking some deep breaths to calm her nerves, but she could feel her heart thumping and when she went to check the time on her phone her hands were shaking. Max was starting in third, with Dommie on pole and Cosmo and Ronnie Finch to the left of him. Lovely. *Nothing to worry about there, then,* she told herself cynically.

As the lights went out and the engines roared to life, she closed her eyes and offered up a silent prayer: *please let Max be OK out there.*

Looking away as the drivers hurtled towards the first tight corner, she waited till they were all through before looking to see where Max had come out. *That was OK, he was still in the front pack. He'd made it through.*

As the minutes counted down, the battle on track intensified, with the front group of drivers constantly taking chunks out of each other, vying to get ahead.

With two laps remaining, Max saw an opportunity and dove down the inside to get into the lead, followed through by Dommie.

Throwing his hand in the air, Cosmo made it clear he wasn't standing for that, and neither was Ronnie, and they both immediately went back in on Dommie, tussling and giving Max a chance to pull a bit of a gap.

With this season's grievances and rivalries foremost in their minds none of those three were prepared to let the others beat them. Entering the last lap, Max's lead was growing with every corner as they squabbled behind him.

Savannah turned to Bambi and clutched her arm.

"Oh my God, he's going to do it!" But Bambi, frozen, to the action, didn't move a muscle. She watched the action in silence, hardly daring to breathe, her eyes fixed on Max.

As he inched out the gap and there seemed no chance of the others catching him, she prayed that nothing would go wrong with the kart. It was all too easy to envisage a wheel coming off, or the engine cutting out, or something else happening to make him lose everything.

But as he came through the last corner and lifted both hands off the wheel in celebration, Savannah and Iona together erupted in loud squeals, hugging Bambi, who found herself in floods of relieved tears.

Hangovers briefly forgotten, they all dashed down to parc fermé to watch Max come in and congratulate him on his first win.

Max was over the moon. Pulling into scrutineering he sat for a moment, helmet still on, letting it all sink in. He never thought he'd get a win at the Nationals, not since they'd seen how tough the competition was going to be.

Pulling up alongside him, Dommie jumped out of his kart and shook Max's shoulders.

"Why are you just sitting there, you loon? You won!"

Max laughed and heaved himself out of the kart. He felt strangely removed from it all, as if the race had just happened to someone else. In a daze, he returned Dommie's high five and, feeling a tap on his shoulder, turned to see Ronnie, who'd beaten Dommie to second place, holding out his hand.

"Well done, Max. Good drive."

Max smiled awkwardly. "Thanks, mate, you too. I was lucky that you guys kept going in on each other, otherwise it would've been a battle right till the last corner."

Ronnie gave a wry shrug. "I know. I guess we all lost our heads a bit out there. I guess I wanted to stop Cosmo winning more than I wanted to win myself." He rolled his eyes. "I bet my dad'll have something to say about that."

Just then, the dads and mechanics were released into parc fermé and Max found himself grabbed and whirled around in the air.

"You did it, Max! You only bloody well went and did it!"

Max beamed at his dad, who had a face-splitting grin

and tears in his eyes. Jake gave him an extra squeeze before releasing him.

"Hey, have you been over to see your mum yet? She's on the other side of the fence. I can hear her shouting for you from here!"

Embarrassed, Max turned to see the three mums all calling and beckoning to him. *Why were parents so excruciating?* Smiling, he ambled over and allowed himself to be hugged and kissed by an ecstatic Bambi. He could see lots of people congratulating his dad too. He didn't think people would be so pleased for him! He'd never seen Aspinall congratulated like this in parc fermé, although he'd probably had so many wins the novelty had worn off for him anyway.

He could see a sour-faced official impatiently waiting to get Jake's attention so that they could do the scrutineering checks. Max tore himself away from his mum.

"Come on, dad, they're waiting for you to take the engine into scrutineering!"

Jake, still grinning, clapped the scrutineer on the back. "Sorry, mate, just got a bit caught up in the moment." The scrutineer relented and gave him a weary smile.

"Just get that engine off and ready to be checked. We've got another race finishing in ten minutes and we need to have you lot out of here first." He added quietly, "And well done."

As Jake, together with the mechanics from the second- and third-place karts, disappeared off to have their engines checked, the crowd dissipated. Max was still surrounded by kids who had come over to congratulate him and excitedly rehash the highs and lows of their own races, and everyone else was watching an escalating row between Frankie and Hugo Aspinall.

They were making so much noise it was hard to miss. Hugo was accusing Ronnie of ruining Cosmo's race and "letting that pikey kid win" and Frankie, whose voice was dangerously low, was standing with his fists clenched looking murderous.

Danny, who'd been hanging round in the empty scrutineering bay, sauntered over and pulled Frankie to one side, whispering something in his ear.

"What?" said Frankie, putting a hand up to the incandescent Hugo's face to silence him. He turned to Danny. "What did you say?"

"You need to put a protest in for Golding's fuel. I think it's illegal. But you need to do it right now. You've only got a few more minutes before they release the karts from scrutineering and you lose your chance. It'll cost £250 to protest it, but I'm sure it'll come back dodgy, in which case Ronnie'll get the win."

Frankie didn't need telling twice. He bloody hated cheats. He was surprised that Golding had used dodgy fuel, but he couldn't see why Danny would make that up, so it was worth a punt. And if he was proved wrong then Danny wouldn't be able to hide behind the excuse of other drivers cheating whenever Ronnie wasn't fastest in future. Turning his back on an indignant Aspinall, he strode over to scrutineering and slapped a wodge of £20 notes down on the desk.

"Golding's using hooky fuel. I want it tested."

Jake looked surprised, then shrugged.

"Fair enough. You'll be wasting your money, though. We use the same fuel as the rest of the team." Frankie glowered, not pleased that Jake was taking it so lightly, and reached back into his pocket.

"OK, then, I'll protest both Golding and Carver's fuel."

With a resigned sigh, the scrutineer passed Frankie the forms to fill in as they went to get the fuel testing kit. They were going to be running behind at this rate, which meant Agra that he could do without.

Once all the paperwork had been filed and the money counted, they all trooped back over to where the karts were parked. The fuel would be tested using an electronic indicator, which dipped into the tank.

Sampling Carver's tank first, the scrutineers nodded and Frankie's eyes narrowed. He was going to rip Danny a new one if he'd wasted £500 on nothing. At least then he'd have to shut up his incessant whining about the competition cheating and find them some more pace.

The scrutineer tested Max's tank next and, to a collective gasp, the readings were significantly different. Jake glanced around the sea of shocked faces.

"What does that mean?" he said.

"It means you've been cheating," smirked Frankie.

As the scrutineers did a second test to confirm the result, Jake stood there with his mouth agape. How the hell could this have happened? He had used the same batch of fuel that the whole team had used! How could Carver's fuel be fine and not his? *Could Lillington have done something?* The scrutineer gave Jake a steely look and shook his head, disappointed.

"Right Mr Golding, we've got some paperwork to complete."

As Jake trailed behind him to the office, his mind whirled with confusion. Shit, this meant they were excluded from the race meeting.

Not only that, but you weren't allowed to drop a round where you'd had a disqualification. All competitors could drop their lowest score in the Nationals, but they would have to keep the zero points from this round. It meant their championship hopes were effectively over.

But, more to the point, it meant everyone would think they had been cheating. How on earth would he break this to Max?

Paperwork completed, he pushed the kart back to the awning, still being congratulated on the win. Shoulders hunched, he just stared ahead and kept walking. Word hadn't got around yet, and he couldn't face starting to explain it to people. He had to find a way to tell Max before he heard it from somebody else.

Frankie ruffled Ronnie's hair proudly. They hadn't had the best start to the season, but it was all starting to come good. And now that cheat Golding had been chucked out, it had evened the playing field a bit. It also helped that Cosmo had scored badly this weekend. Well, not badly perhaps, but he'd finished behind Ronnie all weekend so they'd been able to close the points gap in the championship.

As for Danny, perhaps he was finally earning his money after all. Regardless of him being ruled by his dick, he seemed to be sorting things out now. Especially if Julia's sour expression was anything to go by.

Ousting the cheats went a long way towards making amends, and while Frankie wouldn't trust Danny where engines were concerned, he should perhaps go a bit easier on him from now on.

25
THE MORNING AFTER

Monday morning saw Jake hunched at his desk, staring blankly out of the window.

After wearily packing away, and a slow congested drive home, he had crawled into bed in the early hours only to be woken at 6am to get the train to work. To say his mind wasn't on the job was an understatement. He couldn't stop replaying the events of the weekend in his head.

How on earth could their fuel have been illegal? There were plenty of people in the paddock who did mess around, who were prepared to go to any lengths to win - there always had been - but he'd never even considered it. He'd always believed that if you couldn't win without bending the rules it wasn't a real win at all. How ironic that they had now been branded cheats.

The worst thing had been Max's face when he broke the news to him. From his first win to being a disqualified cheat in the space of five minutes. The poor kid had looked totally shell-shocked. And the problem was, Jake had no answers for him.

All he could say was that they hadn't cheated and that

he didn't understand how this had happened, but that was little compensation.

He felt he'd let Max down enormously. The kid had driven the drive of his life, only to get thrown out because of something Jake was in charge of. He shook his head sadly.

Chase and Carver had both been really supportive. They said they knew he wouldn't cheat, but what good was that?

There was no point him appealing the penalty. They'd tested the fuel twice, right in front of him, and he'd seen the results for himself.

Carver had suggested he consult a solicitor to find out whether there was a technicality that could get him off. Apparently that kind of thing happened all the time. If someone in the office hadn't filled in the paperwork incorrectly, you could get the whole thing overturned. But Jake didn't want to win like that.

Besides the fact that they couldn't afford it, everyone would know that was how they'd got the penalty overturned, and they'd still be considered cheats. Just cheats that got away with it. And what would that teach Max about how to behave?

They would be the only people to know they hadn't cheated. Jake let out a sigh and rubbed his forehead. *What did it matter now?* However it happened, he'd let it happen, and he'd screwed things up. Their championship was over.

Max probably wouldn't even want to carry on racing after this. Even at club level the news would travel fast, and they'd be called cheats wherever they went. It just wasn't fair on Max to put him through that.

Jake logged onto his computer. He'd better at least look like he was getting some work done. As he scrolled through his emails, he noticed a message from his boss titled *Meeting this morning: 9.30am.*

Jake glanced at his watch. *Shit!* It was already 9.45 and he'd just been sitting there daydreaming. He'd already pissed off his boss by putting the phone down on him on Friday, so this was the last thing he needed.

Sending his chair clattering to the floor, Jake dashed off to his boss's office, straightening his tie as he went.

Bambi sat on the bathroom floor, hands shaking, staring at the pregnancy test. After throwing up again this morning it had occurred to her that the weight gain, nausea, tiredness, the fact that she kept bursting into tears: they were all signs of being pregnant.

Dismissing the thought as ludicrous she walked round to the chemist once Max was off to school. She'd do a test just to put her mind at rest. After all, she and Jake had hardly seen each other in the past few months, let alone had time for sex - it was a ridiculous idea!

But apparently it hadn't been such a ridiculous idea, as the double blue stripe on the test now told her. Racking her brains, she could barely remember the last time they'd had any physical contact. It must have been back before the Nationals started, which would, Oh shit, mean she was nearly four months pregnant! No wonder she'd been putting on weight! *Oh God, and the drinking!*

She'd had no inkling she could have been pregnant. What kind of damage might she have done to the baby? She'd have to get a scan booked as soon as possible.

Tears slipping down her cheeks, she sat with her head in her hands. She and Jake had never planned to have another baby. They'd talked about having another after Max was born, but so many years had gone past without it happening they'd both assumed it never would.

The timing really couldn't have been worse. She would have to stop work, or at least have time off, and they were barely managing with both their salaries at the moment.

Then again, after what happened yesterday they probably wouldn't carry on racing, so money would be a lot less tight. They would manage, they always did.

She closed her eyes. Their house only had two

bedrooms - where on earth would a new baby go? They could have a crib in their room for a while, but not forever. And she couldn't ask Max to share a bedroom with a toddler. They'd have to move to somewhere larger; how on earth would they afford that?

Feeling a nudge against her legs she looked at the cat, who was rubbing up against her. Picking her up, Bambi buried her head in the soft fur. She took a deep breath and felt herself start to calm before claws began digging warningly into her shoulder.

This wasn't what Lucifurr had in mind. The cat would tolerate a quick cuddle, but she was hungry, she wanted food. Bambi lifted her head, releasing the cat, and decided she had to pull herself together. She was getting ahead of herself in a panic. The deed was done, and done quite some time ago. She was pregnant.

There was no question of not keeping the baby. They'd always wanted another one, and she must be too far gone to consider a termination even if she'd wanted to. It wasn't ideal timing, but they'd make it work.

First things first, she needed to book herself in for a scan to make sure everything was fine. Splashing some cold water on her face, she looked at herself in the mirror. She hardly recognised the drained, red-eyed, middle-aged woman staring back at her.

Feeling tears rising again she stamped her foot angrily, sending the cat skittering out of the room. Crying wasn't going to get her anywhere. She needed to get off her arse and start sorting everything out. At least this would be some cheerful news for Jake after what happened at the weekend. Well, she hoped he would be pleased, anyway. He would, wouldn't he? But first she needed to feed the cat.

Jake wasn't used to catching a train in the middle of the day. Instead of being packed in with the usual crowd of commuters studiously ignoring each other, he was sharing a carriage with a mum and her young child, and a teenage couple who looked like they were trying to eat each other.

Shouldn't they be at school? he thought irritably, then shook his head in annoyance. Shouldn't he be at work? He looked down at the phone in his hands and wondered again about calling Bambi, but he didn't know what to say. And, after all, this was probably a conversation to have face to face.

Jake was still a bit stunned by the day's events. He knew he hadn't been putting in the effort at work over the past few months, but he'd never thought that they'd let him go. Shout at him, maybe, give him a warning, but not sack him! He remembered that redundancies had been mentioned a few months back, but with everything going on he'd not really taken any notice.

His boss's words rang in his ears."We just don't feel you're committed to the job. Perhaps it's time for you to find a new challenge."

He snorted in a half laugh, drawing an alarmed look from the young mum. *Wankers.* Talk about kicking you when you're down. He'd gone into work this morning thinking that things couldn't get any worse. How wrong he'd been.

They'd given him two months' pay as part of the redundancy package and he wouldn't have to work his notice, which was good, he supposed, but he had no idea what to do now.

Frankly he just wanted to get into bed, pull the covers over his head and stay there for the foreseeable future.

After a slow walk back from the station Jake took a deep breath and unlocked the front door. He couldn't put this off any longer. As if he hadn't let his family down enough already, he now needed to tell Bambi he'd lost his job.

Walking in, he shouted hello but got no reply. Relieved by the brief reprieve, he put the kettle on. As he waited for it to boil he looked through to the dining room and saw it as if with new eyes.

There were boxes of karting components everywhere: an engine under the table, a box of clutches beside it, oily smears on the light switch. There were cables all over the sideboard where all the electronics were charging: the transponder, the on-board camera, the batteries for his power tools, not to mention the piles of tyres stacked up against the wall.

It seemed like karting had taken over their house as much as it had taken over their lives. He hadn't even noticed it happening.

Looking to see whether any of the devices had finished charging yet, he noticed the cat had been sick amongst the wires. Great, he grimaced and went to fetch some kitchen paper to clear it up, a phrase his mum always used to use popping into his head: *It's just another splinter in your bottom as you slide down the banister of life.*

You wouldn't be able to see his arse for splinters at this rate; he'd be Jake with the wooden butt. Pulling a face, he wiped the cat sick off the wires. The revolting job lifting him out of his gloom for a few seconds. He couldn't change what had already happened: they were broke, they'd been branded as cheats and now he was unemployed.

At least the cat sick was one unpleasantness he could spare Bambi.

26
NUMPTIES & NEW MOTIVATION

The good thing about being the notorious Frankie Finch was not having to put up with idiots. Not usually, anyway.

In his manor they'd all learnt a long time back not to piss Fat Frankie off. And, after all, that's what he employed Chris for, to deal with the little annoyances in life. He only ever had to step in if the little annoyances became larger ones, and Chris was good enough at his job to ensure that hardly ever happened.

Unfortunately, motorsport seemed to have introduced a whole new troupe of muppets into his life who didn't know their place in the pecking order, or perhaps they just weren't aware of his reputation.

He glanced at his heavy gold watch and then back at Danny, who was lounging opposite him running his mouth off. *Why was Danny even here?* He tuned back into what he was saying.

"Bruv, she's a nightmare! Who knew she'd be so fucking clingy, eh? I should've known this would happen," he laughed. "The Fox charm is as much a curse as a blessing."

He threw Frankie a grinning wink. "Know what I mean, Frank? All these bored karting wives looking for a distraction. Bet that's why you don't let your missus come to the track too, eh?"

Frankie raised an eyebrow, his blood pressure surging. *What an insufferable prick.*

Oblivious, Danny rattled on.

"It was great to see Ronnie on the top step of the podium at the weekend, wasn't it? Handy that Golding's fuel ended up being illegal."

"True," said Frankie. "I have to admit, I didn't think they'd be running dodgy fuel, but you were right."

Danny chuckled. "Bet you weren't as surprised as they were. Did you see the look on Jake's face?" He gave Frankie a smirk. "It was almost as if somebody had slipped something into his fuel, he looked so shocked."

Frankie looked at him steadily. "Are you telling me that you spiked Golding's fuel?"

"Course I did, bruv! Class move or what? It was the perfect crime. You were busy causing a distraction having that row with Aspinall, and they were stupid enough to leave the kart unattended. I just made the most of the opportunity."

"So, he wasn't actually cheating? We got an innocent kid chucked out?"

"Well, I wouldn't go that far, Frank. Just because I slipped something into his fuel doesn't mean everything was legit to begin with. He was probably cheating in some other way, the officials just didn't spot it. Goes to show it's always worth having a little something in your pocket in case the opportunity arises."

Frankie swilled a slug of whiskey around his mouth and gave himself a moment to think. He might not always have been the most law-abiding citizen in his time, but he'd always prided himself on being a man of honour. He didn't like the idea of somebody being cheated out of a fair win. It didn't sit right with him. Well, unless it was Aspinall, of course, that man would deserve it.

Problem was, there was nothing he could do about it without Ronnie losing the win, and his boy had been so chuffed, he didn't want to take that away from him. Then again, he'd always prefer to win fair and square on track rather than in the office. Frankie heaved himself out of the chair and refilled his glass, not offering Danny another.

He was disappointed his initial instincts about Danny had been right. The kid was as much of a snake as he'd suspected. Not only was he a lazy sponging shirker, he was also a bloody cheat. And he'd thought Golding getting chucked out had actually vindicated Danny. Turns out he was probably the worst of the lot.

Perhaps he should leave the team. He wasn't sure Danny was giving them anything useful apart from awning space; it was Aaron who did all the work. Then again, Britney had said she wanted to come to the next race weekend, Lord knew why, but it meant he'd probably have his hands full keeping her entertained.

Like most teenagers, she spent most of her time looking at her phone, but he suspected she'd get bored after a couple of days at the track. It was probably easier to stay with the team until after then. Besides, which team would he go with if he left? This was a headache he really didn't need.

Fuming and wanting to be rid of Danny, he stood up.

"Time you were on your way, Danny."

Danny looked surprised and pulled himself unsteadily to his feet.

Probably thought he could stay here all night drinking my booze, then have a run at my wife, the arrogant little prick, thought Frankie. Walking him out, he shut the door firmly behind him.

Danny, who'd figured on getting drunk enough to have to crash at Frankie's for the night, pulled out of the driveway, wondering where to go next. He was low on fuel, still had no flat, and he'd exhausted his mates' goodwill after kipping on their sofas for the last month or so.

After a few minutes driving, he spotted a lay-by and parked up. He'd just sleep here for the night.

Hunching against the steady drizzle, he grabbed his duvet, which was stashed in the back of the van along with a suitcase of clothes and a couple of boxes of stuff he'd taken when his landlord turfed him out. He'd sleep across the front seats. It wouldn't be the first time, and it probably wouldn't be the last.

Settling down, arranging the duvet and trying to get comfortable, Danny was a bit miffed. He'd sorted this win for Frankie, the man should be bloody grateful. If he didn't know better, he would think Frankie was pissed off at him for something. The least he could have done was put him up for the night.

Plus, he'd secretly been hoping he'd bump into Frankie's hottie daughter again. He hadn't been able to shake the image of her in those sexy little shorts with her come-to-bed eyes. Slipping his hand under the duvet, he slid it into his trousers and groaned. He might not have bumped into her again, but he could certainly imagine what might've happened if he had.

Jake heard the door slam. He pulled the duvet around him, keeping his eyes firmly shut. There was no point getting up yet. It would only take a couple of hours to trawl the job sites and send his CV off, and he couldn't be bothered with that yet.

He had no motivation. He knew he only had two months' salary in the bank, but that was enough of a buffer to allow him to wallow in self-pity rather than panic about getting a new job.

It shouldn't be, but it was.

With Bambi at work and Max at school, he may as well just stay in bed. He had nothing to get up for. It had been nearly a fortnight since he'd lost his job and he felt stuck in a life-sucking limbo. Plus, he just couldn't shake the whole fuel debacle out of his head.

Throwing the pillow across the room he groaned. His brain was like a dog with a bone; it wasn't going to let him go back to sleep, it would keep turning things over and over until he heaved his arse out of bed.

Swinging his legs to the floor, he ran his hand through his hair and caught a whiff from his armpit. Jeez, he stank. He needed to get himself in the shower. When was the last time he'd showered? His days were all blurring into one, like that weird time between Christmas and New Year when nobody knows which day of the week it is.

Then again, what was the point? He wouldn't see anyone until Max got back from school, so there was no hurry. He'd have a coffee and watch some daytime telly while he woke up.

Padding downstairs, Jake's phone rang. He patted his pockets before realising he was still in his boxers. Where the hell had he left it? He usually charged his phone in the bedroom but he must have drunk a bit too much last night and forgotten.

Jogging into the living room, he turfed the cushions off the sofa until he found his phone wedged down the side. *Three percent battery! Shit!*

If this was a company wanting an interview, the bloody phone would die before he even found out who it was. *What a cracking first impression that would be!*

"Hello?" he said, his voice sounding sleep-soaked and gravelly.

"Jake, it's James Carver."

"Oh, hi mate. Give me a sec, will you, I just need to plug my phone in."

"Is it a bad time? I can call back if you're in the middle of something?"

"Nah, mate," Jake scoffed bitterly as he rifled around in a drawer for a charger. "I've got all the time in the world right now, just no charge on my phone."

"I just wanted to see how you're feeling now you've had a few weeks to come to terms with everything. I know getting excluded was awful, but you can't let this fuel thing get you down. Things like this can happen. You're not the first, and you won't be the last. Give it a couple of months and no one will even remember this. At the next round something else will happen and everyone will have moved onto the next bit of gossip."

Jake scratched at his stubble. "I dunno, mate. The way we're feeling we might pack it all in."

"You can't do that! Max has driven brilliantly; you can't let this put you off racing."

"I don't know," Jake sighed. "Part of me thinks we should carry on for Max, but how can we turn up in the paddock with everyone thinking we're cheats? I don't want to put him in that position, it'll be horrible for him. Even if I had cheated - which I didn't - Max wouldn't have been involved and yet he'll bear the brunt of all the whispering and snide comments. You know how cruel kids can be."

"Look, nobody said it would be easy to go back, but you can't give up at the first hurdle!"

"The first hurdle?" snorted Jake. "If that was just the first hurdle, what the hell else are they going to throw at us?"

Carver chuckled. "How do Bambi and Max feel about the whole thing?"

"We've been arguing about it on and off since it happened. We both feel Max shouldn't have to give up something he loves doing, but it's like throwing him into a lion's den if we do the next round. It also doesn't help that Bambi keeps bursting into tears every time we talk about it."

"And Max?"

"Max is determined to carry on. He doesn't care about the stick he'll get in the paddock, he just wants to get out there and race, to prove himself. I don't think he realises how bad it'll be, how he'll feel when people are calling him a cheat."

"Kids are surprisingly resilient, you know."

Jake smiled sadly. "I know, I've been amazed by his reaction. He's really dug his heels in. He's even said he'll do it without us and pay to race himself if we won't help him." He gave a half laugh. "Not sure how he thinks he'll do that! He reckons it's like bullies - you need to stand up to them. If we give up something we love and drop out, they'll have won."

He shook his head. "I like his attitude, but I just don't know what the right thing is to do."

"Well, I always told Dommie that he should punch a bully in the nose. Not sure that would be the best approach in this case. I think Max is right. You know you didn't cheat. You used the same fuel we did, and there was no opportunity for you to do anything to it, we both know that. The only way this happened was if somebody slipped something into your fuel, or if the scrutineers are in somebody's pocket. Either way, Max is right. If you run away with your tail between your legs, they've won. That would be a serious contender for the title just gone, clearing the way for whoever did this to you to get one step closer to the championship."

"I don't know," sighed Jake. "It's not just that. It's the money as well. We're up to our eyeballs in debt and then I got made redundant last week." He ran his hands through his hair, not improving the way it looked. "Right now, I just feel like sitting here watching Cash in the Attic and forgetting about the whole damn thing."

Carver didn't respond. Jake looked at his phone and saw the battery was dead, he'd been talking to thin air. Oh well. He trudged off to find a charger. It would be ten minutes or so before it came back to life again. In the meantime, he needed some caffeine.

As the Columbian roast started brewing, he inhaled deeply, relishing the aroma. Time always seemed to slow while you waited for coffee to percolate.

Not bothering for the rest of the pot to brew, he poured some into a mug and winced at its tar-like strength. That would teach him for being impatient, but at least it might wake him up.

Perhaps Carver was right, and they should go back and face the music. After all, if Max wanted to go despite everything, they should probably support him. It wouldn't be fun, but Max deserved the chance to finish the season and see if he could get himself a win he could keep. And this time, Jake wouldn't leave the kart unattended for a moment, even if it meant pushing the kart into scrutineering with him or roping Bambi into guard duty.

Carver had warned him that people would do anything to win, but he still found it hard to believe that someone would stoop as low as to spike their fuel. It made him question other things that had happened at club level. Had he just been incredibly naive up until now? Or was he starting to get paranoid? He'd heard people say over and over again that motorsport brought out the very worst in people, but he'd always laughed it off.

Coming to a decision, he took a deep breath. He'd back Max. They would brave the taunts and go back and finish the season. At the very least, he wouldn't give them the satisfaction of dropping out.

Besides, Max deserved that first win. Someone had taken it away from him last time. He would do everything he could to find out who and to give Max the chance to get on that top step again.

All he'd need to do now was convince Bambi.

27
AN UNEXPECTED ADVENTURE

It was 10pm and they were three hours into a six-hour drive up to Scotland for Round Four. Jake glanced over at Max, who was dozing on Bambi's shoulder and she gave him a tired smile.

"It's a long way until we get to sleep tonight, isn't it? Do you want to stop somewhere and grab a coffee, stretch your legs?"

Jake shook his head. "No, let's keep going for now."

He knew he should make conversation, but he had too much going round in his head. Also, every time they talked about the coming race weekend, Bambi seemed to get upset, which wasn't what he needed right now. They'd agreed to finish the Nationals - after all there were only two rounds left - but it was going to be a tough weekend, made worse by the long drive to Scotland and back.

At least he hadn't had to ask for the time off work! One of the few upsides to being unemployed.

Being stuck at 50mph towing a caravan wasn't ideal, and it wasn't doing much to keep him awake either. The only thing that eased the monotony was the surge of adrenaline whenever a juggernaut overtook them, buffeting them in their wake as they hurtled past.

Still, at least they'd got through the roadworks on the M6 so they could get up some speed again now. Bambi offered him a chocolate biscuit, which he gratefully accepted. Perhaps sugar would keep him going. He'd need to stop and have a break at some point, but he wanted to get closer to the border first. If he could last that long.

As he drove, Jake mulled over conversations he'd had in the last few days. He'd been pleasantly surprised by how supportive people had been. Chase had even offered them to run with the team for free this weekend after he heard about Jake's redundancy. Perhaps Carver had had a word with him. Either way, it was a kind offer and one he really appreciated.

Unfortunately, the majority of the paddock wouldn't be so understanding and would be rubbing their hands together at the opportunity to taunt the cheats. Worse still, most people would assume the exclusion was justified. It wasn't going to be a fun few days.

Chase had let slip that Lillington was being a dick about the whole thing, saying he didn't want to be in the same team with a known cheat, that it would tarnish his reputation. He'd even threatened to walk if Jake and Max came back in the awning. Chase had sounded pretty pissed off about that.

Jake had to admit he was touched that Chase wanted them in the team despite the aggro it would cause.

All the same, he'd politely declined. They planned to just do their own thing this weekend and run the kart themselves. They didn't want to cause Chase trouble, and they thought it best to keep themselves to themselves. Jake planned to use the awning on the side of the caravan and run the kart from there.

He wasn't keen to socialise. They were going because Max wanted to go and show the paddock they had nothing to be ashamed of. They knew they didn't cheat so they just needed to hold their nerve and see the weekend through.

After all, things couldn't get any worse, could they?

Jake rotated his shoulders and yawned. It was no good, he would need to have a break soon. Stretching his neck, he heard a sudden, loud bang and felt the van steering go heavy and pull violently to one side. Bambi looked at him, her eyes wide.

He steered onto the hard shoulder with some effort, hazard lights flashing in the darkness.

"Sounds like a blow out. I'd better have a look."

That had woken him up a bit - all traces of tiredness had disappeared now. Using his phone as a torch, Jake checked the damage. Sure enough, the nearside caravan tyre was completely shredded. Jake rubbed his face wearily. *This was going to be fun. At least the blown tyre was away from the road, rather than inches from the hurtling traffic.*

He crouched down, looking for the spare. Frowning, he realised he didn't even know where it was. Did he even have one? And if he did, was it road-legal? Either way, they didn't have much choice now. Was there even a jack? Even if he could find the spare, he wasn't going to get far changing the tyre unless he could jack the caravan up.

After ten minutes or so, Jake climbed back into the van looking glum. There was no jack, so even though he'd found the spare he couldn't change it. To top it all off, he'd let their breakdown cover lapse a few weeks ago, thinking he was saving them money.

Now he'd have to call a local garage out, which was bound to be pricey. After ringing round, he finally found a garage that could replace caravan tyres, but there would be a lengthy wait. The man on the phone couldn't say when they'd be able to get out to him, but it would be at least three hours.

They couldn't stay in the van. Jake went and grabbed the duvet off the bed. It was unnerving being in the caravan as vehicles sped past inches away, making it shudder violently. They'd be sitting at the side of the road for a while so they might as well let Max try and sleep.

In fact, he'd slept through the whole incident so far and needed as much rest as possible as they were due out on track at 8am. That was if they managed to get to the track at all.

Fortunately, it was summer and the weather was dry. If would have been a lot worse to be stuck in winter in the pouring rain.

They settled themselves on the grassy bank by the side of the motorway and huddled together under the duvet.

They'd been sitting despondently watching traffic for half an hour when a truck hurtled past and pulled onto the hard shoulder ahead of them. As it reversed slowly back towards them, Jake got to his feet. *What were they doing?*

The truck's air brake gasped as it came to a stop. The driver's door opened and Dave North jumped down, his Elvis-style quiff getting buffeted by the turbulence of the passing traffic. He jogged over.

"Jake, it is you. I thought so! What's happened, mate?"

They shook hands, both shouting to be heard over the noise of the motorway.

"Blow out. We've got a spare tyre but no bloody jack, so I'm waiting for a garage to come out. They're going to be hours yet."

Dave grimaced. "That's crap, mate. Tell you what, let me see what I can do."

He made a call, pacing up and down the hard shoulder. Jake caught snippets of the conversation and at one point heard him shout that he paid their substantial wages so they could bloody well do as they were told. Jake frowned. *Who on earth was he talking to?*

The answer came shortly when a BRR-branded van screeched to a standstill behind the caravan and three surly young mechanics got out. Without a word, they opened the side door of their van, grabbed their tools and got to work, jacking up the caravan, getting out the spare tyre and replacing it in record time.

Packing up again, the driver signalled to Dave.

"All done, boss!" and in a few minutes they had rejoined the motorway and disappeared into the distance.

Jake and Dave went to inspect their handiwork.

"I don't know what to say, mate. Thanks, you're a life saver! We would have been here all night."

"That's OK. Glad I could help. I wanted to get in touch after the last round, but I didn't have your number. You got shafted. We didn't think for a minute you were actually cheating. You were too much of a threat and somebody did something about it."

Overwhelmed, Jake stared at his boots because his eyes were suddenly swimming. "Thanks, mate, I really appreciate that," he said, clapping Dave on the shoulder.

Dave laughed. "Come on, we've both still got a long drive before we reach Scotland. Let's get back on the road. We'll have a beer and catch up properly tomorrow."

As they got underway again, Jake looked at Bambi and shook his head in disbelief.

"Who'd have believed it, eh? And we thought we had no friends in the paddock!"

"I know," laughed Bambi. "Sounds like those BRR mechanics weren't too keen on helping, though, but I guess whoever holds the purse strings is in charge. Thank goodness they stopped!" She put a hand on Jake's thigh and sighed, closing her eyes with relief. Crossing the fingers of her other hand, which Jake couldn't see, she hoped the weekend would go without any further drama.

They made good time after that, but it was still approaching two in the morning when they pulled into the circuit, bleary-eyed and desperate for sleep. Unhooking the caravan, they parked up at a drunken angle next to Dave's race truck and fell into bed exhausted, relieved to have finally arrived.

After what felt like a few fleeting minutes of sleep, it was time to get up. For a moment Jake considered turning the alarm off and getting a few more hours' kip. *Sod the morning's practice sessions.*

But, after briefly closing his eyes again, he heaved a deep sigh and hauled himself out of bed. They hadn't come all this way just to have a lie-in. Stumbling across to the kitchen, he opened one of the blinds an inch and winced away from the brightness.

As his eyes became accustomed to the light, he saw the track was damp and shrouded in mist.

Chase had said this track was beautiful, surrounded by rolling hills, but there was no chance of seeing those through the fog. He chuckled. *Summer in Scotland, eh?* They'd left home yesterday in stunning June sunshine. Good job they'd brought wet tyres and warm coats.

By lunchtime the mist had cleared, and they enjoyed a few hours of glorious sunshine. But as the afternoon went on, thick clouds rolled in and a steady drizzle started to fall. You could always rely on Scottish weather to give you three seasons in a day!

The fact they didn't know the track, combined with ever-changing conditions, kept Jake and Max so busy they barely noticed what reception they got in the paddock.

Jake overheard a few murmured comments, and of course Danny Fox was smirking like a Cheshire Cat that needed a punch in the face, but he was too tired and too busy trying to get the setup right to take much notice.

It was nearly 6pm before testing was over, by which time Jake was exhausted. A bad night's sleep combined with the stresses of the last 24 hours caught up with him as soon as he stopped.

Plus, it was miserable weather to be running under a pull-out awning. He was damp, cold and starting to regret not taking Chase up on his offer of running with the team

- even with Lillington being a wanker in there. On top of that, a haze of midges had descended that afternoon and Jake was breaking out in blotchy bites all over his hands and neck. He packed everything into the back of the van and headed back into the warm haven of the caravan.

Slumping on the sofa, Jake's eyes felt heavy and he decided to have a quick nap while Bambi cooked dinner. He had just drifted off when there was a knock on the door. He dragged himself groggily back upright. Who could that be?

Bambi opened the door to find Dave and Savannah standing on the doorstep holding beer and prosecco. They greeted them with a jovial chorus of hellos. Jake gratefully accepted a beer; he could do with one after the day he'd had. Settled on the sofa, he and Dave were soon putting the world to rights and roaring with laughter at the horrendous antics of Hillary and her demon children in the awning.

It was good to know the Aspinalls weren't the perfect family they made themselves out to be, and it pulled Jake out of his habitual gloom. He thanked Dave again for stopping and sorting the blown tyre and, after a couple of beers, ended up telling him everything that had happened over the last couple of weeks, from the backlash of the last round to losing his job.

Dave laughed. "Surely you can see that's an opportunity, Jake? How often does life give you a kick up the arse and make you change your existence? You could set up on your own, be your own boss. Why make money for someone else when you can make more and have more flexibility starting your own company?"

He regaled Jake with tales of his own business ventures, and how he'd made his first million working from a box room with just a desk and a telephone in it. As the beer flowed and the night grew dark outside, Jake, who was initially resistant, gradually came round to the idea and they even started talking company names and sketching logos on the backs of petrol receipts.

Realising that Jake was a bit of a technical expert, Dave even offered to get him started by giving him the contract to do the website for his latest property venture.

"It would only be a couple of months' work, but it would help get you up and running."

Full of alcohol and enthusiasm they agreed, shaking on it, and despite everything Jake started to feel there might be light at the end of the tunnel.

28
SCUFF MARKS & SEX PESTS

On Saturday morning Savannah, who wasn't keen to hang out with Hillary, decided to pop and have a coffee with Bambi before all the action started. A bleary Bambi opened the caravan door a crack and peered out. She looked an absolute state: pale and drawn with puffy eyes and still in her PJs.

"Oh goodness!" Savannah said. "Are you alright? What on earth has happened?"

"Come in," sighed Bambi. "I'm just putting the kettle on if you want a brew?"

"Yes, that'd be lovely. Are you OK? This probably isn't what you want to hear but you look dreadful!"

Putting the kettle on, Bambi gave way to tears again and, once she started, she just didn't seem to be able to stop, her shoulders heaving with silent sobs.

Jumping up in alarm, Savannah ushered her to the sofa and produced a packet of tissues from her pocket.

"Come on, have a good cry and then tell me what on earth's been going on."

Feeling ridiculous, Bambi leaned back on the sofa and

blew her nose loudly, letting the last of her sobs subside.

"The last few weeks have been an absolute nightmare with everyone thinking we cheated. Poor Max was absolutely devastated by it all, then Jake lost his job and…" - she paused as the tears started falling again - "I haven't told anyone yet, but I'm pregnant."

Savannah's eyes widened in surprise and she scooped Bambi up in a big perfumed hug, eyes brimming with sympathetic tears.

"No wonder you're feeling emotional! You've had so much on your plate, you poor thing. Haven't you even told Jake yet?"

"No," she sniffed. "I was all set to tell him on the day he lost his job, but then he came home with that terrible news and I didn't want to pile more stress on him on top of everything else. He's been so fed up, I thought my news might be the straw that broke the camel's back, if you know what I mean. I just want to get this weekend done and out of the way, then I'll find the right moment to tell him. I've got my scan on Tuesday, so I'll have to tell him by then."

Bambi leapt up as the kettle started whistling and made them both a coffee.

"I know it'll all turn out OK," she sniffled. "It was just such a shock. We weren't planning a baby. I thought I was a bit old for that kind of thing, to be honest. I mean, there'll be a twelve-year age gap between Max and the new baby." She laughed. "I'll definitely be the oldest mum on the school run." Then, sagging again, "That's if everything's OK when I go for the scan."

Savannah rubbed her arm reassuringly.

"Oh, I'm sure it will be. Just because you had a few glasses of wine before you realised you were pregnant, it's not the end of the world."

"I hope so. Either way, it's out of my control, isn't it? All I can do is the best for the baby now. Who," she added, "is making me horribly sick in the mornings at the moment. If only it meant I was losing some weight! Then again, at least there's a reason why I've been piling on the pounds. I can wear jeans with elasticated waistbands without feeling guilty for the next five or six months!"

Bambi took a sip of her coffee. "I suppose this should really be decaf too, shouldn't it? I need to make some major lifestyle adjustments, but for today I could really do with some caffeine. Anyway, how are things with you and Dave? Is the ex-wife here this weekend?"

Savannah's lip curled. "Yes, unfortunately. Although I don't mind so much now. I was a bit intimidated by her before, but after hearing what she did to Dave I'm ready to kick her arse. I can't believe she treated him like that! Just let her carry on with her bitchy comments, I don't care, I've got skin as tough as a rhino. But I'll tell you now, if she says anything to Dave, I'll go for her."

"Good for you," smiled Bambi. "Dave seems so happy with you, don't let her spoil things. She sounds like a total bitch. It's none of her business who Dave spends his time with. She didn't want him - not enough to stay faithful anyway - but she doesn't want him to be happy with you either. Just ignore her."

Savannah let out a resigned sigh.

"Speaking of which, I'd better go over to the awning and see what's going on. Can't put it off forever, and I don't want Dave thinking I've deserted him!"

They agreed to meet up to watch later, then Savannah re-applied her lip gloss, fluffed up her hair, squared her shoulders and strode over towards the BRR awning. Bambi grinned to herself. *I wouldn't want to be Dave's ex today with the mood she's in,* she mused.

The BRR awning was busier than usual as the Leeches had joined the team. Julia, who was still smarting after her unceremonious dumping, had made things up with Kevin and they had agreed to put her 'blip' with Danny Fox behind them. It hadn't been easy. It had taken a great deal of discussion and not a few arguments to reach this point. Tearfully, Julia had pointed out to Kevin how sorely neglected she'd been in recent months, and how much her self-esteem had plummeted as a consequence.

Unsurprised that her affair had turned out to be his fault, Kevin had duly apologised and resolved to pay her more attention from now on. She was probably right. Moving to a different team was a crucial part of their reconciliation. There was no way they could start afresh with Fox smirking away in the same awning. Besides which, Julia was still sensitive after his rejection.

Compensating for this, Julia was on a charm offensive both with Kevin, who was receiving more compliments and affection than he'd had in years, and also with the Aspinalls, who she swiftly identified as the most influential people in the team and therefore people to get 'in' with.

Her scarlet lipstick a thing of the past, she had reverted to earth-mother mode and was currently chatting away with Hillary as if they were long-lost friends.

Discovering they had so much in common (they both shopped at Waitrose, felt their children were superior to everyone else's, and liked talking about how selfless they were,) they were surreptitiously competing with each other to see who could be the smuggest mum in the awning. Julia was playing the vegan environmental card and Hillary was saying how much she didn't like to talk about all her charity work, both of them eulogising about their precious and talented children, and how blessed they were in their perfect lives.

The pair conveniently skirted around the shortfallings of their own marriages.

Savannah eavesdropped from afar and decided to steer firmly clear. They were undoubtedly kindred spirits and she couldn't be bothered to try and join in with the self-congratulatory circle jerk they seemed to be enjoying.

Plonking herself down in a seat by Dave, she gazed around the rest of the awning. Julia's husband appeared to have fitted in well and was laughing and joking with Ben Redmaine, who seemed to be giving the new family a lot of attention.

Fair enough, he was the front man of the team and new team members needed to feel like they were getting some special treatment. It had probably been the same for Dave when he'd first joined.

Redmaine didn't usually have much hands-on contact with the karts; that's what he hired mechanics for. He mostly did driver coaching and PR when he was around, but she'd seen him with a spanner in his hand this weekend when he was over with Kevin.

Savannah watched the mechanics swarming around Cosmo's kart and, oh shit, she shouldn't have looked over there. Hugo Aspinall had just spotted her looking and given her a lascivious wink. Eugh! She glanced back to Hillary who seemed to have no idea how pervy her husband was with other women, or perhaps she just chose to ignore it.

Looking down she realised her feet were tangled in the straps of a handbag. It was a sensible leather tote, albeit a Mulberry, so it probably cost about the same amount as a small house and, being leather, it must belong to Hillary. As she unfurled the strap caught around her ankle, she spotted a packet of pills in the bag. *That was odd; hadn't Hillary said she disapproved of all types of pill popping?* In fact, if Savannah remembered correctly, she'd been rather sanctimonious about the fact.

Dropping her phone on the floor, she stooped to pick it up as an excuse to take a closer look. Petrodiazapine. What on earth was that? Her interest piqued, especially at the thought of catching Hillary out in a fib, she quickly typed the name into her phone and Googled it.

Wow, those were some serious drugs: used to treat depression, anxiety and stress with a list of side-effects as long as your arm. She felt a pang of guilt at having snooped. Perhaps perfect Hillary's life wasn't quite as peachy as she made out.

Then again, living with Hugo and those two brats couldn't make for the happiest of home lives. Realising Dave had been talking to her, she jumped and slid her phone back into her pocket.

She smiled up at him. "Sorry, I was totally zoned out then. What did you say?"

"Away with the fairies, you were! Could you go and get Parker's helmet bag for me please, love? I think it's in the side locker of the motorhome." He tossing her the keys with a grin.

"Of course," she said, running her hand up his arm affectionately. Dave saw the smile freeze on her face and turned to see what had caused her reaction. Cassandra had just sauntered into the awning, leading her boyfriend by the hand. Dave's eyes narrowed. This was all they needed.

Putting his hand over Savannah's, he gave it a gentle squeeze and whispered, "Just ignore her".

Savannah slipped out of the awning to get the helmet, glad to have a reason to escape. The bitch ex-wife, dressed in skin-tight designer jeans with a bright-white BRR jacket and suicidally-high stiletto boots, had swanned over to Hillary and was greeting her with a great deal of air kissing and ostentatious delight. She turned her charm on Julia, welcoming her to the team as if she owned it.

As Savannah walked away, she was sure she heard Cassandra say, "Looking for someone with more money," followed by bitchy laughter. She bristled. That cow had only come to stir up trouble. She hadn't so much as looked at poor Parker, who was quietly playing on her phone in the corner.

Out by the motor home, Savannah could still hear all the gushing and cooing in the awning and pulled a face. *How had Dave ever fallen for such a phoney? She was such a piece of work!* She sighed sadly, hoping he didn't still hold a candle for her. Either way, Cassandra was Parker's mum, so she would always be in their lives.

Leaning down to get the helmet out of the locker, she felt hands slide around her waist from behind. Dave must've had enough of the ex and come to find her. She wiggled her hips and pushed back against him, smiling.

Then she heard Hugo whisper, "Oh yes! I've been desperate to see you all week, Sav darling, I can't stop thinking about you."

Horror-struck, Savannah jolted bolt upright, catching him in the nose with the back of her head.

Turning to face him she shouted, "What the fuck do you think you're doing?"

Clutching his nose, Hugo tried to sound sexy, but instead just succeeded in sounding a bit nasally congested.

"You don't need to be coy with me, Sav, we both know we've been waiting for this. I've been dying to get you alone all weekend…"

Wide-eyed, Savannah gaped in amazement as he reached towards her again.

"Are you fucking kidding me? Get your piggy hands off me, you nasty little sex pest!" She kneed him hard in the groin and, stepping over him as he lay crumpled on the floor, hissed furiously. "Dave is going to hear about this. And if you ever touch me again, I'll get the police on you for sexual assault."

Hugo, eyes squeezed tightly shut against the blinding pain in his testicles, staggered to a crouch and leaned on his hands, trying to get his breath back. *Fucking bitch!*

Looking down, he saw scuff marks on his immaculate white BRR jacket where he'd hit the tarmac, and that made him even crosser. Red in the face and muttering curses under his breath, he got slowly to his feet. *Fucking little prick-tease, she wouldn't get away with this.*

29
WISHFUL THINKING

Frankie was feeling a bit glum. He'd never known the car to be so quiet. It felt like only yesterday the kids would have provided a constant stream of chatter and demands for the *Disney Favourites* CD to be played on a loop. He'd be careful who he'd admit it to, but he'd regularly sung along to the soundtrack from *High School Musical* at the top of his lungs with them, and he kind of missed that now. How he'd wished for some peace and quiet. *It just goes to show, be careful what you wish for.*

Now, he barely got a word out of his kids. They were constantly plugged into one device or another and only resurfaced when they were forced to.

Britney had been engrossed in her phone, headphones on, for the whole journey. He might as well have been in the car by himself. He'd even been able to croon along to his favourite Frank Sinatra album without any complaint. The only reaction he'd got was a brief raise of her eyebrows when he'd tried to hit a particularly ambitious note.

He never thought he'd look back fondly on the kids

bickering in the backseat, but this journey had made him feel a bit melancholy. The kids seemed totally disconnected from him. They just wanted to immerse themselves in YouTube and online chats with their friends. Maybe that was what teenagers did.

He was quite sure, if he asked Brit, he'd be told that he 'didn't understand', with a side order of eye-rolling and a pained sigh. Perhaps it was the age-old teen problem, but instead of hanging out in the park with their mates and a bottle of cheap cider they were sucked into this digital world. He had no idea what she did on there the whole time.

Frankie parked in the paddock, blocking in two other cars and not caring one bit, and Britney finally glanced up from her technological trance. He'd been chuffed that she'd wanted to come and support her brother this weekend; he just hoped she wouldn't get bored after an hour and spend the whole weekend wanting to go home.

Linda was having a well-earned spa day with the girls, so calling her to come and pick up a bored Britney wasn't an option. Luckily Chris had driven the motorhome up on Thursday night and been here with Ronnie ever since.

If Britney got restless enough, she could always give Chris a makeover. Frankie smirked at the thought of big, tough Chris covered in glittery makeup with his nails painted. If anyone could talk him into that, it would be Britney. He'd known her since she was a toddler and she'd always been able to wrap him around her little finger. He chuckled. The mental image of Chris in full Disney princess makeup would stay with him.

He walked into the awning and shot a glance over at Danny. *Holy shit, he looked like he'd been on a week-long bender.* With creased clothes and bloodshot eyes, he was a right state. He was also jiggling from foot to foot and looked wired as hell. The awning was quiet and empty now the Leeches had left. He'd seen that one coming; there was no way Julia would stick around once Fox had dumped her.

She must have been pretty humiliated by the whole thing. He grinned. *Served her right.* Then again, that woman had more front than a row of houses, so she'd recover fast. At least it meant Fox could concentrate on Ronnie's race weekend, rather than getting distracted by his cock the whole time.

Danny swaggered up with a lazy smile. He was clearly still impressed with himself about spiking Jake's fuel, and hadn't the sense to realise Frankie felt this was crossing a line.

Frankie might be ruthless, but screwing over innocent kids wasn't the way he did business.

He looked over at Britney. Far from showing an interest in her brother or the kart, she was slouched in a chair, back on her phone again, wearing the shortest of shorts. He wished he'd spotted that before they left. She didn't yet realise that showing so much skin would attract boys like flies, especially in the paddock. He could hardly ask her to go and put some tracky bottoms on, though. It was due to be a scorching-hot day and he was just being overprotective. He smiled indulgently. She was his little princess, after all, and he was glad she'd come today. Perhaps they'd get some good father-daughter time when they were watching Ronnie racing.

Frankie walked over to Ronnie and ruffled his hair. "How you doing champ?"

Ronnie ducked away good-naturedly. "Gerroff, dad!"

Frankie chuckled and checked his watch; it must be nearly time for qualifying.

Clapping his hands together, he said, "Right lads, let's do this!" and whistling cheerfully he headed to the grandstand. He had a good feeling about today.

30
CONFRONTATION & COLLAPSE

Everyone turned to stare at Hugo as he stormed into the awning. Face the colour of a tomato, and clearly furious, he cut a slightly ridiculous figure in his dirt-scuffed jacket.

Savannah, who was angry and upset, but hadn't wanted to cause a big scene and distract them from qualifying, had resolved to tell Dave later. But, seeing Hugo, she instantly regretted her decision. She hadn't thought for a moment that Hugo would have the gall to say anything. *After all, he came onto her!*

He was bound to try and give a different version of events, though, and in front of Dave's bloody ex as well. She slipped her hand into Dave's and stood there, her mouth suddenly dry. Dave looked at her, frowning in concern, then caught sight of Cassandra, who was standing with her arms folded looking triumphant. His frown deepened. *What had that bitch done now?*

Hugo strode indignantly up to Dave, bellowing at the top of his voice.

"That prick-teasing slut of a girlfriend of yours! You have no idea what she's been up to behind your back, have you? You've been taken for a fucking ride. She's already looking for her next big meal ticket. Bet you didn't know she'd been sending me sexy messages for weeks, only to play hard to get when she finally gets me alone?"

Dave's eyes narrowed in anger and he seemed to grow taller as he glowered over the irate little man.

"What did you say?" he growled.

Savannah, who's temper had reached breaking point, stepped out fuming from behind Dave.

"What the hell are you talking about? Is this your way of getting back at me after I kicked you in the balls for groping me in the car park?"

Dave looked like he might explode.

"He did WHAT?"

Hugo faltered slightly, but then rallied and triumphantly produced his phone.

"This is what I'm talking about! Look yourself, see what she's been up to." Shoving the screen in Dave's face, he scrolled through page after page of flirty messages between him and Savannah. She'd even sent him sexy photos of her in a bikini. The room fell silent as Dave flicked through the messages. Savannah was mortified. She could see her whole, happy life slipping away in front of her and she didn't know what the hell had happened. She stood frozen in silent fear.

After a few seconds, which felt like an eternity, Dave frowned and looked steadily at Hugo. Holding up Hugo's phone, he tapped on Savannah's number. The awning hushed as everyone waited and then a phone started to ring. Looking around to see where the ringing was coming from, their eyes rested on Cassandra, whose smug smile was rapidly fading.

Dave walked over to her, took the handbag off her shoulder and pulled out the ringing phone. He shook his head and laughed bitterly.

"You desperate bitch," he said. "You went to all the trouble of doing this to try and split us up."

Cassandra tossed her hair over her shoulder. "You old fool, you think she loves you?"

"Yes, actually, I do."

Turning to Hugo, who was paling as he realised he'd not only been taken for an idiot, but he'd just got himself into deep and very public trouble with his wife, Dave said, "And as for you, I suggest you back down, little man. Coming in here all puffed-up and indignant because she'd rejected you! What exactly were you planning to do? Bite my ankles?"

He towered over Hugo, his face dangerously angry. "You owe Savannah an apology."

He passed the phone to Savannah, so she could see what had been done in her name. She read through the texts in horror, spotting photos which had clearly been stolen from her Facebook feed. Cassandra must have been stalking her online for weeks. Scrolling through all the suggestive messages, she realised why Hugo had come and manhandled her, and who had set all this up.

Shaken and angry, she turned on Cassandra in disbelief.

"You went to all this trouble? You got a new phone, got his number," - she nodded her head towards Hugo - "you pretended to be me and egged him on? Why? All so that Dave would think I'd cheated on him? That I was doing to him what you did? Were you so desperate to hurt him? So desperate to break us up? Haven't you done enough to him already? And as for you," she said turning to Cassandra's boyfriend, who took a step back, "how can you show your face here? You were his friend, but as soon as you get the opportunity you shack up with his wife and then parade around in front of him? You should be ashamed of yourself!"

He held his hands up defensively, moving away from Cassandra. "Hey, I didn't know she was going to pull a stunt like this."

Savannah moved up close to Cassandra's horror-struck face.

"You know," she snarled, "after everything you did to Dave, you're still going out of your way to try and make him miserable." Punctuating her words with sharp pokes to Cassandra's chest she continued. "You screwed up, and you screwed him over. Now leave him the fuck alone. I've got his back now. If you go after him, you go after both of us, and I'll tell you now, you're going to have a hell of a fight on your hands if you want to take me on."

Dave, who had been watching Savannah in astonishment, broke the silence with a heartfelt laugh. Grabbing her wrist and pulling her into his arms, he beamed at her.

"Christ, I love you," he said before enfolding her in a passionate embrace.

Everyone else, who'd been frozen to the spot by the unfolding events in the awning, started shifting uncomfortably. But suddenly they were galvanised into action by Ben Redmaine shouting. "Come on, everyone! We've got to get out on track. Karts down to the grid sharpish, now!"

The awning swiftly became a hive of activity: tyre pressures being set, engines tested, drivers quickly zipping up their suits and putting their helmets on. All except for Savannah and Dave, who stood in the middle of the room, arms around each other, grinning.

Julia, standing with a stony-faced Hillary, put a consoling hand on her shoulder and asked sympathetically (if a little smugly) if she was OK.

Shrugging Julia's hand off, Hillary turned to her and icily replied, "I don't know what you're looking so smug about. At least my husband hasn't been flirting with the team boss all weekend," before stalking out.

Well! thought Julia, huffily. *I know she's just had a shock but there was no need for that, I was just being kind. No wonder her husband is looking elsewhere.*

Dave still had Savannah in his arms.

"I'm sorry I've got a psycho ex-wife," he murmured. "I

had no idea she would do something like that."

Savannah leaned her head against his chest. "My heart just dropped when I saw those messages. I didn't know what the hell was going on! How did you know it wasn't me who'd sent them?"

"I trust you. Besides," he chuckled, "it wasn't your phone number. I memorised that the first time you gave it to me, so I knew as soon as I saw it that something strange was going on."

She laughed, shaking her head. There were certainly advantages to him being the kind of bloke who still memorised a girl's phone number. Here's to old-fashioned guys. They were the best. She grinned, slipping her hand in his. "Come on, let's go and watch."

Frankie needed to calm the fuck down. Things had gone well today; they'd qualified second and had scored a win and two third places in the heats, earning them good points for the championship. They'd had good pace; they'd be in a sound starting position for the final tomorrow, and there hadn't been any drama. In all honesty, there really was no reason for him to be feeling this pissed off.

The problem was, with only them in the awning, he'd been getting the undiluted attention of Danny Fox all day, and it was becoming increasingly apparent that he was a total waste of space. Aaron was doing all the work. Again, he'd found himself questioning what he was paying all this money for.

Danny's contribution to the race weekend seemed to be strutting around the paddock with his chest puffed out, crowing to anyone who'd listen about how he'd known the Goldings were cheating all along, and precious little else. He'd overheard him saying, "Otherwise they just couldn't have been that fast as a newbie," while shaking his head self-righteously, as well as; "We all know why he was so quick now" and "Why do people do it? They're just cheating their kids at the end of the day".

Frankie knew he should be able to tune out the bollocks, but it was winding him right up. The last round had been over a month ago. Surely it was old news by now? And Danny's constant gloating particularly rankled since Frankie knew what had really happened.

He'd seen Jake around the paddock, looking drawn and tense, and almost felt sorry for the guy, but he'd shrugged it off. You had to be ruthless in this game, and to beat Aspinall to the championship they were going to need every last point. If Golding quit, there would be one less front runner to contend with. He would never have condoned Danny's actions, but he had to admit it had done them a massive favour.

All the same, his temper kept simmering away under the surface, only just under control.

A couple of times he'd nearly told the addicted little runt to fuck off out of the awning and leave them alone. He knew it was Danny's awning, but he was the one paying the money and he couldn't see Danny standing up to him. It was only Britney that held him back. She'd confronted him this morning, asking him why he was being so mean to Danny all the time. *Couldn't he be nice? Just for her?*

Sighing reluctantly, he'd conceded. His little princess had never been to the track before and he wanted her to enjoy it. So, for Britney's sake he swallowed down his annoyance and kept schtum. They only had to get through this weekend, then he was dumping Fox Racing for good.

He'd seen Danny and his daughter talking quite a bit, so perhaps there was some benefit to having him around. At least Britney wasn't bored. She seemed to be taking a real interest - perhaps she was quizzing him about having a go herself? He'd have to ask her later. After all he couldn't think what else she'd have to talk to Danny about.

The paddock was packing up for the evening, Aaron meticulously cleaning and checking over the kart, getting it prepped for the morning. The kids were out of their race suits and busy playing on bikes, scooters and with footballs, any on-track animosity forgotten.

It was the parents who persisted with their grudges, almost relishing the animosity and wanting to turn it into more bitter feuds.

The awning emptied rapidly, and soon only Aaron, Frankie and Chris were left. Gesturing to Chris, Frankie stepped outside. He wanted to run the whole Danny situation by him and get his take on it. Chris was a safe pair of hands and always made a good sounding board, and Frankie was concerned: was he letting his emotions get the better of him?

The thought had him rattled. Frankie had always prided himself on being calm and clear-headed whatever the situation and he wasn't used to doubting himself, but business was different. There were no emotions involved, nor were his kids. With the extra complication of wanting to do his best for Ronnie, he just couldn't get it straight in his head. Every time he thought about the team situation, he found himself more and more wound up.

Sitting in Frankie's car, Chris listened silently to the whole story without comment. Once Frankie had got it all off his chest, he considered for a few moments before answering.

"To be honest, Frank," he said, "it seems to me, that the only thing you're paying Fox for is awning space and hot air. You don't trust him with your engines, you don't trust his opinions on setup or strategy, and frankly he's a fucking liability. If what he did to Golding ever comes out, he's going to be toxic to be associated with, and you don't need that aggro. I reckon you get shot at the end of the weekend. Distance yourself as far as you can from him. You also need to decide whether you'll be running with another team for the last round, or whether we're running ourselves."

Frankie stroked his chin. Chris made a lot of sense. And he was right. Frankie had some decisions to make. He didn't want the hassle of having to run out of a crappy pop-up gazebo for the last round. For starters, Aspinall would rip the piss, and he could really do without that. That only left him with the option of joining another team, but which one? Certainly not BRR, although that would make Aspinall blow a gasket, he thought, the side of his mouth stretching into a grin. *It would almost be worth it.*

Feeling better now he'd made a decision - or at least part of one - he and Chris headed towards the bar. Frankie needed a cold beer to soothe the stresses of the day.

The paddock bar was lively and humming with conversation as everyone let off steam after a busy day. Danny Fox was in his element. Elbows resting on the counter, he was relaxed, the buzz from his first beer having taken the edge off his craving for another hit, and he was chatting loudly to Chase when Britney walked in and slid onto the stool next to him.

She took a long swig from his bottle of beer, smiled at him, and leaned in close to his ear, making him shiver.

"Get me a beer, Danny." she murmured.

The side of Danny's mouth twitched, and he clicked his fingers at the barman. "Another couple of beers here, bruv."

Danny appreciatively took in Britney's long, tanned legs and toned midriff and whistled to himself. She really was a cracker and, after all, he was the catch of the paddock. Who could blame her for fancying him? Slipping his hand onto her knee, he leaned across to whisper something in her ear when he felt a hand on his shoulder.

"Are you for real, mate?" said Chase, eyes wide with concern. "I would be seriously careful if you know what's good for you."

Danny snorted. "Fuck off, granddad. Who invited you to the party anyway?"

Britney giggled in admiration. He was such a rebel, and so much cooler than the immature boys at her school.

Danny looked pleased with himself and turned his back on Chase, who shook his head and went to join another table. "I'm not sticking around to watch this car crash," he muttered.

Danny turned his full attention back to Britney, who was watching him from under heavy lidded eyes.

"So, what made a gorgeous girl like you come to a racetrack? Are you thinking about getting behind the wheel?"

She shrugged with a little smile.

"No, I just like the scenery," she said, holding his gaze and lightly biting her lower lip.

Blimey, thought Danny, *she's totally hot for me.* The initial buzz from the beer was starting to wear off and, despite the ravishing company, he was starting to crave a better hit. Grabbing her hand, he led her over to a table in a dark corner. Making sure her back was shielding him from the rest of the bar, he pulled out a small bag of white powder, dipped his van key into it and snorted it. Checking over her shoulder to make sure nobody was watching, he repeated the process with the other nostril, then offered some to her.

Britney was keen to impress. After all, he was the reason she'd come this weekend, and she didn't want him thinking she was a baby. So, she flicked her hair back defiantly and copied him, snorting it back, her nose wrinkling and eyes screwing up as she felt the acrid burn at the back of her throat.

She heard Danny chortle and murmur, "That's my girl," and when she re-opened her eyes his face was close to hers and he was staring intently at her. All of a sudden, the butterflies in her stomach had gone, and she felt amazing, her whole body tingling! Every nerve seemed to be alive and, with a new-found confidence, she leaned forward and kissed him.

High on cocaine and desire, they were both oblivious to the public setting. Feeling invincible, Danny pulled her onto his lap, their kiss deepening and becoming harder and more desperate. He slipped one hand under her top, fumbling for her bra clasp, and the other cupped her arse as he pressed himself into her. Her bra now undone, he slid his hand around and over her breast, making her gasp into his mouth as he pinched her nipple. He desperately needed to get her out of the bar and to somewhere more private. He racked his brain for a place to go. *The grandstand!* That would be empty at this time of night, and it was dark enough that anyone walking by wouldn't spot them in a corner.

But it was hard to tear himself away and he didn't want to spook her by making a move too quickly. He'd give her a few more minutes and then she wouldn't question going outside with him. She was putty in his hands.

Suddenly Danny felt a rush of cool air as she was torn away from him and he was grabbed by the neck and slammed against the wall. Confused and angry, with a raging boner, he struggled to orient himself. He found himself staring into the cold, angry eyes of Fat Frankie Finch.

"Oh my God dad, you're totally embarrassing me!" whined Britney, her words slurring, as she tugged at his sleeve trying to get him to let go of Danny.

Frankie, keeping one hand on Danny's throat, grabbed Britney's chin, studying her.

Turning to Danny, his voice like cold steel, he growled, "What the fuck have you given her?"

"What are you talking about? I haven't given her anything?" stammered Danny. He tried to shrink himself further into the corner, but it wasn't far enough, as Britney chose that moment to throw up, spectacularly spattering vomit all over Danny's trainers.

"Oh, for fuck's sake, you silly bitch!" he shouted, then rapidly shut up as he saw the murderous expression on Frankie's face.

Frankie turned to Chris, who was supporting a limp

and now quietly crying Britney. All the fight had gone out of her after being sick and she looked young, ill, and like she needed to get to bed.

"Take her back to the motorhome and make sure she's OK, Chris. Find out what she's taken. I need to have a word with Mr Sicky Shoes here." Grabbing Danny by the hair, he dragged him, struggling, through the bar to the emergency doors, kicked them open and went into the dimly lit alley outside.

Holding Danny up against the wall with one hand on his throat, Frankie gave him a short, sharp jab in the nose, breaking it. He let Danny drop, his head hitting the pavement with a smack. Danny looked dazed and panicked.

Frankie leaned over him. "I've had enough of you, Fox. I'm going to teach you why you don't lay your hands on my little girl, you fucking nonce." Straightening, he delivered a sharp kick to Danny's ribs, which made a satisfying crack. Danny groaned and rolled, trying to crawl away as he clutched his side, but Frankie wasn't having any of it. His anger, which had been brewing for so long, had finally found an outlet, and he was enjoying himself.

Frankie dragged a whimpering Danny to his knees.

"SHE'S-FUCKING-FIFTEEN, YOU-SICK-FUCK!" Frankie shouted, punctuating each word with a sickening punch to Danny's face. Danny slumped, coughing bloody drool onto the floor, along with a tooth. *Good!* Thought Frankie. *He won't be so pretty after I've finished with him!* Danny curled into a foetal position, trying to shield his face and stomach, but there was no stopping Frankie; he was livid. Red-faced with rage, Frankie continued punching and kicking Danny until he was an unresponsive, bleeding mess on the floor.

Then he leaned down and, looking into Danny's swollen, half-closed eyes to make sure he was paying full attention, Frankie growled, "If I ever see you at a track again, you'll regret it. Next time I won't tickle you, I'll fucking kill you! Consider this your one and only warning."

Frankie stood, placing his foot on Danny's throat as he regarded the mess he'd made of his face. "UNDERSTOOD?" he roared, eliciting a weak nod before delivering one last mighty, devastating kick to Danny's battered face, knocking him out.

Frankie then walked calmly back into the bar, closing the emergency doors behind him. He ignored the crowd of shocked faces and walked into the toilets to wash his hands. Drying them with paper towels he paused to ensure his manicured fingernails didn't have any blood beneath them. All good. He regarded himself in the mirror and saw the man he used to be looking back at him. It was good to be back. He'd had enough of trying to be respectable; it didn't get you anywhere. *It was about time the paddock realised what happened when you fucked with Frankie Finch.*

He strolled back through the bar and out the front, heading back across the paddock.

He'd wasted enough time on that duplicitous little pervert. He needed to go back and check on his princess. Poor Britney, he didn't dare think what might've happened if he hadn't shown up when he did. Rage still coursing through his veins, Frankie marched back through the dark, deserted, paddock, his mind racing.

Suddenly he faltered as he was hit by a sharp pain in his chest. Gasping in shock, he tried to keep walking, thinking it would pass, but his chest felt like it was being squeezed in a vice. He couldn't breathe, the pain was so bad. Stumbling heavily, he put his hand out to steady himself before he sank to his knees and collapsed.

Jake opened a can of cider and stretched out on the sofa. It had been a long, tough day and it was good to finally relax. He watched Bambi as she stirred a risotto on the stove, and smiled. She looked tired and drawn but she was still his gorgeous girl.

The last month had taken a toll on all of them. He'd

have to find a way to take them off on holiday once the season had finished. She could do with a treat; in fact, they all could. Catching him watching her, she frowned, wrinkling her nose. "What are you up to?"

Jake shrugged, smiling.

"Just thinking how gorgeous you are!"

Bambi chuckled softly, rolling her eyes.

"Yeah, right! I don't think I've ever looked such a state."

"I think you look lovely, positively radiant."

She snorted. "Hardly." She stared back at the pan she was stirring. *Perhaps this was as good a time as any to tell him.* Taking a breath, she turned to Jake and said shakily, "Actually, there's a reason I might be looking radiant…"

She stopped as the caravan shuddered with a heavy thump and they looked at each other in alarm.

"What the hell…?" said Jake, his unease quickly turning to anger as he sprang to his feet. "If that's Danny Fox messing about I'm going to give him what for. He's been going out of his way to make life difficult all bloody weekend."

Flinging open the door, he grabbed a torch and stormed outside ready for a confrontation. Bambi stood in the doorway, peering into the darkness, her heart pounding, but all she could hear was urgent muffled voices. *What on earth was going on?*

Then Jake shouted, "Bambi, quick!"

Stumbling down the steps in the dark, she rounded the corner of the caravan to find Jake stooping over a collapsed Frankie Finch. Her first thought was that Jake must have hit him.

Her second thought was about Frankie's reputation and how Jake hitting him would be a huge mistake.

"Call an ambulance, I think he's having a heart attack," said Jake. Bambi bolted back inside the caravan, struggling to unlock her phone with shaking hands.

She paced nervously back and forth as she waited for

the call to connect.

"Ambulance, please," she said to the operator as she hurried back to where Jake was crouched beside a white-faced Frankie. "Er, yes, he's breathing, but I think he's having a heart attack. We're at Castle Borgue racetrack." She paused. "Yes that's it." She gestured to Jake, trying to get his attention. "How long as the pain been going on?" Jake shrugged and Bambi frowned in frustration. "We don't really know. We think he's only just collapsed, we've just found him." She listened to more questions squinting with concentration as she struggled to understand the crackly voice on the other end of the line. "It's hard to tell, we're in the dark. He looks pale, I think, and he's sweating quite a lot." She paused again. "Age? I don't know. Mid-forties. I'd guess?"

"Oy!" wheezed Frankie, "I'm only fucking 38!"

Bambi laughed nervously. "You heard that, right?" Then turning serious again, "Sorry, I didn't catch that, the signal's really patchy - could you repeat it?" Frowning, she looked down at her phone and walked briskly away. "Hello? Can you hear me?"

She called back over to Jake, hating the quiver in her voice.

"My phone cut out! The signal here's terrible and I can't get a connection. They took my number, but unless I get a signal they won't be able to call me back." She rubbed her face anxiously. "What do we do? Will they send out an ambulance?"

"I have no idea," Jake said, getting his own phone out of his pocket. "I've got no signal either. We can't just sit here. The hospital can't be that far away!" He looked panicked for a moment, then glanced down at Frankie, whose breathing was shallow and who seemed to be drifting in and out of consciousness. "I'll drive him," he said.

"What, in the van?"

"What choice have I got? I'm not sure he'll make it if

he has to wait for the ambulance, and that's if one is on its way!"

Between them they heaved Frankie, who was even heavier than he looked, especially as a dead weight, into the front of the van and Jake raced out through the gates of the paddock. Following the sat nav to the nearest A&E Jake drove like a rallycross driver down narrow back lanes, glancing across at Frankie who was slumped in the passenger seat.

"How you doing there, Frankie? You holding up OK?"

Frankie opened his mouth in a silent groan. He didn't look good. Praying that the roads would stay empty, Jake floored it all the way - hoping he wouldn't have to beep his horn to try and clear traffic out of the way - he wasn't sure Frankie's heart could take any sudden unexpected noises.

After fifteen frantic minutes of driving Jake finally saw the hospital at the end of the road and felt a surge of relief. *Thank Christ for that.* "We're nearly there, Frankie, hang in there." He glanced across; he was sure that Frankie was looking even greyer than before.

Frankie was wheezing, trying desperately to say something, but Jake couldn't hear him.

"Save your breath, mate, we're nearly there."

Swinging the van across both of the ambulance bays, Jake pulled on the handbrake and jumped out, shouting for help. Frankie looked terrible and Jake couldn't tell if he was breathing. Paramedics and hospital staff came running out and, within seconds, Frankie was the centre of frenetic activity and had been wheeled swiftly into the hospital.

Jake was left standing in the silent car park. He leaned back against the van and let out a long breath, his head falling back and eyes closing with relief. He'd done it. He'd got Frankie here in time. At least, he hoped so.

Hearing sirens wail in the distance, he forced himself to his feet and tried to gather his thoughts. He'd better move the van out of the ambulance bays and find somewhere to park it.

After failing to find a large enough space in the hospital car park, Jake gave up and parked on a side street. He walked back to the hospital, but had no idea how to find Frankie. Waiting at reception, he stood in a line behind a motley crew of walking wounded who were all having Saturday nights worse than his and felt guilty for his rising impatience. When he finally reached the sliding window, he asked the tight-faced receptionist where he could find Frankie Finch and was told tersely that he'd have to take a seat and wait for news.

Jake sat on a hard, bottom-numbing plastic chair, which must have been designed to discourage malingerers from hanging out in A&E, while he sipped a weak coffee from the machine, which tasted of the plastic cup.

He suddenly jolted in panic. *What about Ronnie? Had the kid been on his own, wondering where his dad was all this time?* Stepping out into the cool evening air, he called Bambi. He was relieved to get through and to hear she'd gone straight over to Frankie's motorhome and let that big bouncer guy know what was going on. Apparently, he was looking after the kids. He'd also rung Frankie's wife, who had been flying up that evening anyway, and she was coming straight to the hospital. That was good; he'd wait till she arrived then he'd head back to the track.

"Mr Golding?" Jake heard his name being called and hurried back. *Typical*, he thought. *You could wait for hours and it was always when you stepped outside that they called you.*

According to a young nurse with a freshly scrubbed complexion, Frankie had undergone emergency angioplasty to unclog his coronary artery, and he was now out of theatre. He wasn't up to visitors yet, but she could take him to a different waiting room. Jake followed her through an endless labyrinth of grey corridors until they eventually reached the right ward. He wondered whether they made the corridors all look the same just to confuse people, and had a vague suspicion that the nurse had taken him around and back on themselves a few times just to disorient him further.

Frankie was still coming round from sedation, which was probably a blessing since Jake didn't know what he'd say to him. It wasn't like they were the best of mates. All the same, he didn't want to leave until he'd seen that Frankie was OK. He sat himself down in a different but identical hard, plastic chair and looked wearily at the clock on the wall. He leaned his head back and closed his eyes for a moment.

Waking with a start, Jake realised he'd dozed off. Blinking sleepily, he wiped a trickle of drool from his chin and rubbed his face. He looked across to the nurses' station to see what commotion had woken him up. A short, fierce woman, wearing leather trousers and sky-high heels was having a few choice words with the ward nurse in a heavily accented cockney screech.

He smiled to himself. *That could only be Frankie's wife.* She was demanding to see her husband immediately. Yes, of course she knew it was the middle of the bloody night! He'd had a heart attack and she needed to see him!

The nurse calmly explained that Mr Finch was recovering from surgery and needed to be kept calm. Mrs Finch could see him but, she stressed, only for a few moments because he needed his rest.

Jake scrambled to his feet, making the nurse glance up in alarm.

"So, he's all OK? Nothing to worry about?" The nurse nodded patiently.

"Thank Christ for that!"

Linda Finch turned to him, mouth agape.

"Oh my God, are you the hero that brought him in?"

Without giving Jake time to answer, she enveloped him in a tight, perfumed hug and gave him a big kiss on the cheek.

"I can't thank you enough. Frankie would have died

without you, you totally saved his life!"

Looking up at him she whispered, "I can't tell you how frightened I was," her voice faltering and eyes filling with tears. Jake patted her awkwardly on the back, not sure how to react to this onslaught of emotion from a woman he didn't know. He was relieved when she pulled away.

Linda Finch seemed to get hold of herself. This wouldn't do.

"Oh my God, what am I thinking! I'm standing here chattering and my Frankie's just got out of surgery! I must go and see him." She dabbed her eyes with a tissue, checked her reflection in a compact and quickly applied some lipstick. Then she drew herself up to her full height, fluffed her hair and, with her chin in the air, strode into the room.

Jake took a deep breath and smiled to himself. He was willing to bet she'd have a few choice words for Frankie once he'd recovered.

He was relieved everything had turned out alright. It could so easily have ended differently. If he'd ignored the thump against the caravan, or if they'd waited for an ambulance to arrive, then Frankie might not have made it.

Back in the van, Jake drove wearily to the track, parking up in the silent, pre-dawn paddock. He unlocked the caravan as quietly as possible and fell into bed exhausted, throwing a possessive arm over the gently snoring Bambi.

31
A HOSPITAL HANGOVER

Jake was blundering through a frustrating dream maze of hospital corridors when his alarm blared rudely. It was almost a relief to wake up, but jeez, he was knackered. He'd only managed to snatch a couple of hours' sleep and he had a long day ahead. Rubbing at his crumpled face, he swung his legs over the side of the bed, feet hitting the cold vinyl floor of the caravan. The icy shock was nearly enough to send him scuttling back under the toasty warmth of the covers, but he forced himself to get up and put the kettle on.

How could the floor be that damn cold in the middle of summer? Pulling open the blind, he peered outside eliciting a mumbled groan from the half-asleep Bambi. Jake could see the paddock was shrouded in thick, grey mist behind which was a brightness suggesting it would be a warm, sunny day. Spying his reflection in the window, he saw a creased face, eyes heavy with dark bags. *Oh well. Might as well get on with the day.*

As the morning progressed, even in his sleep-deprived daze, Jake noticed a peculiar atmosphere in the paddock.

Aspinall didn't seem his usual belligerent self and Jake hadn't seen any sign of his busybody wife. Fox was noticeably absent too, which was a relief, and of course Frankie wasn't there as he was still in hospital. Everything seemed strangely quiet.

The first race of the day was the pre-final, which went well for Max, giving him a front-row start for the grand final, but less so for his old teammate. Dommie earned himself a one-lap penalty for sideswiping Finn, who he was thoroughly fed up with. He hadn't been able to shake off Finn who, instead of working together, kept constantly trying to overtake him, slowing them both down and preventing them from catching up to the front runners.

After a few laps of this, Dommie's temper had snapped and he'd sent Finn spinning off into the barriers. Seeing the results, Jake felt relieved they weren't in the Apex awning. The atmosphere there must be pretty grim with the on-track trouble and both kids now starting from the back of the grid for the final.

With a couple of hours to wait until the last race of the day Jake would dearly have loved to go for a nap. The adrenalin from watching the pre-final had worn off and he was seriously flagging, but since they were running on their own, he knew he couldn't really afford the break.

He settled for a strong black coffee; that should perk him up a bit. After all, he only had to get through a few more hours, then they could set off home. At least he didn't have to get up for work in the morning, he thought with a wry smile. Being unemployed did have some benefits.

As he'd suspected, the day turned out to be a real scorcher. Jake was working away on the kart under the awning with Bambi sat in a garden chair, sipping an iced tea and sharing the small patch of shade, when Savannah burst around the corner, buzzing with excitement.

"Oh my gosh!" she gushed. "Have you heard about

Danny Fox?"

She paused, eyebrows raised in a silent question. Lowering her voice and clearly relishing the scandal, she said, "Apparently, he was caught getting off with Frankie Finch's fifteen-year-old daughter in the bar last night. Got the absolute crap kicked out of him when the dad walked in and found him all over her!"

Bambi gaped in astonishment.

"Seriously? What was he thinking?"

"I think it was his trousers that were doing the thinking."

"Sounds like it." She turned to Jake. "That explains a few things, though. Maybe that's what caused the heart attack."

Jake nodded, adding grimly, "And would explain where those blood stains on his shirt came from. They asked me about that at the hospital and I didn't know."

Savannah's eyes widened. "Hang on! Who had a heart attack?"

Bambi smiled. "That was our excitement for the night. Frankie collapsed outside our caravan last night and Jake had to take him to hospital. My knight in shining armour," she added, winking playfully at Jake, who rolled his eyes and turned back to the kart a little pinker in the face.

Savannah plonked herself down in a chair.

"Blimey, it's all been going on, hasn't it? Aspinall's in the doghouse with his wife too, not to mention with the rest of the team. I'll tell you the full story about that later. It all kicked off in our awning yesterday and I haven't seen any sign of Hillary since, thank goodness."

"It must be something to do with it being the end of the season," Bambi laughed. "Everyone seems to be losing their heads! I suppose that explains why we haven't seen Fox around the paddock today. I wonder where he is now?"

"I have no idea. Sounds like he must have been in a pretty bad way once Frankie had finished with him. I bet he's long gone by now. I don't think he'll be showing his face for a while."

Heading down for the final, Jake spotted the looming, grim-faced figure of Chris Slaughter, who gave him a respectful nod. The big man had a sombre Britney and Ronnie in tow, as well as their mechanic, who looked frankly terrified of messing anything up.

Ronnie turned to Chris, who nodded gently. Walking up to Jake, Ronnie squared his little shoulders, gave him a level look and held his hand out.

Voice thick with emotion, he said, "Thanks for looking after my dad last night." His voice broke and he cleared his throat. "Appreciate it." His eyes shone with tears, but he kept his chin up and defiantly refused to look away.

Jake shook his hand, a bit taken aback, and said, "No problem, glad I could help." He patted Ronnie awkwardly on the shoulder, adding,, "I'm sure he'll be back on his feet in no time." Ronnie gave him a curt nod and wiped his nose on his sleeve before putting his helmet on and striding briskly towards his kart for the final.

The race was scrappy from start to finish, as finals often are, especially towards the end of the season. The driving standards did nothing to improve Jake's already jumpy nerves. Aspinall got into the lead early, only to be sent spinning off the track and into the gravel when Parker tapped his rear bumper. Jake chuckled quietly. *Hugo wasn't going to like that.* Ronnie, understandably, didn't have his head in the right place and kept making mistakes, meaning he dropped further and further down the field.

With one lap to go it was a three-way fight for the win between Parker, Max and Dommie, who'd taken advantage of a first-turn incident to make his way quickly up through the field. It was a hell of a drive, but Carver often said Dommie performed at his best when he drove angry.

The action was relentless, with each driver desperately trying to get in front of the other two then hold position. Jake's stomach was churning as he watched, hoping they would all cross the line without any incidents, and could hardly believe it when Max edged ahead at the final corner and took the chequered flag to win.

Jake closed his eyes. He felt sick. He was as proud as hell of the way Max just drove, but they had to get through scrutineering before he'd officially won it, and after what happened last time he was unable to shake a horrible sense of dread.

What if he'd messed up and Max came in underweight? Or something was mechanically wrong with the kart? What if they got disqualified again because it didn't suit somebody for him to win?

At this point he didn't have a lot of faith in anyone in the paddock, and since they didn't know who'd sabotaged them the previous round, he suspected anyone and everyone of foul play. As they opened the gates and let the mechanics into parc fermé, Jake muttered a silent prayer that everything would be OK.

As it turned out, he needn't have worried. The scrutineers were extra cautious after the previous fuel issue and checked everything they could think of, but unable to find any issues they finally gave everyone the okay to leave. Flooded with relief, Jake scooped Max up in a grateful hug.

Gossip travels fast in the paddock and, thanks in no small part to Savannah, who had decided Jake needed some positive PR, the news about Jake's heroism the previous night had spread like wildfire. By the time he left parc fermé, he found himself surrounded by a crowd of people congratulating him both on the win and for saving Frankie's life.

One person who wasn't feeling magnanimous was Hugo Aspinall, who could be heard blustering indignantly at one of the officials about his son being smashed off the track and demanding what the hell they were going to do about it?

With saintly tolerance, the official checked and informed him that they weren't planning to do anything about it. Hugo, by now the colour of a beetroot and absolutely livid, barged his way out of parc fermé muttering, "Get out of my fucking way".

Impatient and angry, he pushed through the throng knocking Bambi - who was waiting outside the fencing for Max and Jake - to the floor. She sat dazed for a moment, unsure what had happened. The fall hadn't really hurt but it was a shock and, what with being both hormonal and emotional after Max's win, she burst into tears. God, she felt so bloody useless at the moment.

Grabbing Hugo by the shoulder, Savannah swung him round and slapped him hard across the face. Hugo goggled at her, astonished, his cheek stinging. The whole crowd fell silent to watch this new drama unfold.

"She's pregnant, you inconsiderate prick," Savannah shouted furiously, hands on hips. "Is that how you get your kicks when you're not groping people? Knocking pregnant women to the floor?"

Jake, who had turned to see what the commotion was about, stared open-mouthed for a second before striding towards the group, his expression thunderous. Reaching them, Jake landed a hefty punch to Aspinall's jaw, sending him reeling backwards onto the tarmac and receiving a smattering of applause and a few cheers from the gathered crowd. Kneeling down by Bambi, who was still sitting on the floor, he cupped her chin and tilted her face up to look at him.

"Are you OK? Is it true? Are you really pregnant?" Bambi snivelled a bit and nodded.

An ear-splitting grin spread slowly across Jake's face. "This is the best day ever!" he beamed, helping her to her feet and wrapping her in a gentle hug. Max, who'd been excitedly discussing the race action with Dommie had totally missed what'd just happened. He only saw his mum and dad kissing with everyone watching.

He rolled his eyes and shook his head at Dommie, who grimaced in solidarity. *Parents were so embarrassing.*

The head scrutineer came up and tapped Jake on the back, who drew reluctantly away from Bambi.

"I hear double congratulations are in order. A race win, and a new baby on the way."

Jake smiled, shaking the mans outstretched hand and shrugging ruefully. "I know I shouldn't have hit Aspinall. He'll probably have my licence for that, but it was worth it."

The clerk looked at him questioningly, his eyes wide. "Don't know what you're talking about, mate. I didn't see anything, and I'm pretty sure nobody else round here did either." He winked at a slack-jawed Jake before walking off, whistling cheerfully.

32
A NEW BEGINNING

A couple of weeks later, Jake sat in the shed at the bottom of the garden, which was newly converted into a smart little office, and gazed happily out of the window. He'd been watching the rather rotund Lucifurr stalk a pigeon, until Bambi startled it into flight as she crossed the lawn with two slopping mugs of tea. The cat slunk under a hydrangea looking annoyed.

Still suffering from morning sickness, Bambi had taken some of her annual leave to help Jake set up the business. They enlisted the help of some friends and, within a couple of days, they'd cleared all the junk out of the shed, insulated it, wired it for electricity and given it a smart new coat of paint. Both Jake and Bambi were very aware that with a baby on the way and only a small house, a separate office would be essential if the business was to succeed.

Dave had been as good as his word and had given Jake the contract for his new website, so he'd been able to start earning almost straight away. Having to work on his laptop at the kitchen table hadn't been ideal, but now they had the new office sorted he could knuckle down and really concentrate.

Jake found himself feeling more enthusiastic about work than he had done for years.

It had been an easy decision. Once Bambi was ready to go on maternity leave, she'd join the business and run the design side of things, saving Jake a fortune in agency fees and giving them both more flexibility for when the baby came. Also, now she'd told work about being pregnant, they were encouraging her to take all her overdue holiday time off, so she'd cut down her hours and would be helping out for one day a week from now on.

They still only had one client and needed to get more in, but that contract was enough to keep them going for the first few months. Jake had been approached by plenty of friends to do their websites over the last year or so, he'd just never had time. Now Bambi was getting on the phone and spreading the word, putting together proposals and turning those offers of work into something more concrete.

It was exciting; she just hoped she could get enough work coming in. She had another three months before the baby was due and wanted to achieve as much as possible before then.

When they'd had the scan, the hospital told Bambi she was just over 22 weeks pregnant. Seeing the grainy image of the baby, they both started to feel excited about this unexpected adventure. Even Max, who had been decidedly unimpressed about the whole having a baby idea, became enthusiastic when he saw his baby sister on the screen.

Perhaps being a big brother wouldn't be so bad. After all, he'd have someone to boss around...

Jake put down his cup of tea to answer his mobile.

"Hello?"

"Jake, it's Frankie Finch."

Surprised, Jake raised his eyebrows at Bambi, partly wondering where Frankie got his number from. "Frankie! How are you?"

"Much improved. Thanks to you. I wanted to call and thank you. I appreciate what you did for me that night. I would've been done for if you hadn't come out and found me. And let's face it, I wouldn't have blamed you for leaving me to die, the way I've treated you this year. You've not had an easy run of it."

"Well, I wouldn't say that," said Jake, embarrassed, as he recalled briefly considering doing just that.

"Anyway, thanks to you and those doctors, I'm on the mend. Linda's put me on a strict diet of greens and chicken, not to mention chewing my ear off constantly, so I've got no choice but to get better. She's not letting me out of her bloody sight now," he chuckled. "She's even making me walk to the shop to get the paper every bloody morning so I'm getting some exercise. So, in short, I owe you, Jake. If there's anything I can ever do for you, you let me know, understood?"

To say Jake was gobsmacked was an understatement. He laughed drily and said the first thing that came into his mind. "Well, you could get our fuel exclusion overturned."

"Ah," said Frankie, and paused long enough for Jake to regret blurting that out. Had he just pissed Frankie off? He certainly didn't need that right now.

Frankie continued. "That was the next thing I wanted to talk to you about, actually. I might be able to help you out there. Turns out you weren't cheating, which I'm sure you know," he laughed heartily. "I found out later that Danny Fox spiked your fuel in parc fermé. When I got out of hospital, I made a few calls and the club have found CCTV footage of him slipping something into your tank. I made sure the officials were sent a copy and they've agreed to reinstate your win."

Jake gaped, not sure what to say. "Wow, that's amazing, thanks! I bet Fox is unhappy about that."

"Frankly Jake, he's got much bigger problems to worry about right now. Like owing me money. Plus, he's had an unfortunate accident, meaning he'll be out of action for quite some time."

"Yes, I did hear something about that," said Jake.

"I bet you did. Nothing stays quiet in the paddock for long, does it? Let's just say he didn't get anything he didn't deserve."

"That's pretty much what I'd heard, to be honest. After what he did, I'm surprised his accident wasn't worse. Is your daughter OK?"

"Yeah, I think she was pretty shaken up, but she's a tough cookie. Chip off the old block, that girl. It was a hell of a weekend for her, what with me ending up on the operating table too. Not sure I'll get her at a karting track again any time soon, and that's no bad thing." He laughed. "Anyway, you'll get a letter through in the next day or so confirming your exclusion has been overturned. If it doesn't arrive, you let me know. Somebody convinced Danny to write a full confession to accompany the CCTV footage, so they have no choice but to reinstate the results. I suspect the footage might find its way all over social media as soon as the paperwork's finalised, too. I think everyone in the paddock needs to see what he's done."

"Thanks, Frankie, I really appreciate that. Especially as it means Ronnie losing the win."

"Don't mention it. If he's going to win, I want him to win on track. Besides I've got a good feeling about the next round."

Jake grinned, a huge weight lifted from his mind. "Well, I have to say it's been a difficult few months, what with the whole fuel debacle, then losing my job. But with your news, plus Bambi expecting, and starting a new business, things are starting to really look up. By the way, if you know anyone who wants a website doing, just send them my way." Jake laughed, figuring he'd have to get used to dropping that into every conversation until the business was established.

Frankie was quiet for a moment, and Jake grimaced wondering whether he'd been a bit too cheeky. After a pause, however, Frankie said: "I'll do that, Jake. I owe you a favour, and I've got a lot of business contacts. I'm sure I can have a word and send them your way. I'll make a few calls, twist a few arms."

Jake put the phone down dumbfounded. Blimey, he hadn't expected Frankie to take that seriously. He chuckled and shook his head. Web developer to the mob, eh? He'd better do a bloody good job.

33
THE BIG FINISH

The final round of the British Championships was at Foxcombe circuit, a grey ribbon of tarmac nestled between the undulating hills of the Cotswolds. Surrounded by picture-postcard villages, swarming with tourists eating cream teas, it was a surprising place to have a racetrack, and because of its location the circuit was only allowed to run nine race weekends a year due to militant local councillors imposing noise restrictions.

August had been particularly warm and, unfortunately for everyone attending, as they approached September this weekend was forecast to be the hottest of the year. The hottest, in fact, since the fabled heatwave of 1976, according to the news, although they seemed to say that every year. The paddock was dusty and unforgivingly torrid.

By Saturday morning, everyone was suffering from the heat except for those in the air-conditioned BRR awning. Being pregnant, Bambi seemed to be feeling it even more than usual, sweating profusely and very pink in the face. There was nowhere she could go to escape; even the van's air con was ineffectual against the sweltering sun, simply circulating hot air around the cabin.

She and Jake had decided against running with the team again that weekend and there was precious little shade thrown by their pull-out awning. Adding to that, the sea of tarmac just reflected and intensified the heat and the caravan was as scorching as a tin can on a beach. It didn't even seem to cool down at night. The best she could do was sit in a patch of shade, her feet in a bucket of water, fanning herself with a race programme.

Heatwave aside, the Goldings were all looking forward to this round. Cosmo had the championship pretty much sewn up, but there was still a scrap to be had for the best of the rest, and they were hoping Max could finish in the top three. That would be a great result for his first year, and they'd get to go to the big awards dinner at The Dorchester.

Now their fuel penalty had been revoked, the paddock felt like a much friendlier place. This had been helped enormously by the video of Danny tampering with their fuel tank going viral on social media, and everyone had come out in indignant support for them. Jake had lost count of the number of people who'd come over to sympathise and express their outrage. It was a pity they weren't that supportive at the time, he thought wryly.

Ronnie Finch had joined Apex Motorsport for the last race of the season and the Finch family were there in force to cheer him on.

In return for Linda allowing him to come back to the track, Frankie had promised her he'd take a step back and not get stressed in any way.

He was on a strict diet prohibiting red meat, alcohol and his beloved cigars while his cholesterol improved, and she wasn't letting him out of her sight. She'd almost lost him, and she was going to make damn sure he didn't have another heart attack whether he liked it or not.

Being under Linda's constant scrutiny hadn't made Frankie any less of a menace, however. When Lillington had been overheard bleating to Chase about him bringing undesirable elements into the awning, Frankie had given him a stern look, slowly drawing his finger across his throat and sending Lillington scuttling back to his corner in fear of his life.

Turning back to Linda, Frankie had received a disapproving look, to which he'd responded with a wink, murmuring chirpily, "Just playing the game, love, nothing to worry about."

Aspinall was so far ahead in the championship that he only had to score a handful of points to secure the title. He'd easily accomplished this in the heats on Saturday, so in effect didn't even need to race on Sunday - the championship was already won. Frankie had known this would be the case, but it still irritated him beyond belief, especially when Cosmo came in from his last heat unzipping his race suit to reveal a t-shirt emblazoned with the words *British Champion* front and back.

Cocky little sod, thought Frankie sourly, feeling the familiar tightening in his chest and taking a few calming breaths.

As he stood there glowering and thinking uncharitable thoughts, one of the scrutineers clapped him on the shoulder and thanked him for uncovering the fuelgate scandal. Earnestly pumping Frankie's hand, the man admitted that, without the pressure he put on the club to look at CCTV footage, they would never have uncovered the truth. Laughing, he held his hands up defensively. After all, how could they have known? They were just doing their jobs? But there could have been a huge miscarriage of justice.

Judging by the new-found reverence in the man's tone, Frankie also suspected word had got around about Danny ending up in hospital. Perhaps that little toerag had been useful for something after all. Finally, people in the paddock were starting to realise Frankie Finch wasn't a man to mess with. Maybe things wouldn't be quite as skewed in Aspinall's favour next season.

As everyone packed up after the day's racing, a party was getting underway in the cool of the BRR awning. In anticipation of Cosmo's win, Hugo had stashed a couple of crates of champagne by the air-conditioning units so they would be chilled to perfection.

The awning was filled with the popping of corks and the cheers of a team who'd just clinched their first championship. The mechanics, who would never turn down free alcohol, were celebrating hard and getting rowdier by the minute.

Savannah and Dave raised a dutiful glass to their teammate's success, then slipped out, Dave having pinched a couple of bottles to drink with the Carvers and Goldings. Why not share them with people they actually liked? There was ample champagne to go around, and they'd both had more than enough of having to spend time with the bloody Aspinalls.

Hillary, who didn't usually drink, had her arm twisted into accepting a well-deserved glass of fizz. *After all, it's not every day your son becomes British Champion,* she thought smugly. Hugo, seeing her with a glass in her hand, slid over and had a quiet word, suggesting that perhaps she should limit it to one glass.

Throwing him a spiteful look, Hillary downed the whole glass in one go and poured herself another. He was in no position to tell her what to do!

She felt the warmth of the alcohol spread deliciously through her body and wondered why on earth she didn't drink more often. This felt fabulous!

As she drank, becoming louder and increasing combative, Hillary decided now would be a great time to get a few things straight with Hugo. She'd had just about enough of him and his philandering and proceeded to tell him loudly how much she'd enjoyed having the house to herself for the past few weeks. He could damn well keep staying at his club from now on. Pouring herself another glass, she announced to Hugo that she would be divorcing him and taking the house in Mayfair. By the time she'd finished with him, he'd have nothing, not even the little reputation he currently had left.

Mortified, Hugo mumbled an apology to everyone, explaining that his wife was taking medication and really shouldn't be drinking. Speaking slowly and calmly he tried to soothe her and, steering her by the elbow, asked one of the mechanics to drive her back to the hotel. She shrugged him off furiously.

"You don't get to touch me any more, you vile little man. I've put up with you and your sweaty hands all over me for nearly twenty years and I've had enough." She stamped her foot angrily, unsteadying herself and grasping the mechanic's arm to regain her balance. "You think I don't know what you've been up to all these years? Letching over every pretty face. Unwanted hands all over them, brushing up against them to get cheap thrills like a dirty old man. And everyone knows you've been shagging your poor secretary for years. I only ignored it until now because it took the pressure off me to have sex with you."

She stared at him triumphantly. Hugo closed his eyes in defeat. There was nothing he could do to stop this car crash. He'd just have to wait until the alcohol had worn off, then try and pick up the pieces of his marriage.

Tilting the bottle of champagne, Hillary was surprised to find it empty and she looked around for another. She felt liberated. She'd been holding back this resentment for so long, it felt amazing to let it all out. As she sought out a top-up, her eyes settled on Julia, who was staring at her, mouth open. Hillary felt a flash of anger and she spun on her heel and advanced.

"And what are you gawping at, Miss Goody Twoshoes? You think you're so bloody perfect, don't you? You sanctimonious bitch! What with your veganism and your precious oh-so-perfect child, but everyone knows you were fucking that coke-head Fox. And once he'd finished with you, he moved onto a fifteen-year-old girl. It must have been your flat chest that attracted him to you! Either that or the fact that you were all over him. After all, he's never been known to turn down an easy lay."

Julia gaped indignantly, but Hillary wasn't finished.

"Then again, I suppose it's understandable. My husband might be a PHILANDERING SON OF A BITCH (she shouted this bit over her shoulder at Hugo, who looked despairingly at the floor) but at least he's not gay."

She paused for dramatic effect, aware the whole awning was gripped by the unfolding spectacle.

"Surely you know? It's blindingly obvious to everyone else that your husband and Ben Redmaine can hardly keep their hands off each other. I suppose that explains you throwing yourself at Fox - you have to get some action somewhere, don't you?" She smiled nastily. Julia glanced desperately at Kevin, waiting for him to leap to her defence, but he just pressed his lips together apologetically and a little sadly. And with that, Hillary drained her glass and stormed out victoriously. A terrible silence followed her exit. Everything was quiet except for the hum of the air conditioning.

"Um, sorry about that everyone," stuttered Hugo. "Drinking really doesn't agree with her. It's the medication she's on." Then, turning to one of the young mechanics, he said, "Could you do me a huge favour and see if you can get her back to the hotel? She can't be driving in the state she's in, and I think she'll take it better coming from you than from me right now."

He sighed, rubbing his forehead wearily. "Just look after her, will you."

The mechanic nodded and, taking a determined breath, went after her.

Everyone let out a collective sigh of relief that the drama was over, but the party atmosphere had been ruined. No one felt like celebrating any more, and they awkwardly and quietly finished packing up before dispersing.

Hugo, who'd had a truly shitty day sat in the corner on his own, nursing a half-empty glass. He hadn't envisioned all this when he'd dreamed of Cosmo becoming British Champion. He wasn't sure what to do. He couldn't face going back to the hotel and seeing Hillary and was contemplating sleeping in his car. The last thing he wanted was to continue the row with the mood she was in.

Eventually, feeling the weight of the world on his shoulders, he heaved himself up and plodded across the paddock to his car. But when he reached it, he was surprised to see Hillary's matching Range Rover still parked next to his. He halted. So, the mechanic hadn't managed to get her back to the hotel after all. With a resigned sigh, he walked off to scour the paddock to make sure she was OK.

After half an hour of walking around in the dark, Hugo heard urgent noises coming from behind an awning. Peering reluctantly round the corner, he spotted Hillary's great white arse shining in the moonlight. The BRR mechanic was thrusting enthusiastically into her, her head thrown back in ecstasy, hands braced against the wall.

Hugo exhaled heavily. Oh well, he supposed he had asked the mechanic to look after her. Feeling conflicted but resolved, he pulled his phone out of his pocket and videoed for a few seconds. He didn't feel great about doing it, but if Hillary followed through on her threat of suing for divorce then at least he'd have some counter-ammunition. It was lucky Hillary had got herself that tattoo on her bottom in her one moment of wildness during her gap year; that should make the evidence pretty indisputable.

Shoving his hands glumly in his pockets, he headed away from the crescendoing groans back towards his car.

34
SWEAT & NAUGHTY SCHOOLBOYS

Sunday was already hot and humid before Jake got out of bed, the stale air in the caravan cloying and sweaty.

He'd had a restless night, tossing and turning, never seeming to cool down despite all the windows being open. So, instead he lay there, uncomfortably warm, listening to all the nocturnal noises that don't usually penetrate the sanctity of your bedroom: the screech of an owl, the bark of a fox, strange rustling sounds that could have been anything. Hedgehogs? Rats, mice?

By the time the sun rose at about 5.30am, he gave up trying to sleep and, creeping around the caravan to avoid waking Bambi and Max, took a cup of coffee and went to sit outside. The day was already warm but there was a slight breeze, which brought some welcome relief.

Sitting in a garden chair, scrolling through the latest news on his phone, he heard a car engine start and glanced up. He was surprised to see a dishevelled Hillary driving out of the paddock. Wow, they must have really been celebrating last night if she was only just going to bed now. He scoffed at himself. Why was he being so judgemental?

He probably would have been up all night celebrating too if Max had won the championship yesterday.

He tried feeling pleased for the Aspinalls, but without much success. He couldn't help being rather sour about the season. Everything had gone in Aspinall's favour this year, almost as if Cosmo been chosen as champion before the season started. The golden boy hadn't been able to put a foot wrong. No matter how badly he'd behaved, his conduct just hadn't been seen, at least not by the people in authority.

The other drivers had all received penalties and yet he'd been able to smash people around, swear, shout and generally behave horribly all year without any consequences. Jake had heard rumours of officials being given massive backhanders to turn a blind eye. He had no idea whether that was true, but judging from the outcome it seemed plausible. Whatever Cosmo did, no action was taken.

Carver had mentioned Cosmo had also got away with various issues in scrutineering. In the previous round, he'd been under the minimum weight and left parc fermé with his control tyres on, both of which carried an automatic exclusion. And yet, somehow, he'd got away with both. Some people just had charmed lives.

Or was that the benefit of having money to throw around? Maybe he'd been naive to think it was ever going to be a fair competition. Looking back on everything now, the odds had been stacked against them from the start.

He took a sip of coffee. Well, whatever had happened, it was all done and dusted now. With the championship sealed, the rest of them were competing for second place, and in a way that was nice. It took the pressure off. He couldn't imagine how stressed he'd be feeling now if Max was still in with a shot of the title. He'd no doubt have had an even worse night's sleep!

After Max's points were reinstated, he was in second place in the championship ahead of Ronnie, but there was only one point separating them. Then there was a larger gap to Parker and Eden Leech in fourth and fifth, with poor Dommie trailing in about eighth place after his two exclusions and various other penalties.

With today's pre-final and grand final still to go there was everything to play for, and not just the last silverware of the season. If Max had a DNF or a penalty, he could easily drop out of the top three, which would be gutting after all their hard work.

He hoped Max could play it safe and make it through the day without any incidents.

Hours later, as they walked down to the grid for the last race of the season, Jake couldn't help feeling nervous.

The pre-final that morning had been hard-fought but fair, and had finished with Carver in the lead, Ronnie in second and Max in third place ready to start the grand final. Cosmo, now that he'd clinched the championship, just seemed to be putting in minimal effort. After all, there was no point him getting caught up in the hard racing around him and risking any kind of penalty; he just had to see out the weekend.

Standing on the grid, Jake was surprised when Frankie came up and offered his hand. Even when he was being friendly, Jake still found Frankie intimidating, but he just wished both boys good luck.

"May the best man win," he said magnanimously. Then, spoiling it, he added in an undertone, "And by that, of course, I mean Ronnie." He winked and Jake smiled along with him, but it didn't do anything to help his nerves.

He might have a newly fledged friendship with the rather frightening Frankie, but he didn't want to do anything to get on the wrong side of him. The last thing he wanted was for Max to accidentally take them both out of the race, and in doing so out of the championship too.

The warmup lap was soon over and the lights had gone

out, the occasion telling on the drivers as they fought hard for every position. With seeded numbers up for grabs, every point mattered and all the grudges that had built up over the year spilt over onto the track. Every driver was desperate to finish ahead of their rivals.

Coming onto the penultimate lap, Dommie, who was battling for third, was sideswiped by Cosmo and went spinning off into the barriers. Cosmo, who had forgotten his instructions about keeping his nose clean, stuck two fingers up as he drove away.

That meant there were yellow flags out on track while they cleared the kart, preventing any overtaking. As the drivers crossed the line to start the final lap, the flags cleared and they were able to race again.

Ronnie was in the lead with Max right on his bumper, Cosmo having dropped back after his contact with Dommie. Going into the first left-hander, Max managed to edge his way ahead only to get overtaken as the track curved back round to the right. They battled hard for every corner, neither willing to concede. Racing along the straight, they were side by side coming towards the last corner, and it was a game of chicken to see who would brake last and get ahead. Jake closed his eyes, praying they would both get through without a horrendous accident, and as he heard both karts race past him towards the finish line, he opened his eyes slightly to see Max, just inches ahead, take the chequered flag.

Roaring with delight, he celebrated wildly, grabbing the nearest person and hugging them as he jumped around the grandstand. Unfortunately, that person was Frankie Finch who, even though he'd just been pipped to the win, had to wryly smile at the raw emotion on Jake's face. He shook his head. "Well done, Jake, that was a good, clean fight. Gutted we didn't win it though. If we'd only had one more lap…"

Pulling into parc fermé, Max and Ronnie climbed out of

their karts and shook hands, grinning widely. It almost didn't matter who won with the thrill of the racing still coursing through their veins. Taking their helmets off, hair all sweaty, they excitedly relived all the moves they pulled on each other in their battle.

Cosmo, who'd finished third, pulled up next to them. As he got out of his kart Max and Ronnie both eyed his race suit, which was the usual BRR suit except with British Champion written front and back instead of the regular BRR logo.

Seeing them looking, Cosmo pointed at the words and drawled, "Well deserved, eh? Well deserved!"

The boys raised their eyebrows at each other.

"If you say so," said Ronnie, deadpan. He nudged Max. "I think he means your win, Max."

Smiling, Max played along. Turning to a frowning Cosmo he said, "Thanks, mate, what a win, eh? It was well-deserved, wasn't it? Appreciate you saying that."

Ronnie nodded seriously, adding, "Very sporting of you to say that since you only came third."

Grinning, they turned their backs on Cosmo and went back to their conversation.

"I wasn't talking about that…" blustered an irritated Cosmo, who was soon soothed as he found himself surrounded by sycophantic BRR mechanics and his dad, who wanted to take him off to be interviewed by a reporter.

The scrutineers, relieved to have reached the end of a hard season and a long, hot weekend came over to chat with everyone.

"Come on, lads, let's just check your restrictors and we can all go and get a nice cold drink."

Cosmo's mechanic pulled a face and groaned. "Seriously? It's the last race of the season. We won the championship yesterday."

The scrutineer gave him a stern look, all trace of a smile gone. "Restrictors now, please."

Jake, still grinning at Max's win, happily took the restrictor out of his engine, had it measured and was given the all-clear. Putting everything back together, he looked back at Max, who was chatting happily with a group of other kids, all sweaty and grimy and excited. Jake mused that, despite everything, perhaps this crazy journey had been worthwhile. It had nearly bankrupted them, driven him mad with frustration and made them miserable some of the time, but on days like this, seeing the joy on Max's face made it all worth it.

Frankie ambled over to see how Aaron was getting on and stopped for a chat with Jake. All of the stress and antagonism of the season had ebbed away, and they were left, perhaps not the best of friends, but with the forced brotherhood of people who'd shared one hell of an experience.

Out of the corner of his eye, Jake spotted one of the BRR mechanics run out of parc fermé like a scalded rabbit. Strange. *What was going on there, then? Come to think of it, it was odd that Cosmo wasn't out of scrutineering yet. They were usually just waved through like they had diplomatic immunity.*

He and Frankie exchanged a puzzled glance and then shrugged. *Who cared?* The season was done, and they'd been cleared to go. As Jake turned to leave, an apoplectic Hugo barged past on his way back into parc fermé.

Frankie smiled slyly at Jake. "Looks like this might be about to get interesting. Wonder whether golden boy's luck has finally run out?"

Jake laughed. "Fat chance of that! He's had everything go his way all season!"

"Never say never," said Frankie enigmatically raising an eyebrow. They both stood and listened intently, trying to hear what was going on. They could only catch the odd word, but somebody - they guessed Hugo - was doing quite a lot of shouting.

As they stood eavesdropping, Ben Redmaine rushed into scrutineering too and Frankie and Jake reacted like naughty schoolboys who'd been caught listening outside the headmaster's office. Stifling guilty laughter, they continued trying to listen in. If anything, the shouting seemed to be getting louder. If only they could hear what was going on!

Frankie suddenly came to his senses. He shook his head.

"Why the fuck am I just standing here? We were top three. We've got just as much right to be in scrutineering as they have!" And with a wink and a grin he strode back in to see what was going on. Jake hesitated. He still had the kart with him and while he was curious, he felt a bit of a tit standing there snooping by himself. He could hear Frankie's cockney twang joining in with the arguments and chuckled to himself. *Trust Frankie to stir things up even more.*

Reluctantly, he decided to take the kart back to the awning. He didn't have mechanics to put everything away like the other dads did, and he couldn't stand around gawking any more, it was just too awkward.

If anything interesting happened Frankie would be sure to let him know. Either way, he reflected happily as he pushed the kart back through the sunny paddock, they'd won today and got second place in the championship, and nobody was taking that away from them.

It'd been a great end to the season. He'd go back and have an ice-cold beer and put his feet up until the podium ceremony. He could pack everything up afterwards.

Bambi was in a shady sun lounger eating an ice cream by the time Jake got back. He smiled as he ran his eyes over her burgeoning bump and thought how much he loved her. She'd put up with so much this year and didn't need all this stress, especially being pregnant. Grabbing himself a beer, he went over to give her a sweaty kiss.

She swatted him away good-naturedly.

"Ugh! Get off! I'm so hot, don't even think about touching me!" she laughed, fanning herself. "I've been lying here dreaming of air con and chilled margaritas. I don't need reminding that I'm teetotal, pregnant and a hot, sweaty mess right now."

He grinned and pulled up a chair next to her.

"The problem is, now you're eating for two you take up all the shade and there's none left for me."

"Oy!" squealed Bambi, thwacking him with the race programme. "Just for that, you can sit in the bloody sunshine!"

Jake chortled, his beer making a satisfying hiss as he opened it. If only all the race weekends could feel as relaxed as they did right now.

Taking a long swig, Jake closed his eyes and savoured the moment. The relief at the season being over was sinking in. Max had done a brilliant job. He might not have won, but second place was pretty damn good for your first season.

Just then, the tannoy hissed and crackled into action, announcing the podium presentation would take place in five minutes. Bambi and Jake glanced at each other and smiled. He gave her a hand to heave herself back out of the chair.

"Ugh," she laughed. "My dress has totally stuck to me I'm so sweaty."

"Stop it, you're turning me on," laughed Jake, slinging his arm lazily around her shoulders and kissing her on the head as they strolled towards the podium.

Even though they'd said five minutes, it was more like twenty minutes later that the officials made their way up onto the podium to start proceedings. As the other classes were called out, they all clapped and cheered, especially the kids, who were dripping wet and bedraggled from having a water fight after the final.

As they got to the cadet race, Jake spotted Frankie on the other side of the crowd, and who waved and gave him a double thumbs-up. Jake grinned. *It was great to see everyone in such a good mood.* It just went to show how much strain they'd all been under throughout the season. At least it wasn't just them who'd had found the pressure difficult.

The race director was giving a speech about what a fantastic season it had been. *Was he ever going to present the trophies?*

Jake scanned the crowd. Cosmo wasn't there, but that was no surprise. He never bothered turning up to a trophy presentation if he wasn't on the top step and after all, the championship awards would be given out at the formal dinner later in the year.

Finally, it was time for the cadet trophies.

"And in third place in today's race we have one of this year's rookie racers: Eden Leech!" The crowd clapped and cheered as Eden went to collect his trophy and Julia pushed her way to the front of the crowd to take photos. Jake frowned. *What the hell? Cosmo came third, why was Eden up there? He'd finished in fourth! Did this mean there really had been a problem with Cosmo's kart in scrutineering?*

Shit, or had Max been disqualified for something and he hadn't realised? He hadn't even thought to check the published results. Would that explain why Eden had been bumped up to third? The beer started to churn uncomfortably in Jake's stomach.

"And after a hard-fought final a driver who has performed brilliantly all year - in second place today, Ronnie Finch." Jake was flooded with relief as he realised that must mean Max's win was still secure and he clapped and whistled as Ronnie mounted the podium, hair still dripping from the water fight.

Frankie had made his way through the crowd to where Jake was standing. "What happened to Aspinall, then?" Jake shouted over the noise of the crowd.

Frankie grinned: "Illegal restrictor."

"No way!"

"Yep! I reckon he's been running it all year and getting away with it. Got excluded from the meeting." He turned to Jake and grinned broadly.

The race director continued. "And our winner today, a driver in his rookie year at the Nationals…"

Jake turned to Frankie, his eyes widening. "But if Aspinall's been excluded, he's lost all the points from this round…? Does that mean…?"

"… who has raced his heart out and turned in a really impressive performance. Please put your hands together for today's winner, and this year's British Champion, Max Golding!"

The crowd erupted around Jake, who stood there clutching Bambi's hand, absolutely stunned. Max, who had no idea what was going on, stumbled up the steps looking puzzled and was handed the trophy. As he took his place on the top step, Ronnie leaned over to explain what had happened.

Realisation dawning, Max's face was an absolute picture, turning from confusion to shock to absolute joy. Rushing back down the steps, he raced towards Jake - who was already pushing his way through to the front of the crowd - and ran into his arms. The two of them, tears streaming down their faces, held each other tightly.

Bambi, smiling broadly, took a sneaky photo of the two of them on her phone before wiping her eyes and going in to join the hug.

This year had been one hell of a rollercoaster ride, but she wouldn't have changed it for the world.

THE END

OTHER TITLES BY TM THORNE

FRANKIE FINCH BOOKS

Notorious:
Danger, Deception, Desire

Accused:
Stardom, Scandal, Survival

Driven:
Racing, Rivalry Revenge

Caged:
Rock, Ransom, Retribution

Made:
The Frankie Finch prequel (short story)

THE LONDON VAMPIRE SERIES

Spooked

Jinxed

Enthralled (short story)

Find out more at www.TMThorne.com

Printed in Great Britain
by Amazon